For My Brother

THE BUTTERFLY GIRL

Frances Paige was born in Glasgow between the Wars, but has lived in the North of England for many years. In her forties she took up first painting and then writing with great success. She is the author of nearly thirty novels, including the popular 'Sholtie' series.

FRANCES PAIGE

The Butterfly Girl

This edition published by Grafton Books, 1999

Grafton Books is an Imprint of
HarperCollins*Publishers*
77–85 Fulham Palace Road,
Hammersmith, London W6 8JB

1 3 5 7 9 8 6 4 2

First published in Great Britain by
HarperCollins*Publishers* 1995

ISBN 0-26-167352-1

Set in Linotron Palatino

Printed in Great Britain by
Caledonian International Book Manufacturing Ltd, Glasgow

One

1968

Van sleeked down, or tried to sleek down, Sam's hair. It was difficult to decide whether he had inherited his black frizz from Eb, his father, or herself.

'I used to plait your father's hair for him,' she said. 'He liked it that way.'

'That's for girls.' Sam looked sullen. He had seen no photographs of Eb since Van didn't possess any, but she had decided early on that Sam ought to know about the existence of his father, even though he had never seen him.

'No, it's a fashion for some men.'

'Only black men.'

'Your father was black.' Was she too open? Ritchie, her father, had advised her to 'come clean' with Sam when she went to live with them. 'It will complete his sense of identity.' Ritchie was a painter, a famous painter. Although not bookish like Anna, Van's mother, he had a great fount of natural wisdom. She had tried, therefore, to introduce to Sam as he left babyhood, the facts of his birth, that his father was West African, that she had left him before he was born.

'I don't want to go to this old school.' Mention of Eb invariably made Sam unsure of himself.

1

She looked at the little scowling face. He had Eb's brown eyes, but her mouth, his skin was smoothly olive. He was a beautiful child. Everyone said so. Everyone wasn't as brusque as Bessie, their maid, who had said once in her kitchen, 'Aye, he has a good touch o' the tar brush, that yin.'

'It's a lovely school,' she said, straightening his red tie, buttoning the navy blue blazer with the badge on the pocket. That and the grey shorts were the uniform of the private school he was going to for the first time this morning. 'Granny's school when she was a little girl.'

Anna and Ritchie were paying the fees. Van hadn't wanted that. There were Corporation schools further down Great Western Road, but she had been won over by Ritchie pointing out that this one was nearer. 'You don't want him jumping on and off buses at his age. He can walk easily to the Botanic Gardens.' The school was in Queen Margaret Drive.

'They'll wonder where my daddy is.' His eyes were liquid brown, the whites faintly yellow, heavily lashed.

'Tell them you have a grandpa instead. He'll take you sometimes if he isn't painting.'

'He's always painting, always up those stairs.' He was truculent. 'That's what Granny says.'

'Oh, he'll come down for *you*. But this time, since it's your first day I'm taking you. Try on your cap.'

He lifted it from the table, jammed it on by the stiff peak. It rose slowly from his head because of the thickness and liveliness of his hair. They were standing in front of a mirror. They both watched it slowly rising. He giggled, and she caught him in her arms, giggling too, wanting to weep. 'It'll flatten down in

2

no time,' she said, holding him close for a second. 'Just don't bend forward.'

They made their way down the broad staircase of her parents' house, passing the leaded landing window, 'real old Glasgow stained glass,' she could hear her mother's proud reminder, the thick carpet soft to their feet, 'Templeton's finest Axminster from Wylie and Lochhead.' Mother had renewed the same pattern when she inherited the house from Granny Rose and had come to live in Glasgow. Each year a man came and changed it round to even the tread and replace the parts which were worn. It was a warm ruby colour, a happy contrast with the oak-panelled walls.

Bessie was in the kitchen when they went in and she widened her eyes in pretended astonishment. 'Well, well, who's this fine young gentleman then? I've never seen *him* before in this house.'

'It's Sam, Bessie.' The boy laughed. 'You know me, Sam who lives here.'

'Sam?' She looked mystified. 'I've never seen a Sam in this house, no' wi' a blazer and rid tie.'

'She's teasing.' Van laughed. 'It's Samuel Carradine Laidlaw. It's on his birth certificate.' She had put in Eb's name although he had said he hadn't wanted anything to do with the coming baby, that he had enough trouble looking after himself . . .

'Och, aye,' Bessie's face broke into a smile, 'I've got you now. Well, if that's the way o' it, there's a wee present here for someone wi' that name, something to carry his sandwiches and mebbe some Foreign Land biscuits.' This was Bessie's favourite pun directed at the estimable Glasgow bakers, Mac-Farlane Lang. She lifted a small red knapsack from her table. 'To match your tie. It'll haud your books as weel.'

3

'Oh, that's awfy nice,' Sam said. Occasionally he lapsed into Bessie's idiom. 'Isn't it, Mummy?'

'It's very kind indeed. You shouldn't have wasted your money, Bessie.'

'An' why no'? Here, son, pit it on your shoothers. That's right. Now away you go oot o' ma kitchen, and see you listen to whit your teachers tell you then you'll no' miss anything. You'll never make it up if you miss the beginning.'

He was jaunty, walking along Great Western Road with his knapsack on his back, cheerful when she left him at the gate of the small school in the charge of a kindly teacher. She told herself it was nothing at all, mothers surrendered their children at school gates every day of the week. Then why are you bloody well crying? she asked herself, as she walked back, turning left at Byres Road where she had promised to do some shopping for Bessie. A coffee here with Anna would have made short work of her weepiness, she thought. She was always so practical when it came to other people's affairs.

Anna's Achilles heel was her still evident love for her husband, touching when you considered she was now fifty-five years of age. She was vulnerable where Ritchie was concerned, but hard-headed with everyone else, except Jean, her twin sister in Kirkcudbright. The Siamese twins, Ritchie called them.

He and Anna were at Arenys de Mar, their house near Barcelona. It would be a combination of painting and pleasure for them both. Ritchie was working on a mural for a new concert hall, and Anna would be pottering about the city. Although she rarely worked when she was in Spain, the Spanish influence was strong in her work. Her pewter mirrors with their encrusted and decorated frames had become her

4

hallmark in Glasgow. Ritchie's name, of course, was internationally known. It was a strange decision, Van thought now, to move from their home in Renton, near London, and come to live here when Anna's mother had died.

Van didn't understand roots. There had been Renton as a girl, then Clerkenwell with Eb, now Glasgow and Clevedon Crescent, a refuge they had offered her when she became pregnant. To Ritchie, she felt, it had been a natural and spontaneous gesture; for her mother it had been a conscious decision, a wish to let bygones be bygones, to forget her disappointment in Van's life-style, to drop her prejudices. She valued that gesture, knowing how much it had cost. I wish I were gifted, she thought, as she went into the fish shop to get the finnan haddie Bessie had requested. 'I could speak their language then.'

She treated herself to a coffee in the upstairs tearoom which she and Anna frequented. Today was a milestone in her life. Now that Sam was at school, she would have to think seriously of her future. For his sake, she must give him a sense of security for a few years by staying on at Clevedon Crescent. That ruled out any residential job, but there must be plenty of children's homes around where she could work during the day . . .

The thought of her future was still in her mind when she got back to the house laden with shopping.

'Did you no' see the letter for you?' Bessie said.

Van hurriedly dumped the shopping on the kitchen table. 'Yes, but I had to get rid of this first.' She turned and went out again. Her name had stared up at her from the Benares tray on the hall table as she had passed.

She saw it had a London postmark as she opened

it with trepidation. The only people she knew there were Eb, a few neighbours who had lived near their flat, and Adelaide, his sister, whom she had once been so attracted to when they had both lived in Renton.

'Dear Van,' she read. 'I found your address amongst Eb's things.' She stopped reading for a second, her heart beginning to beat faster. She looked down again.

He never talked about you, but sometimes, when he got really ill, I think he regretted what happened. When we had him moved to a home, he said, 'Van wouldn't have let this happen.' Well, what could I do about it? I was married with two kids of me own. I couldn't keep a cripple like that in a two-roomed flat, could I?

Well, I'm sorry to tell you he died last week. I would have let you know, but as I said, I only found your address when I had to go through his things. He was thirty years of age, my brother, and had gone steadily downhill with the polio since you left. But he didn't try. He was full of self-pity. That's what the matron in the home said when she sent for me. 'Ebenezer never tried to help himself, that was the trouble.'

Well, he's gone. He was always selfish, but likeable with that big smile of his. I often thought you were too good for him, and never blamed you for clearing out. Strangely enough, he was devoted to my two kids. His face used to light up when I took them to see him, smiling all over his face.

He never told me what made you leave, and to tell you the truth I was too busy to find out where you were, what with having my first, and Bert, my hubby, in and out of work all the time.

There's nothing I can give you of Eb's. He hadn't paid his rent, and when he was moved to the home the landlord kept everything there was in lieu of money. I remember the good times you and me had in Renton when we were girls. Your mother was always kind to me although I knew she didn't like me. I'm sorry I once took money out of her purse.

All the best, Addy.

Van went back to the kitchen. When they were sitting over their half finnan haddie each (poached in milk and butter between two plates on top of a pan of water), Bessie said, 'You're looking as if somebody stole your scone. Was it that letter?'

Van got up and went to the sink to rinse her plate, her back to the room, and Bessie. 'Yes. It was to say that Sam's father had died.'

There was silence behind her, then the noise Bessie made with her tongue behind her teeth which could express every emotion in the book. 'Oh well,' she said, 'maybe he's better oot o' the road. He was never any good to you anyhow.'

'Oh, Bessie . . .' Van turned to her, tears streaming down her face. 'That's a terrible thing to say.'

She went into her arms as she had done when she was Sam's age.

Two

Anna had wanted a swimming pool ever since she had been entertained at Manuel Folguera's house quite near their own. It had been necessary to come to terms first of all with the image which rose in her mind along with the jealousy. But that was a thing of the past. It was six years ago since Ritchie had left her to live with Maria Roig in her apartment in the Barri Gòtic.

If anything that temporary desertion had strengthened their love. 'There's nothing like giving yourself a good fright to make you come to your senses,' Ritchie had said. 'When I realized I might have lost you for ever, that was the end of it.'

'You like your pool,' Ritchie said now. His bathing shorts were dry. Except for a cursory dip they would remain so. He wasn't fond of swimming, but he professed to take a Nero-like pleasure in watching Anna in the water.

'Yes.' She smiled up at him. 'It's more than just swimming. Water round me, sliding through my fingers, wallowing in the stuff. It's an emotional release.'

'I don't need it.' His eyes were hidden behind his sunglasses. His beautiful eyes, she thought, his painter's eyes, missing nothing.

'It's because you're a lazy devil. You don't know the meaning of stress. You don't need any emotional release.'

'I get it in its proper place. Bed.'

'You old goat. What about your painting?'

'That's a tussle with life, how to express . . . its meaning.' He laughed. He hated discussing his motives. The juices ran out in words, he said. 'But when it comes right, when you solve it, it's as good as bed.'

'Then we're both happy.' In a sudden little burst of joy she swam away from him in her fast methodical crawl, covering the length of the pool twice before she came back to him.

It was early September but the sky was already purple-blue with heat. She wouldn't go to Barcelona today. This was too delicious. In Glasgow already the trees in the Botanic Gardens near their house would be looking tired, there might be a snell wind. 'Has the post come yet, Ritchie?' She stood breast-high in the water underneath him, her arms outstretched, moving them slowly, turning her hands like the blades of oars.

'I don't know. Would you like me to go and see?'

'Would you? I'm expecting a letter from Van telling me how Sam got on at school.'

'She'll miss him. He filled her day. Housekeeping was never Van's strong point. I think she helps Bessie out of kindness. She can't bear being waited on.'

'I'm like Mother. I can. Bessie knows where she stands. There's no servility in her. She's part of us.'

She swam away from him, under the water this time. Down there, swimming level with the blue tiles, you could imagine yourself in a tropical sea. They should go to the Caribbean sometime, but they

9

couldn't spare the time. The nearest she had got to underwater interest was swimming amongst the lobster pots in nearby Calella, a strange sub-world of green fronds and rocks and the giant shapes of the wicker cages.

She emerged to see Ritchie waving a letter. 'From Van, and I've got one from Mish. I wonder if he's married that girl yet?'

'You're like a fussy mother,' she said, climbing out to take her daughter's letter and subsiding on a lounge chair with a towel round her shoulders. 'Karin's not pushing him. I wonder how Sam got on . . .' She was opening the envelope as she spoke.

'Dear Mother,' she read. Even the handwriting was awkward. Van was left-handed, what Bessie called 'corry-fisted', and she couldn't write in a straight line because of her myopia or astigmatism or a combination of both.

'Did Sam cry?' Ritchie said, looking up from his letter. 'Mish has a Rothko on show in his gallery. Good for him!'

'Marvellous.' Mish was shrewd. If it wasn't a Rothko it would be a Léger. You could bet on Mish. 'No, *she* did.' Anna looked up from her perusal of the letter. 'Eb's dead.' The bluntness of what she'd just said shook her. She noticed her hand trembling. 'Dead. Can you believe it? She's had a letter from his sister, that girl Adelaide.'

'Poor soul. He never got much out of life.'

'I've known some people with polio who got quite a lot. I see them at that home in Cardonald I visit. Cheerful. Helping each other.'

'Hard-hearted Hannah. You never liked him.'

'It's no good pretending. Maybe his illness made

10

him selfish, but he took from Van all the time, then threw her out when she was pregnant.'

'Van left him.'

'He didn't want to know about the baby. He couldn't take the responsibility. Well, don't let's go into it. It's over and done with.'

'She'll feel this badly. I wish we'd been at home.'

'Yes, I wish we had.' Anna felt her eyes fill with tears. She remembered that time she'd gone up to London from Renton to see Van and found her living with Eb Carradine. She hadn't liked him then, in spite of her sympathy for his condition. He'd asked for that sympathy with his whining remarks, his quick change to ingratiation, his huge melon smile.

Most of all she had disliked how he had treated Van as a servant. 'Couldn't you have bought some wine, Vanny? I'm sure your mother is used to wine at dinner. A nice lady like her.' Melon smile. Greasy plaits. She was ashamed now of her too-perfect politeness during that visit. 'He hadn't much of a life,' she said, keeping her face averted. 'I wish we could have done something for him.' She was glad when she looked up and saw Manuel with his friend, Juan, coming through the garden towards them.

She got up, welcoming the intrusion, and as she threw her robe around her, used the end of the belt to dash across her eyes. 'Just in time for drinks! Are you going to swim?'

'No, thank you,' Manuel said. Each of them kissed her cheek in turn. 'Juan's been shopping for a special occasion. He likes me with him to advise him, although I do not take any part in the cooking.'

'Wise man,' Ritchie said. He was already pouring out drinks for them. 'Sherry with ice?' They nodded.

'Some day, Juan,' Anna said, 'I want you to write

11

out a book of recipes. It would go like a bomb, you know. Most people think the Spanish eat only paellas.'

'What's the special occasion?' Ritchie asked.

'Look at his eyes, like a sheep,' Manuel laughed. 'To celebrate this last mural of yours, of course! It's the best yet. Each year I say this man is at his peak and then he surprises us again.'

'You nearly gave me up when I had that block, remember?'

'Ah, yes. There were extenuating circumstances.' His eyes slid away from Anna's. 'May we expect you on Sunday?'

'Yes, thank you,' Anna said. 'I'm sure Sunday's all right. But we might go home earlier this time. I'll phone Van tonight. We've had a letter from her this morning. Sam's father has died.'

'That is very sad. She has great sensitivity, that daughter of yours. She doesn't express it through her hands like you two, but her heart is tender.'

'Nevertheless,' Juan said in his prim voice – privately Anna and Ritchie called him 'Mrs Folguera' – 'it's tidier. She now knows where she stands.'

'Everything relates to housekeeping with Juan.' Manuel smiled fondly at him.

'Perhaps. But now there is a space in her life. When one door shuts another opens. You know that saying?'

'Yes, it's universal,' Anna said. 'You may be right, Juan.'

'Is it a large party, Manual?' Ritchie asked. He loved parties, he adored being deprecating about his work.

'Quite large. And why not? You are a large painter. Maria will be there with her new man.' There was a

12

hint of mischief in his eyes, in his folded plump cheeks. 'Some industrial magnate from Madrid where her daughter goes to school. That child will break hearts. She's quite beautiful.'

'Just like Maria?' Anna said. Manuel looked at her in appreciation and they laughed together. Juan smiled primly and Ritchie busied himself with the ice bucket.

Manuel's parties were always enjoyable affairs. The space and lack of furniture in his salon enabled it to accommodate up to fifty people with ease. There were hardly any seats except several large sofas, but the marble ledges beneath the windows were strewn with cushions, and for those who wanted to lounge there were the chairs round the pool.

It was there that Anna met Maria with a portly middle-aged man, possibly in his fifties. His teeth flashed as he spoke. He wore a white dinner jacket and had a broad gold band on his finger, set with a large diamond.

'Ah, Anna!' Maria never changed. She was a few years younger than Anna, her complexion was flawless, her heavy gold hair still immaculate, the same exquisite smallness and neatness, a work of art in a jade-green dress, backless, almost frontless. Her smile had become more effusive since her affair with Ritchie six years ago. They had both agreed, without discussion, to ignore it. Anna could afford to be generous. 'As beautiful as ever.'

'I can return the compliment, Maria.' They kissed. This is a different lass from the Glasgow girl in her twenties, Anna thought, observing herself. It was brittle, but it was fun, a pantomime. And she had grown to like Maria. Underneath the little girl appearance there was a shrewd woman who had to be admired, and who had a sense of humour.

'I've been so looking forward to introducing you to my friend, Señor Bellido. He has been anxious to meet you.'

Señor Bellido bowed and kissed Anna's hand. She smiled at him. 'It's usually my husband people want to meet.'

'In my case I like to see the power behind the throne. Besides, Maria has been telling me you are quite as gifted, but in another direction.'

'Oh, I'm just a craftswoman. I work in pewter, mostly.'

'This has interested me very much when Maria has told me.' He narrowed his eyes. 'I have several . . . outlets in Madrid. I like unusual pieces. Anything English, you understand.'

'I'm Scottish, but the work I've been doing for the past few years has a Spanish influence. I tag along with Ritchie, you see.' She laughed.

'"Tag along"? I like it.' He turned to Maria. 'You know that expression?'

'Yes. It means "follow at his heels".' Her pale coral mouth rose at one corner.

'Ah, I see. A perfect union. Isn't that really beautiful? An example we should follow.'

'I think it may be the Scottish temperament, Largo. Steadfast against all onslaughts.'

'Maria has a sense of humour, señor,' Anna said. The two women smiled at each other. I like you, Anna thought. The sign of maturity. I can like this woman who was in bed often with my husband and made me frantic with jealousy.

Some other guests joined them, people whom Anna knew slightly through Ritchie, the cognoscenti.

14

While she laughed and chatted she had a sudden wish to be with Jean in her stone house in Kirkcudbright, sitting at the fire talking their heads off. 'I'll leave you two to have a good chinwag,' John would have said, going off with his doctor's bag, a little more worn each year, but happy in his life and his wife. Anna felt a wave of homesickness.

Three

Van had found something she was good at. She had, in her own opinion, so few accomplishments, that she was proud of her driving competence. It was as if her diffident nature left her when she sat at the wheel of a car. She became, it seemed, a different Van, an assured young woman. She always took care to dress to suit the occasion, a suede jacket, sometimes a checked tweed skirt, sometimes trousers, a good silk blouse, a scarf tied round her hair, her face made up.

She was following the tendency on the distaff side of her family to paint their faces. It had probably started with Granny Rose, living up to her name, but Aunt Nancy, Aunt Jean and Van's mother had followed her example. It helped your morale, she had found; even garage men were different.

Men were generally critical of women in cars, especially garage men. The only one who didn't take up attitudes was her father. Ritchie rejoiced in any accomplishments of his women, especially those which were generally considered to be in a man's domain. He was lost in admiration that Van could change a wheel.

When her mother had telephoned from Barcelona and offered to come home, the idea had struck.

16

'Thanks, Mother, but, honestly I'm all right. And since you said I was to be sure and use your car, I've just had the idea of going to Aunt Jean's for a few days. Sam's school has been closed down because of measles.'

She thought Anna had sounded relieved. There was a man whom she had met who was interested in her work. He came from Madrid. It seemed quite an opportunity. Don't dream of missing it, then, Van had said. She was proud of her clever parents. Besides, she knew Anna had never approved of Eb, and it might have tried her honesty to mourn with her daughter, at least, overtly.

Now, driving through the placid autumnal countryside en route for Kirkcudbright, she was philosophical. Eb was dead. No more bitter tears. And Sam, the good thing that had come out of that relationship, was sitting beside her, his eyes bright and watchful. He loved being driven in 'the motor' – Bessie's word. Besides it gave him a chance to tell Van all about his first week at school.

'Do you like the other boys and girls?' she asked him.

'Yes, Charlie's the nicest. He said he would bash Graham for me.'

'What for?'

'Graham said I was a nigger. What's a nigger, Mummy?'

'It's a silly name. Don't pay any attention to him and he'll soon stop it.'

'Will I tell the teacher?'

'No, don't clipe.' 'Tell-tale-tit, your tongue shall be slit . . .' the children at her old school used to sing. English children wouldn't have heard of the word 'cliping.' 'To be classed as a clipe at school,' she remembered Anna warning her when she lived in Renton, 'was the worst possible thing.'

'Is it like nigger brown? Bessie's got a skirt that she says is nigger brown.'

'In a way. Have you heard of Martin Luther King?' She knew he was too young. He looked bored.

'I don't want to hear.' He put his hands to his ears.

'It won't take long. In the south of the United States of America – your Uncle Mish lives in the north – the children who haven't white skins aren't allowed to travel in the same buses. Dr King was a good man, and he didn't like this . . .' She decided to stop. He was only five. When you had an only child you were inclined to burden them with concepts which took an adult to understand. She said in a bright voice, 'Look, is that a deer racing across that field?'

His head popped up. 'Yes, it is! It is!' He jumped up and down in the seat beside her. 'I've seen it in my picture book. Wait till I tell Granny and Grandpa! A real deer, with horns!'

'Antlers they're called.'

'Antlers,' he repeated, 'horns with branches.'

'This is Robert the Bruce country,' she said. 'Do you remember Granny's song, "Scots wha' hae . . ."'

'She learned me it.' He sang loudly, '"Scots wha' hae, Scots wha' hae . . .".'

'"Wi' Wallace bled." When you're older I'll tell you the story. Or maybe Miss Clewes will tell you at school. It's about Robert the Bruce and William Wallace fighting the English in battle.'

'Did my father fight in a battle?'

'He wasn't able to fight. He wasn't well enough. He was in a wheelchair most of the time.'

'Was that why he didn't come to see us?'

'In a way.' She had better change the conversation,

18

first race and colour, now Eb, who had never wanted to be a father. She fumbled in the glove compartment, brought out a chocolate bar and gave it to him. 'Don't get it all over yourself. Dainty little bites. Look! Do you see that big bird sailing in the sky? It's called a kite.'

He peered. 'It's floating, not sailing. Why are you crying, Mummy? I can see a big tear.'

'It's something in my eye.'

Aunt Jean and Uncle John gave them their usual warm welcome. 'You don't mind me coming on such short notice?' she asked Jean.

'Mind? And why should I mind when it means that I get a chance to see this fine big schoolboy as well?'

Aunt Jean was as beautiful as ever. Her hair had a wing of grey now, but she still wore it loose with a band. Her face was thinner, which made her eyes look larger. She looked like an artist, a Rossetti woman. That was Father's expression.

Uncle John was thinner too. He worked too hard although Alastair, his daughter Sarah's husband, was there to help him now. Mother said John was a work-horse, and if he weren't careful he would die in harness like his father, old Dr Whitbread. 'If I were Jean I'd make him slow down,' she had said, and Ritchie had smiled at her. 'It suits her. She's just as busy herself.'

Jean was a well-known painter now, more fey than Father, 'a chip off the renowned Glasgow Girls,' he had said, 'like your mother.' 'I'm not in the same street as Jean,' Anna had said. 'Mine is a lesser discipline.' She deferred to her twin sister in artistic prowess.

Over tea, Jean said, 'I'll say how sorry I am about

19

Sam's father and that's about it. I only knew him at second-hand from Anna.'

'Have you finished, Sam?' she said. The boy was moving restlessly in his chair. 'On you go, then, and see the goldfish in the kitchen. They're waiting for you to feed them.' Sam got down and trotted away.

'He'll like that.' Van kept her head lowered. 'Maybe Mother was glad . . . that Eb had died.'

'Don't say that!' Jean's eyes flashed at her. 'Your mother did her best. Her heart ached often. She told me. She castigated herself.'

'I didn't know that. But I loved him, Aunt Jean. It was when he didn't want the baby that I had to go away. He depended on me, but he didn't want me to be dependent on him in any way.'

'You did your best.' Jean never harangued. 'More tea?'

'Yes, thank you.'

'You knew about Frederick Kleiber, who was my tutor at the Art School?' She lifted the teapot.

'Yes, Mother told me. Oh, I've suddenly realized . . . I have Sam, but your child, *his* child, was born dead.'

'That's it.' She passed Van her cup. Her face was calm, her eyes dark. 'That's the way of things. But when I married John we had Sarah and Roderick, and that made up.' She shrugged and smiled. Her eyes didn't reflect the smile. 'But I can see now that our . . . affair, Frederick's and mine, might not have lasted anyhow. I don't think he was the faithful kind like John. And he was married. He never knew about the baby. He died before –' Sam came rushing in.

'Where's the packet of food, Aunt Jean?' He was jumping about with excitement. 'Where's the –'

Jean got up. 'I'm a silly soul. Come and I'll get it.'

Van followed them into the kitchen where Jean was showing him how to feed the goldfish. 'Not too much, Sam. If you give Goldie the whole packet he'll burst, and Roderick would be annoyed. They're all his.'

'How is Roderick, by the way?' Van had coached Sam in the car. She was proud of him. 'By the way' was his own addition.

Jean spoke seriously, smoothing his hair. 'It's very kind of you to ask, Sam. He's doing quite well at school, thank you.'

'Does he learn good things at his school?'

'Yes, a lot. Carpentry, and gardening, and he's good at sports.'

'He's very old to be at school.'

'Well, it's a special school. He lives there. I tell you what. Tomorrow we could go and see him after we've seen Sarah's little baby. You'd like that, wouldn't you?'

'I'm not keen on babies. They cry a lot. Mummy was crying in the car, like a baby.' He giggled. 'But I'd like to go and see Roderick. He lifts me up and *burls* me, whoosh! Round and round!'

'Yes, he's strong.'

When Jean looks like a Madonna she's saddest, Van thought. Who wouldn't be sad if they had a mongol son of twenty-three years of age incarcerated in a home?

'Off to bed, then, Sam,' Van said, getting up. 'You're going to have a busy day tomorrow.'

It was about nine o'clock when John came in. Jean never ate until he arrived, but she had regaled Van and herself with sherry. The difference between Aunt Jean and Mother, Van thought, is that I find it easier to talk to Jean. She voiced this when they were both

21

feeling mellow on their second glass. 'Why do you think it is?'

'A step away. I can be more objective, and also you know that I wouldn't pass on what you and I say to each other. Although,' she smiled, 'sometimes I think Anna knows. We're very close, always have been.'

'She was glad I was coming. She had someone to see who might be buying her work.'

'That's what she would say. She would know you had to talk about Eb, and she feels badly about him. Underneath that hard shell of hers she's as soft as butter. Tell me, are you planning your future, now that Sam's at school?'

'I'll try to get a job. I want to work with deprived children – or adults, for that matter. I haven't any skills.'

'You have compassion, that's better.'

'Maybe. If I got anything that would keep Sam and me, I'd like to move out of Clevedon Crescent. I *take* all the time. I want to be independent.'

'Well, that's not a bad thing to be. But don't rush it. Remember, Sam comes first.' She turned as the door opened, her face lighting up. 'John! Did you have a hell of a day?' She got up and kissed him.

'One hell of a day.'

The two sisters were lucky, Van thought. Both had husbands who adored them. Father and Mother still behaved like lovers, making her feel like an interloper. Sometimes she heard stifled laughter coming from their studios upstairs, and mother's face would be flushed when she came down. Once when there was a loud, what Bessie called a 'dunt' on her kitchen ceiling, Bessie had looked up from her ironing and said to Van, 'There's some hanky-panky going on up there!' She had smiled and shaken her head, 'What a pair!'

'Tomorrow afternoon we're going to see Roderick, darling,' Jean said. 'Would you like to have lunch with Sarah? I'll phone and ask her.'

'Of course. I'd like to have a *snack* with them. They don't have much. Sarah says it's better for Alastair's digestion.'

'She's determined to make him live for ever,' Jean said, 'now that he's a daddy.' Lucky Sarah, Van thought, with a husband who was willing to assume his responsibilities. Or was it that she had chosen wisely, like Mother and Aunt Jean?

But there had been good times with Eb when they had gone to bed together and she had helped him to love her in the way he wanted. 'Don't worry,' he had said, 'I couldn't make a girl pregnant if I tried . . .'

At half-past ten, when they were having coffee at the sitting room fire, there was a knock at the door.

'Don't tell me a patient has had the nerve to come at this time of night,' Jean said. She looked at John. The firelight was playing on her warm dusky skin, a shade lighter than Sam's, her eyes were beautiful, brilliant, deep blue. Wise.

'Sit tight,' John said. He got up and went out.

They heard voices in the hall, another man's voice, then the sound of the study door shutting.

'I hope it isn't a poor wife who's gone into labour,' Jean said. 'That's one thing you can't time.'

After a few moments they heard John's voice and the other one in the hall again, then the outside door closing. There was a pause, silence, and Van felt a creeping apprehension under her skin as she waited. The door opened, and John stood there, determinedly unaffected. It didn't come off. She saw his eyes.

23

'Now, don't get alarmed, Jean. They can't find Roderick. That was the police. It looks as if he's run away.'

Jean was on her feet. 'When did they miss him?'

'At supper time. Six thirty. They've searched the grounds thoroughly.'

'It's eleven o'clock! We must go right away! Help them to look . . .' Her voice broke. 'Oh, silly, *silly* boy!'

'Try not to worry too much. He's mischievous, doesn't think. He'll have gone for a walk.'

Jean turned to Van, speaking as if to calm herself. 'He gets bored, you know. Who wouldn't with that régime? John,' she wheeled back to him, 'we must go. Right away.'

'Yes, of course we'll go. We'll have to see the matron. They have three policemen searching. Mac-Pherson assured me they would find him soon.'

'I'll get your coat, Aunt Jean,' Van said. 'Maybe you'll find him back when you get to Dumfries.'

'Will you phone Sarah?' John asked her. 'Alastair will have to cover for me.'

'I'll do that.' When she came back with Jean's coat, she was standing in John's arms. She turned to Van, 'I'm quite hopeful, really.' Her face was anything but hopeful. 'I know Roddy. He's mischievous, easily bored . . .'

'He'll be there when you get to the home. You'll see.' She helped her on with her coat. 'On you go.'

She saw them out and went straight to the telephone. She and Sarah would have to stay put, Sarah with a new baby, she with Sam asleep upstairs. She tried to be cheerful when she heard Sarah's voice. Sarah was the same as always.

'He's up to his tricks again. Poor Mother . . .'

24

Four

Jean didn't weep as they drove the thirty miles to Dumfries, but her tension was obvious in her continual smoking. One cigarette succeeded another until the interior of the car was like a Glasgow fog. Her eyes stung, John coughed.

'I know how you feel, Jean,' he said. 'Someone like Roderick is always special to his mother. But don't forget I share it. I've a feeling we're going to find him sitting with the matron with that cheeky grin on his face.'

'If she punishes him I'll kill her! I'm sorry Mr and Mrs Walker are no longer there. Their son, Jimmy, had Down's syndrome, and they made it a home rather than an institution. Her voice changed. 'If it hadn't been for that bugger, Tim Logan . . .'

'Jean!'

'That's what he is. Threatening to make a court case out of Roderick indulging in a bit of horseplay with that precious Alice of theirs.'

She noticed John's silence, because she knew in her heart that the incident had been more than horseplay. At seventeen Roderick's sexuality had got the better of him. She would never forget that Christmas Eve at the Logans' when Anna had been in Tim Logan's study, and they had heard the girl's terrified cries, 'Mummy, Mummy! Come quickly! Roderick's hurting me!' The only good thing about that episode was that it had interrupted her father's leering advances towards Anna.

She tried to speak calmly. 'Of course, neither of us is stupid. No one knows the power of sex better than I do . . .' Long ago, in that dark wood, their bodies bared, paired, exulting in each other. And afterwards, sitting in that boat in the quiet loch, looking at the beauty of Frederick, her lover, looking, although she didn't know it, for the last time . . .

He didn't comment, changed the subject. 'Still, it must be difficult to be in charge of young adults. But I can tell you now, Jean,' the darkness of the car loosened his tongue, 'I've often worried about him being incarcerated with other young men, but I've tried to keep my mind open. And although you may not think it, I know as much about the power of sex as you do.'

'I'm sorry. I know you do. But the régime has been stricter with Mrs Lawson. She keeps them busy. All their free time is carefully controlled. I don't know how he managed to get away. Oh,' her voice rose, 'do you think he'll be trying to make his way home? Shouldn't we be scanning the road all the time?'

'I *have* been. Were they ever taken for walks further afield, do you think?'

'I know there were organized expeditions and picnics.'

'He'd keep off the roads. He's not daft, our Roderick.'

'No, he's not daft.' She sighed, 'Just not so wise. And unlucky.'

'Ten to one we'll find him back when we get there. Just you wait and see.'

But they didn't. Mrs Lawson, a stern-faced woman of about sixty, was determined not to be blamed.

'It's distressing for you, I know, but I can assure you he's been happy under my dictum. I've always been strict, but fair.'

'We know that.'

'He was popular too, not good with his hands, but he made them all laugh with his antics. He had a happy nature.'

'He *still* has, Mrs Lawson.'

The woman bristled. 'Oh, I wasn't inferring, Mrs Whitbread, but he was, is, one for practical jokes. Quite a card, really.' Her thin smile expressed reluctant admiration. 'He even made *me* laugh.'

That would be difficult, Jean thought. Mrs Lawson had the hatchet face which deserved the cliché-ridden adjective.

'You've searched the house thoroughly?' John asked. 'The attics, for instance?'

'Every inch, Doctor. And everywhere in the grounds. It's my belief he'll turn up for his breakfast tomorrow morning as right as rain and think of it as a good joke. That's the trouble wi' they yins,' her polite diction failed her for a moment, 'no real sense in them, if you'll excuse me saying it.'

John persuaded Jean to go home with him after they had sat until two in the morning. Mr Mac-Pherson, the policeman in charge of the search, had come back to the home and said they had called it off for an hour or two until dawn.

'Have you looked in the general direction of Kirk-cudbright?' Jean asked him. Her face was drawn, her beauty gone.

'Oh, yes,' he assured her, 'and all round for a cir-cumference of ten miles or so. If I were you I'd go back with the doctor and snatch a few hours of sleep yourself, then maybe you'll find your worries are over.'

John put his arm round her. 'Mr MacPherson's right, Jean. We mustn't be selfish. We're keeping Mrs Lawson out of her bed as well. She has the other inmates to think of.'

They didn't talk much on the way home. Jean was slumped beside him, exhausted with anxiety. When he drew up beside the house, he said, 'Come on, then. I'll tuck you up in bed then bring you a cup of tea.'

'You're good to me,' she said, getting out. 'I don't deserve it. But the worry, John, the terrible anxiety, in case . . .'

'He's my son, too, remember.' He put his arm round her as they went into the hall and guided her towards the staircase.

The next day passed somehow. Mercifully Sam had found an old tricycle of Roderick's in a shed outside, and he occupied himself in cycling up and down the drive, incessantly ringing the bell. Van stayed beside Jean, trying her best to reassure her by remaining calm herself.

At lunchtime Mrs Lawson telephoned. They hadn't found Roderick.

Jean's face ran with tears as she turned to Van. 'I can't bear this any more. I'll have to go and see.'

'Right,' Van said, 'let's get the car out. I'll drive you.' John had been called out to an urgent case.

'It's my fault.' Jean was making no effort to wipe away the tears. 'I gave in to having him incarcerated at that home. If I hadn't let Tim Logan hold a knife to my throat . . .'

'You weren't to know Roderick would set off on

his own like that. He's never done it before, remember. But we'll have a good talk with Mrs Lawson, find out exactly what's going on.'

'She hasn't a good heart like Mrs Walker. But that doesn't exonerate me, nor John. He should have stood up to Tim Logan at the time. He's too bland, too forgiving.' Everyone was being blamed. She was no longer weeping.

Van helped her into a jacket which hung in the hall. It was like dressing an infant. This was not the positive Aunt Jean whom she knew. She was certainly in no fit state to drive. Then it was Sam's turn to be persuaded to get off the tricycle and come with them. They had decided they would leave him with Sarah.

'I'm not into babies,' he said, looking obstinate.

'You'll get into them when you see this one.' She coaxed him into the back seat. Jean was already in the front, silent, tense, waiting for her to start.

'We'll be there in no time,' Van said, getting in beside her. She didn't reply. She was twisting her hands in her lap.

The continuing tenseness still puzzled Van, even allowing for the circumstances. But as she drove she remembered her mother once saying, 'It's the old story with Jean and Roderick. The sickly lamb.' And at the time she had thought of the illustrated cards she used to collect for good attendance at Sunday School. There had been one of Jesus holding a lamb, and the tender expression had moved her. And there was Blake's 'Little Lamb, who made thee?'

They stopped at what was still known as 'the doctor's house'. John had lived there before he married Jean, now Alastair and Sarah were happy and busy there with their small family. It was a stern double-fronted villa with a surgery tacked on to its side and an ugly cement path leading to the door flanked by rhododendron bushes.

Sarah didn't seem to mind its lack of charm. She was a practical, level-headed girl, like her father in temperament and looks with her sandy hair and nut-brown eyes. And with his charming smile, Van thought, when Sarah opened the door to them. She put her arms round Jean immediately in a warm hug.

Jean said apologetically, 'This is me, Sarah, going to pieces. Anything to do with Roderick . . .'

'Don't you worry. You know Roderick. He'll turn up like a bad penny. He'll have curled up somewhere and gone to sleep. They'll soon find him.'

Sam had been led away on a tour of the house by Sandy, aged three. 'They'll go to Janet in the surgery,' Sarah said. 'Sandy loves washing bottles.'

Jean was more cheerful when they left. 'I'm blessed with Sarah,' she said. 'She has the same calming influence as John has. And that marriage of hers with Alastair was made in heaven.'

A girl like Sarah would never make the wrong choice, Van thought. What did she think of *her* unmarried state? And then she remembered the sympathy she had shown when Van had told her of Eb's death. 'Life hasn't been easy for you.'

She wondered now, driving towards Dumfries, if circumstances were ruled by temperament, rather than the other way round. Her adolescence had been turbulent, certainly from her mother's point of view. From her own it had seemed for the most part like trying to come to terms with all the sadness in the world, and at times it had overwhelmed her.

She said to Jean, 'When we get back to the house I

think you should phone Mother. She'll want to know what's happening.'

'Yes, I know. I was hoping I would have good news. You know what Anna's like. She would drop everything and come straight here, and I don't want her to do that.'

'She'll be more upset if you don't tell her.'

'It's a wonder she hasn't guessed.' Her expression lightened. 'We could always tell what the other was thinking. Mother had the daft idea that twins should share a bedroom, twin beds and all that,' she gave an unexpected giggle, 'although as you know there was plenty of room. Nancy was in solitary state. She said she always felt left out. Oh, yes, there's a strong bond. We knew it, tried to deny it by refusing to be dressed the same . . .'

Van encouraged her to talk. 'I expect you told each other all your secrets.'

'About men? Yes, but I kept dark about Frederick Kleiber because I knew she would say I was being stupid. But it didn't stop me. I went ahead, and we loved . . . and he drowned, and I had his baby . . . and it died. I would have died too if it hadn't been for Anna. For a time I only lived on her strength.'

'She was the same with me when I got pregnant. And she didn't like Eb, never liked any of my friends. They both sustained me – Mother with her clear-cut intelligence thought I'd been stupid; Father would have loved me if I'd robbed a bank.'

'Men just love regardless, if they're any good. When I told Anna I was pregnant she decided we should tell my father first and then let him break the news to Mother. We went to his office in St Vincent Place, the two daughters of the boss. He had a frump-ish secretary and she was all admiration. If only she knew, I thought. I'll never forget his face. The blood drained out of it, and with it his youth. I've often thought that was the beginning of his heart trouble. He was a fine man, your grandpa, a true Highlander, reticent, mystic. Sometimes I think you're a bit like him.'

'I wonder if he liked William Blake too.'

'He wasn't a great reader – I don't know – but he could draw like an angel.'

'That's where you and Mother get your gift. It's escaped me. Looking back I see now that I felt inferior. Mish was like them. Perhaps that's why I was a rebel. But I was looking for something, the truth, maybe.'

They had arrived. 'Well, here we are.' She glanced at Jean and saw that all her anxiety had returned. She fumbled with the door of the car, and Van went quickly round and opened it for her. She half fell out in her haste.

'Don't complicate things by breaking your leg,' Van said.

'Cheek.' She gave Van an affectionate, quivering smile.

Mrs Lawson stood at the open door. She must have seen them arriving. One look was enough. 'I'm sorry, Mrs Whitbread. There's no news yet. Didn't the police telephone you?'

'Yes, they did earlier – or I telephoned them, one or the other. But I was hoping there might be . . . or he . . .' Her voice faltered.

'Come in and have a seat for a minute. You look worn out.'

'Yes, thanks, Mrs Lawson, we will have a seat for a minute. We'd like to know the expeditions the boys are taken on, routes, that sort of thing . . .'

The woman felt Jean's eyes on her. She ushered them in, talking as she did so. 'We have voluntary helpers who take them, of course. In here please.' She opened the door of her sitting room, and after she had seated them she rang a bell on her desk. In a minute or two a young girl came in. 'Tea please, Annie,' she said crisply.

'Yes, Mrs Lawson. Tea for three.'

Jean spoke immediately she had left the room. 'Do you think those voluntary helpers could tell us anything?'

'They've *been* questioned.' The woman looked down her nose.

'I just wondered if we could see the one who was in charge the day Roderick . . .'

'It was Mr Peters. He was taking them bird-watching. The boys make far too much noise, he says, they scare the birds, but he hopes *some* of them might take an interest.'

The girl came in with the tray and put it on Mrs Lawson's desk. 'Is that all, Mrs Lawson?'

'Thank you, Annie. Would you see if Mr Peters is on the premises?'

'Oh, he is! It was his day, but the police said . . .' She looked at Jean with sympathy. 'I'm that sorry about your lad. We all liked Roderick.'

'Annie!' Mrs Lawson frowned. 'Mr Peters, please.'

They were having their tea when there was a knock at the door and a middle-aged man came in. He looked puny, but spry in his movements as he came forward to shake hands when he was introduced. 'No tea, thanks, Mrs Lawson.' He refused her offer when she had given him a seat. 'I don't drink the stuff. Bad for the liver.' He turned to Jean. 'This must be a very anxious time for you, Mrs Whitbread. I'm sure it will turn out all right in the end. He's a strong, healthy young man, Roderick, the leader of the pack. But he'd frighten the birds off the trees from here to the Isle of Man with the racket he kicks up.' He laughed at his little joke.

'I suppose you've told the police all you know?' Jean's smile was half-hearted.

'Oh, yes.' He produced a map. 'I brought this. Do you mind, Mrs Lawson?' He spread it out on the table, and beckoned to Jean and Van who got up and bent over it. 'Here's where we stopped,' he said, pointing. 'About four miles out of Dumfries. I parked the brake in the lay-by and we all walked up the lane on the left. We didn't cross the road. It's too busy and some of them can't be trusted.' He gave Van and Jean a quick look. 'I know the special thickets where the birds are to be found, and I gave them picture cards of the particular ones we were looking for. But they get bored soon, that's the trouble, push each other about. You have to be quite strict with them. You'll bear me out, Mrs Lawson?'

'Kindness and firmness.' She nodded.

A thought struck Van. 'Did Roderick always stay with the others?'

The man laughed. 'Roderick! Here today and gone tomorrow. He liked to hide and then pop up and frighten them. You know how he laughed. My, he enjoyed himself! He used to appear suddenly from behind a bush, his thumbs in his ears, waggle his fingers and yell, "I'm a magpie!" or some such non-sense, hop about. He didn't like being told off. He became sullen, trailed behind us. He was like a bad wean.' His Dumfries accent highlighted the words. Jean turned her head away quickly as if the picture disturbed her too much.

34

You had to remember, Van thought, that Roderick wasn't a child, he was a young man of twenty-three, who could appear suave and grown-up with his polite phrases one minute, and revert to childhood with his unruly behaviour the next. It was his lack of consistency, the randomness of his thinking which was typical of his affliction.

When she had been at school at Renton she had worked in her spare time in a similar home to this, generally during her school holidays. There had been two boys with Down's syndrome who were also paraplegics, much worse than Roderick. She remembered trying to convey to Ritchie how she felt about them, 'as if I were bleeding inside,' she had said, and going on although feeling embarrassed, 'until, one day, under the grimaces and head-turnings I saw . . . their soul . . . looking out at me, a kind of beauty.'

Ritchie had understood. He had nodded. 'Yes, truth, beauty, one and the same.' Mother had never gone further than compassion, except where her sister was concerned. She listened again to Mr Peters talking to Jean.

'. . . and then Donald said to me, "Sir, we've lost Roderick!" I was dumbfounded. I'd been telling the boys about different birds as we walked along, and getting them to pick flowers and try to identify them, and when Donald said that I realized I hadn't *heard* Roderick for some time. It was quieter.

'Well,' he looked smug, 'I think I acted quite correctly, Mrs Whitbread. We stood together, I counted, "One! Two! Three!" and then we all shouted his name at the top of our voices. They were laughing, they thought it was a game. I daren't leave them to go and look for myself or I should have had more than one missing lad on my hands. Wilful, they are, very wilful. Usually when I get home I say to the wife, "I'm ready for a rest, Dora, after that."'

Jean looked impatient. 'So you gave up shouting, eventually?'

'Yes, I had to. We retraced our steps towards the main road, calling out his name every few minutes, then I bundled them into the brake and drove back as quickly as I could to report to Mrs Lawson. I couldn't have done anything else, could I?' He looked reproachfully at Jean.

'So you don't know how long you'd been walking without Roderick?' Jean asked.

'Not really. But as soon as the police came I went back with them and showed them exactly where we'd been. They searched the area thoroughly. I helped them. You can imagine how anxious I was. In my care . . .'

'Of course. You stuck to one side of the road?'

'Oh, definitely. As I said, we walked up the lane on the left from the lay-by. The boys were always being warned about traffic. The cars go so quickly, and some of them are deaf.'

Van said to Jean, 'Do you think there's anything else, Aunt Jean?'

She turned her anguished glance at her. 'I've been trying to put myself in Roderick's place.'

No one knew Roderick better than his mother, Van thought, how his mind worked. She had given him constant loving care all his life. 'How far, for instance, could he walk?' Van prompted Jean. 'Was he a good walker?'

'When it suited him.' She looked at Mr Peters. 'You were on the Kirkcudbright Road?'

'Yes, but only four miles out of Dumfries.'

She turned to Mrs Lawson. 'Did he ever talk about

. . . walking home, for instance, trying to get back to our house?'

'Oh no, he was happy here, I assure you.' She bridled. 'Besides, it's miles to Kirkcudbright.'

'As happy as he could be. But he was like one of your birds, Mr Peters. He couldn't have liked being caged. He was a free spirit.'

Mrs Lawson's mouth was a straight line, but Mr Peters had leaned forward, as if Jean's remark had started a train of thought. 'Strange you should say that. One of his tricks was pretending to fly. I remember that. He would open his arms like a bird and say he was going to fly away home.'

Mrs Lawson made an impatient movement in her chair. No one spoke.

In the silence Van saw Roderick clearly as a child. Performing. 'Show me what they teach you at school,' John had said, and she and Sarah had sat together trying not to giggle. It had been in the sitting room of Aunt Jean's house with its flowers and dried grasses, its Victorian prints and Mother's pewter pots.

'A song with actions!' Roderick had announced, and bowed deeply. She and Sarah pinching each other, not meeting each other's eyes. And that voice, out of tune, the soulful expression on his piggy face.

'My pigeon house . . . I open wide . . . and let the pigeons fly . . .' Arms waving, stubby hands floating. 'Mummy, Sarah's laughing . . .'

'They fly over hill . . . and then over dale . . . And light on the tallest tree . . .' Pointing dramatically, and then that terrible bit which had made she and Sarah red in the face as he skipped, lumbered, rather, round the room, arms held stiff . . .

'He loved high places,' Mr Peters said. 'It was just

a gentle slope we were walking on, but even then I remember him bounding up it like a gazelle – well, not exactly like a gazelle – and then he was gone. I can't believe it.'

'I think we'll go home now,' Jean said. 'There might be some news.' She looked at the end of her tether. As she got up her mouth was trembling. Then, remembering the man: 'Thank you very much, Mr Peters. You've been very helpful.'

'As long as you don't blame me . . .' He was also on his feet.

'No, I don't blame you. We appreciate all you've done.' It was Roderick's voice, Van suddenly thought, the polite phrases.

'It was a social commitment on my part, trying to help –'

She interrupted him. 'I understand. Thank you for the tea, Mrs Lawson.'

'I'm sure we all do our best.'

'Coming, Van?' Jean turned to her. They took their leave abruptly. There was nothing Van could do but add her thanks.

On the outskirts of Dumfries Van saw a telephone box. She stopped the car on a grassy patch beside it. 'I've an idea,' she said. Jean only looked at her. Her distress seemed to come in waves, making her unable to speak.

'I was thinking of that song of Roderick's, "My Pigeon House". He loved singing it.'

'Don't, Van.'

'I'm sorry. Do you think Sarah could cope with Sam for an hour or more?'

'Sarah copes with anything. She's like John. And she has a good woman in the kitchen. Why?'

'I don't know the district around Dumfries as well

as you do. Is there a high place, a hill, near here?'

'Nothing spectacular like Screel Hill or White Coomb but they're miles away. It's mostly gently rolling pasture land. Why?'

'I didn't want to say anything to Mr Peters, but he said Roderick loved high places. We'll drive slowly towards Kirkcudbright and see if we spot a hill, for instance. It needn't be a mountain. It's just an idea, but supposing Roderick really believed he could fly, and he looked for some high place and hid until they got tired looking for him?'

'Oh, he's not stupid! He knows he can't really fly.'

'Of course he knows *logically*, but say he skipped away on his own with that idea and hid, and got cold . . . he's very addicted to chills and catarrh, isn't he? And supposing he even got a bit delirious so that his mind wasn't working as it should, and he walked on and came across some kind of crag, for instance, and thought, if I stretch out my arms I could fly away home . . .' The words sounded desolate as she said them.

Jean looked at her. 'Mr Peters didn't say just how long he looked for Roderick. And then he had to drive back to the home, tell Mrs Lawson and wait for the police. And then go back again. That could have taken quite a time. Then night comes. You're right! Roderick runs a temperature very easily. I've always had to watch his chest. You can die of exposure, *he* could . . .' She seemed to have difficulty in breathing. 'All that time! Go and phone Sarah!'

'No, we haven't found him, Sarah,' she said in response to her anxious query, 'but we have an idea. We think Roderick might have climbed a hill near where they were taken for a walk.'

'Climbed a hill?' Sarah sounded mystified.

'The man who took them for a walk says Roderick was always pretending to be a bird. Sarah, do you remember that song with actions he used to do. "My Pigeon House"? Flapping his arms?' She heard a muffled sound at the other end.

'Yes, Van,' her voice was thick with tears, 'I remember. It's an idea . . . oh, poor wee Chink!'

'I know it sounds stupid, but we think that if there was a hill near where he went missing, he might have climbed it, and it got dark and . . .'

'You're going to look?'

'Yes, it's just an idea. I'm phoning in case you get worried. Would you tell your father . . . ?'

'Tell him what?'

She tried to be as logical as Sarah. 'I'll park the car where the walk started in a lay-by. Uncle John will see it there. And if there's a hill of any sort, say, across the road, we'll look.'

'That's good enough. Father will know it, or he can find out from the home.'

'I'll get back to your mother now. She's half-mad with worry. She's better to be doing something.' She hung up.

Five

'Here's the place Mr Peters showed us on the map,' Jean said. 'There's the lane running up to the left where he led them. You can see there's a wood further on. The police will have searched all round there.'

'But supposing he crossed the road?' Van looked at her. Jean met her glance, then put her hand on the door, 'Let's get out.'

They stood together, feeling the windstream from the traffic on their faces, holiday-makers and commuters from Dumfries hurrying home to their cottages in the pretty villages around. There was the occasional lorry.

'And there's where he might have made for.' Van pointed. 'Do you see that hill?' It rose steeply in the distance, dark with clumps of bushes and the occasional gleam of rock, an eruption in the gently undulating landscape, a freak of nature. 'Quite a distance, though.'

'But if it gave him the idea? *Your* idea about flying? He didn't think. He did everything on impulse.'

'Let's cross, then.' Van locked the car doors. 'We'll have to be careful. They come round that bend at a hell of a lick. Wait!' She put a restraining hand on Jean's arm. 'Okay, come on, run!' She felt like Jean's mother.

There was a fence surrounding the field on the other side, and they had to clamber down a ditch, then up again before they could get through it. Luckily it wasn't barbed, and they held it up for each other while they squeezed through. If an irate farmer suddenly appeared, Van thought, they would tell him the truth. It was serious now. Roderick had been missing since yesterday. He could die of exposure, especially with his weak chest. They struck diagonally across the field towards the hill.

'I feel we're on the right track,' she said to Jean, as much to reassure herself as her aunt.

'I'm going on your intuition. It's the only hill around.' They walked on. The going was easy, except for the occasional cowpat.

'It's a long way, though.'

'Oh, he's strong,' Jean said. 'A grand walker and runner. I remember us taking him to Dumfries to be measured for a new suit and the tailor said he had the physique of a man. That was for Wendy's wedding. He was only sixteen.'

'He's a handsome lad,' Van said, thinking, the pity of it . . .

The ground was beginning to slope gently upwards under their feet; they had to cross more fences, more fields. The detail of the hill became clear as they drew nearer. On the right flank there were two dense thickets separated by a bare grassy space. The hill was in fact a rocky promontory, but over the years it had been invaded by vegetation. It would be difficult to climb. They were walking doggedly now, in silence for most of the time. Was it a stupid idea to think of him remembering that old song and acting on it? But, supposing he had, would he lose his enthusiasm halfway up and curl behind one of those huge rocks jutting out like giants' stepping stones? The questions went on and on in Van's head. Was it cruel to lead Jean on what might well be a wild-goose chase?

She stole a look at her. What a beautiful woman she was in spite of the signs of suffering on her face. The deep line scored on one side of her mouth only accentuated its beauty. She had an unique quality. No wonder Mother admired her. Anna was chic, Jean was beautiful. 'I'm glad you're wearing sensible shoes,' Van said.

Jean laughed. 'Oh, you soon learn that living in the country. Anna and I were the doo's dab when we were living in Glasgow. That's one of Bessie's choicer phrases. We used to pride ourselves on our smart shoes – the fashion was for high heels and stubby toes which didn't really fit the shape of our feet. But fashion was more important than comfort. Oh, we were proper townees in our tailored suits made by mother's court dressmaker in Hillhead,' she laughed. 'Hats and gloves were *de rigueur* for smart young ladies in the thirties.' She fell silent suddenly.

'I'm a townee, but not smart.'

Jean ignored her remark. 'We should have told John what we were doing. Why didn't I think of that? He's always so thoughtful.'

'Don't worry. I told Sarah to tell him where we were.' She didn't say what she had also said to Sarah about Jean's anxiety.

It seemed as if a bond developed between them as they walked, more slowly as the ground became rougher. They had much in common, Van thought, both had had a child conceived out of wedlock, as some people still said, but she was luckier in that Sam had survived. On the other hand Jean had the compensation of a loving husband.

43

She thought of Eb when she had first met him, and how her overwhelming compassion for him had turned to love. She had liked his appearance, his shining copper-black skin, his wide smile, his tiny plaits of hair which were such a source of pride to him. She had admired his jaunty courage.

It was only as time went on that she had realized it was a front which he used to charm. He was self-pitying and selfish, ungrateful. She had forgiven him often, returning from work, tired, realizing the frustration he must feel to be confined in a wheelchair most of the time. It was not until later that she had recognized that much of the imprisonment was deliberate, a play for sympathy.

But she had forgiven him wholeheartedly until that day when she told him she was pregnant. She remembered the sulky face, the turning away of his head. 'I've enough to do to take care of myself.'

In between her shifts at the home for battered wives she had walked the streets in despair, wondering what she should do, thinking of her mother and father. They'll die if they know, she had thought, but it wasn't true, nor had it proved to be true.

'Are you tired, Jean?' she asked.

'No, no. Walking's my favourite pastime. Fresh air blows through your mind. That's how I walk up my paintings. Do you know what that means?'

She nodded, remembering how *she* had walked and walked before she'd had the courage to telephone her mother. She turned to Jean. 'You said you didn't tell anyone for five months when you were pregnant with Frederick's baby?'

'That's right.' She met her glance. 'And then only Anna. I couldn't tell Frederick. He was dead.'

'At least you couldn't know what his reaction might

have been. I had no doubt about Eb's. He told me to get the hell out, so I kept on working in the hostel. The matron soon spotted that there was "something wrong with me". Isn't that Scottish?' She laughed. 'She'd had plenty of experience. But she was quite willing for me to go on working as long as I could. She'd learned to be tolerant.'

'Compared with Sarah you do see life.'

'She's fulfilled with Alastair and the children but in my case I was the only inartistic one in a talented family. I had to find something of my own. Maybe that was why I had Sam. Something of my own.'

'I'm fond of you, Van.' Jean squeezed her arm as they walked.

'I'm fond of you.' She laughed. 'My declaration of love.'

'You're quite a girl. Remember I told you Grandpa Mackintosh was something of a mystic?'

'Yes.'

'I think you're the same. This idea of yours about Roderick wanting to fly, for instance. Children have that. I remember Anna and I trying it out after we'd been taken to see *Peter Pan* at the Alhambra. We jumped from the table! But I had a dream once that I had *soared* off the table and flew round the room. Anna was mad with jealousy!' She laughed and sighed.

They had reached the base of the hill and they stood looking upwards. Near at hand the ascent didn't look as difficult as it had seemed further away.

'There's a path running between the rocks,' Van said. 'Do you see it? Just a sheep path. What do you think, Jean? Should we start looking first, or go right up to the top?'

'I don't know.' She was white, miserable. 'I'm

afraid now, and yet I've a feeling that we'll find him. As long as he's . . .' She turned to Van. 'What do *you* think?'

'Suppose we follow the path as far as it goes? We'll keep our eyes open. It isn't so far to the top and that will be a good vantage point. We'll be able to scan the hill carefully from there.' She felt as miserable as Jean, and yet buried deep in her mind there was a sureness. This was the place. She stifled the same fear as she knew Jean had.

They looked carefully as they climbed, taking a side each. If they saw a likely rock which might have concealed Roderick, they left the path to make sure. But there were no traces. Judging by the sheep droppings they were the only creatures who ever ventured up here.

They reached the top before they realized it, and stood for a moment to get their breaths back. The wind dragged Van's hair from her scalp, and Jean, with hers flying, looked like Catherine Earnshaw. The view over the gentle Galloway landscape held their gaze for a minute or two, the smooth hollows where farms nestled, the fields dotted with sheep or cows – at any other time they would have been soothed by them. Jean left Van and walked over the grassy summit. She was soon back.

'No sign,' she said. Van nodded once. The top was only the size of a large room. There was nowhere to hide, only a cluster of small rocks like a miniature stone circle, each about a foot high.

'Let's stand and look down very carefully, going over every inch.'

They quartered the hill with their eyes. Van could see the path they had followed winding its way between the limestone rocks. From here, if they had by any chance missed Roderick on their way up, they would now be bound to see him.

'Where are the two thickets we saw from the foot?' Jean asked.

'Oh, yes. I'd forgotten.' They looked again, and both saw them at the same time, on the right flank of the hill. The path had veered away. Van turned to Jean, her premonition strong again, a sureness, almost a compulsion. 'Supposing he did try to fly. From here. From this summit. But directly above the thickets. In line with them.' She turned round. 'See where that flat stone is embedded in the grass? It would make a good taking-off place.'

Jean had turned too and now looked at Van as if infected by her sureness. 'If he did, he might roll into one of the bushes.' Her voice was suddenly strong. 'Right. You take the nearest one I'll take the lower. Come on!' She was away.

Van stood for a second watching her scrambling over the rocky scree. She looked footsure. If she twisted her ankle on top of everything . . . She began to clamber down herself, slipping and sliding, and when she got to the nearest thicket she saw Jean was still making her way down.

The clumps of bushes Van had reached were a mass of prickly thorn and brambles growing low on the scree. It was a dense, impenetrable mass. No way could someone as big as Roderick get through it, unless he had rolled there. Now the whole idea seemed ridiculous to her, but nevertheless she set herself to search thoroughly. She found no gap, no broken branches, although she poked all over with a stout piece of rotten wood she had found.

When she emerged, she looked down and saw Jean had now reached the lower thicket. She stood on a flat rock and watched her push her way into it, determination in her movements, not taking time to look up. It seemed easier in access than the thicket Van had searched, less dense although bigger. She scrambled down to join her, slipping and sliding on her hunkers until the soles of her shoes were like glass. Once she caught her foot on a trailing bramble, and nearly fell. There was an eerie silence now, she noticed, the silence of coming dusk overlaid with a sad autumnal feeling, the approach of winter. 'The sedge is wither'd from the lake, And no birds sing.' It was atmospheric, ominous.

A sudden loud cry from Jean seemed to crack Van's eardrums and echo against the rocks. Her heart shook with fear. Jean never screamed like that. Her voice was pitched too low.

'Van! I've found him! I've found him . . . found him . . . found him . . .' A kite, disturbed, wheeled in the sky and sailed away.

She fell several times in her hurry to reach Jean. She ran crouched, once she tripped over a projecting rock and felt a dull pain in her kneecap, a sickening pain. There was no blood.

'Coming, Jean! Coming!' She kept on shouting reassurance, until panting, she reached the thicket and began to push through. The pain in her knee seemed to have transferred itself to the back of her throat.

The broom, which seemed predominant, was thorny, but there were patches of moss between the bushes, hardly any rocks, a hidden green and yellow house divided into rooms. In one of those rooms Roderick was lying on his back with Jean kneeling beside him. For a moment Van thought he was dead.

'Is he . . . ?' She knelt down also, and then she

heard the stertorous breathing, the rattle in his chest. She noticed that the fat cheeks divided by the pug nose had a spot of colour in each of them. His hands, thrown out on either side were covered with dirt and scratches, his clothes were torn. His face had escaped injury except for an ugly scratch across the low forehead. It was the familiar face of Roderick with all the signs of his affliction in the deep little eye sockets, the porcine cast of the features. She saw snot had dried under his nostrils in a crust, there was a day's growth of stubble on his chin, and that his lips were blue.

'He's breathing!' Jean said, looking up. Her joy was so great and yet contained so that her expression remained calm. 'Run and get John! Hurry! Go back to that phone box! Oh, Van we've found him.' She was tucking her jacket round Roderick as she spoke.

'Have mine too.' Van took off hers and spread it over Roderick's legs. 'Oh Jean, isn't it great? Great!' Words were useless. She put her hand on Jean's shoulder. 'I'm off. I'll be as quick as I can.'

Her knee had swollen badly, but the going was easier the further down she got. 'Hurry, hurry!' she kept on saying to herself. 'Don't think of anything else but getting there . . .'

When she was at last on level ground she saw a man's figure in the distance and knew it was John. She waved and he waved back, beginning to run. He covered the distance between them while she was still struggling on, because of the stiffness in her knee. 'We've found him!' she said when they met. 'Jean's with him!'

'Is he alive?' He caught her arm, hurting her with his grasp.

'Yes. You'll have to hurry . . . Did Sarah . . . ?'

'Where?' His face had the same contained joy as Jean's. She turned and pointed to the hill. 'A quarter of the way up. The big thicket on the right. You have to leave the path.'

'I see it. My car's beside yours. Get back to the kiosk and phone for an ambulance. Give them directions.'

'Right.' She forgot her knee as she half ran across the level fields, even when clambering over the fence. The pain came back when she tried to run across the road in the first space in the traffic, and with it a pumping heart.

She drove back to the kiosk in less than five minutes. This time she didn't have to fumble for pennies. 'Dial 999 for emergencies,' the notice said. She was reassured by the calm voice of the man who answered.

'Right. Got it! Just past the first kiosk on the A75 out of Dumfries. We're on our way.'

She sat in the car, waiting, her head bowed, her heart and her swollen knee pounding together. When she had waited five minutes she got out of the car and stood with her back to the door. Her heart had steadied now and she was ready to speak calmly to the ambulance driver when he drew up behind her and jumped out.

Six

Roderick had bronchial pneumonia. John stopped attending surgeries and sat by his son's bedside with Jean. He was necessary to her. She was distraught, filled with guilt, he told Van, because she had allowed him to be incarcerated in the home in the first place.

She had made the decision herself, he told Van one afternoon while Jean was resting. The district nurse was with Roderick. 'I had to wait, give her time. I knew if I pushed her she would blame me. But, basically, she's sensible. It's only her love for Roderick which clouds her common sense at times.'

Sam was back from Sarah's, and Van took over the management of the house, although Grace, the housekeeper, was efficient and kindly. There was a steady stream of visitors, letters, flowers, telephone calls. Anna rang from Barcelona every night.

When Van did the shopping, there were invariably questions about 'the doctor's boy' from assistants and acquaintances. Some merely enquired about his welfare. Others were more curious, but Van kept quiet about Roderick's bid for freedom.

Christine Logan called with flowers and was closeted with Jean for a long time. Her husband didn't come with her, but the strong bond which had existed between the two women seemed to have been mended. Bunty, her married daughter, came with her, a buxom young woman not unlike Sarah with whom she had shared a passion for horses in their younger days. Van remembered her terror of Sarah's horse, named Satan, aptly, in her opinion, but in retrospect she knew he had been as meek as a lamb.

Bunty sat with Van while her mother was with Jean. 'We were warned off by Father after the incident with my sister, Alice. I suppose you've heard about it?'

Van nodded. Anna, she remembered, had had nothing but contempt for Tim Logan. Perhaps she had another reason. 'It's all in the past now.'

'Still, you can imagine how your aunt felt. Sarah and I had been friends till then too.'

'I'm sure she didn't bear you any grudge. You grow away from girlhood friends sometimes. I had one called Adelaide. I thought there was no one like her at school. She was the sister of Sam's father. Still is.' She smiled. Bunty's answering smile was uncertain. She hadn't the character of Sarah.

Sarah came often and they would sit with Roderick while Jean attended to essential chores. 'Mother looks as if she's sleep-walking,' she said, 'the danger of too much.' There was more to Sarah than first met the eye.

Van was appalled at the change in Roderick because of his illness. His boyhood had left him, the fat cheeks had been honed to the bone, the pug nose was more prominent, his small eyes had lost their red rims, as had the edge of his nostrils. The significant features of his mongolism had disappeared, except for the low forehead and the constantly drooling mouth.

'Well, Vanessa,' he said when he saw her. 'Long time no see. How goes it?' She and Sarah laughed. At least he hadn't changed in his comical colloquialisms.

'Very well, Roderick. You're looking much better. Your mother tells me your temperature's down.'

He nodded sagely. 'You can't get rid of me as easily as that. Isn't that right, Sarah?'

'Yes, that's right, wee Chink.' She had called him that since he was a child.

'Is Aunt Anna joining the party soon?' he asked Van. His little eyes twinkled.

'Yes, as a matter of fact she is. Today.' She had said on the telephone, 'I've got my plane ticket.' Van hadn't been surprised, and had said she would meet her at the station.

'The more the merrier . . .' His voice faded, his eyelids with their short white lashes dropped over his eyes. Jean came in.

'That'll be enough, girls,' she said, 'I don't want him tired.' Her beauty had come back to her, the hair was heavy, luxuriant, her dusky skin glowed.

Alastair was with John when they went downstairs. He had been punctilious in visiting some time every day to have a professional look at Roderick. He was a serious young man, red-haired, long-chinned, a typical Highlander.

'Well, Van,' he looked up, 'John tells me you've done sterling work.'

'Nothing at all,' she said, smiling. 'Anyhow, the boss is arriving today.'

'Your mother?' He grinned.

'Roderick's really on the mend, isn't he?' she said.

'Yes, the pneumonia's clearing up, thanks to John,' he glanced at him, 'but of course the lungs are still packed full.'

53

'Always were, more or less,' John said.

'Wee Chink used to say, "That damned catarrh!"' Sarah sat down beside her husband. 'Quoting you, Father.' Alastair's arm went round her shoulders.

'Anyhow, you've been a great support, Alastair,' John said. 'I doubt if I would have trusted my own judgement.'

'Come off it. You taught me all I know. Well, darling,' he spoke to Sarah, 'we'd better get back. You've got the kids and I have the surgery. Don't dream of coming in tonight, John. Stay with Jean and try and persuade her to let up a bit now that the danger's over.'

'I think I'll take advantage of your kind offer, old chap.' John looked gaunt.

'How's your knee, Van?' Alastair asked.

'That was a wonder ointment you gave me. Quite cured. Well, I'm driving to Dumfries to pick Mother up at the station. I'd better get off. Tell Jean to leave everything till I come back, John. 'Bye, Sarah. You've been so good having Sam.'

She went upstairs. He had been put to bed for his afternoon rest, enticed by a new picture book she had bought him. 'I'm going to meet Granny,' she said. 'Do you want to come?'

'Oh, yes, yes!' He sprang out of bed, comical in his underpants.

'And Sarah says you can stay with them again if you like. Or you can have the camp bed here.' He would have to vacate the little boxroom for Anna when she came. They were cramped for space at the cottage.

He considered. 'I'll stay at the surgery house, I think, Mummy.' He was pulling on his short trousers. Van tucked in his shirt. 'I like packing

54

Bessie's bag. And Miss Thompson needs me. She has a lot of bottles for me to wash.'

'Okay.' Van took down the red canvas bag from a hook behind the door and put in it his pyjamas and toothbrush. They would have to get home now. The crisis was over, and they had disturbed this house long enough. Besides, Sam had to get back to school. She would drive Mother to Glasgow with them, if she wanted to leave.

She was surprised to realize that Eb's death had faded in her consciousness because of the immediacy of Roderick's disappearance and illness. But she would go back to Clevedon Crescent now, with or without Mother, and try to plan her future. Eb was physically gone, but he had been gone for her since he had rejected her, pregnant with Sam, over five years ago.

Anna, city smart as always, stood out amongst the other people on the station platform. Van's theory about her was that if the house went on fire she would emerge properly dressed, face made up, hair in place. Ritchie, on the other hand, would be more untidy than ever, his curly hair like a halo, he would have a scarf round his neck and an old anorak. Even at official functions which he had to attend, his bow tie was always askew, his white dickie bulged.

Sam rushed into Anna's arms. 'I wish *I* could be in a train!' he greeted her. 'That's what I'd really like. You're lucky, Granny.'

'Poor little soul,' she said, hugging him. She put an arm round Van with Sam still clinging to her waist. 'You look tired, Van. God knows what your aunt will look like.'

'She's fine, now. I think Roderick's on the mend.

So does John. The car's round the back, Mother. Sam, let Granny walk. And you're crushing her suit.' Anna had a wardrobe of smart uncrushable suits with appropriate blouse, hat and gloves for each one. 'You look lovely, Mother.' But Jean had the extra beauty, the strangeness. Her own appearance, she knew, left a lot to be desired. She had inherited Ritchie's liking for what he called casual clothes, words designed to make Anna see red.

In the car Anna said, 'You should have let me know about Roderick far earlier. I would have come before if I had known he was so ill.'

'It was Aunt Jean, Mother.' And wickedly, 'She said you would come storming away from Barcelona and start ordering everybody about.'

'She never said that!' She looked genuinely astonished. 'Jean *needs* me. She always needs me.'

'I did my best. But you'll have more time for your chinwags now.'

'I'm only staying a couple of days if I find everything fine. Ritchie's at Clevedon Crescent. He came away from Barcelona with me.'

'But Bessie's there.'

'He needs *me*. He can't be long without me. His painting suffers.'

'My, you're a great one for being needed. Are you sure it isn't you who needs to be needed?'

'You're smart, Van,' she gave her an admiring glance, 'I'll say that. Not smart smart, but really on the ball.' Mother used to say that *her* mother, Granny Rose, was an enigma. Now Van was thinking the same thing of *hers*.

They dropped Sam off at Sarah's, which meant also that they had to go into the house to let Mother see the new baby. The sight of Sarah, legs apart under an enveloping white apron, bathing the child, twisted Van's heart. She thought of Eb and her eyes filled. Envy was a waste of emotion. So was regret. She watched Anna accept the freshly bathed infant, wrapped in a towel, regardless of the smart suit. The eyes she raised to Van were wet, like her own.

'Anyhow, you have Sam,' she said when they were once again in the car. After that she talked about Barcelona and the interesting people they had entertained, and Ritchie's new work. That subject absorbed them until they turned into the old High Street. It would have been no good remarking on the married love and security which surrounded Sarah. Mother had never had any time for self-pity.

'You'll do Aunt Jean good,' Van said as she drew up at the door. 'At times I thought she would break down.'

'Jean was never moderate in her reactions. That's her style.' She looked quite proud of her twin sister as she said it.

Grace opened the door before Van could insert the key John had given her.

'You needn't have –' She stopped. Grace was holding a handkerchief to her mouth. Her eyes above it were shocked.

'Oh, I was hoping you'd come soon, Mrs Laidlaw.' She had always given Van the benefit of the doubt, possibly for her own comfort. She glanced from her to Anna. 'And your mother . . .' The handkerchief went now to her eyes. Her hand was trembling. 'You're never going to believe this. Oh, dear . . . come in . . .' She stood aside for them to come into the hall.

'What's wrong?' Anna asked. Her voice was sharp.

Grace beckoned them nearer, looking meaningfully

57

up the stairs. 'It was just after you left, Mrs Laidlaw,' she was whispering, 'and your Aunt Jean was . . . up there. I heard her cry out, "John, John!" I'll never forget that voice. It went through you. The doctor was having a look at the paper – you know how he likes – and I was clearing up after the young doctor and –'

'What has happened?' Anna interrupted her.

'Roderick's deid. His heart failed him. Just like that, and him sitting up and taking notice, quite jeco. Of course, it's always been weak, and maybe all the upset, and him ill, gave it too much to do, like trying to . . . shove through glaur . . .' Anna was halfway up the stairs.

Van put her arm round the woman and led her into the kitchen. 'I'll make you a cup of tea, Grace,' she said, 'you just sit down. It must have been a terrible shock for you too.' She crossed to the sink to fill the kettle. She hardly knew what she was doing, or saying. The water ran over her hands. She had to empty some of it out.

'Aye, but think of that puir woman, your aunty, not to mention the doctor! And them that happy that he was on the mend. Oh, dearie, dearie me.' She was using her handkerchief again.

Van felt nothing. It wasn't only Grace who could suffer from shock.

Once again, when Grace wasn't there, she became head cook and bottle-washer. Either John or Anna was with Jean. Sometimes Anna brought her down to the sitting room where her aunt greeted Van politely, like a stranger. She was calm. She didn't weep.

The postmortem passed, and then the funeral, at which the Logans were noticeably absent. Still Jean hadn't wept. John had gone back to work. Alastair was carrying a double load willingly, but John had said to Van that it couldn't go on.

She talked more with John than she did with her mother. Her uncle's practical common sense had reasserted itself. His grief was well hidden.

'It shouldn't have been a surprise to us. It's just it coming as it did. Jean had accepted long ago that he wouldn't live to an old age. I think it's the lost years when he was at the Castle Home which she can't accept.'

'She will. It's just . . . she's dramatic in her reactions. An artist.'

'You understand her.' He smiled. 'Life's funny. You came to see us because your . . . Sam's father had died. Jean told me that you'd want comfort. We had plans,' he smiled sadly, 'to take you out of yourself.'

'I've had comfort in a way. I've seen I'm not the only one to suffer loss. Maybe working in institutions where there's so much sadness has helped. You'll know the feeling too, when a patient comes in, and you listen and think: what am I grumbling about?'

'Knowing and feeling are different. But, yes, it helps. Which reminds me, I'm due for the evening surgery. Put your feet up and listen to the wireless.'

'Maybe I will.'

'And have a sherry. Pour out three glasses and call the sisters downstairs.'

'I'll do that.' She went into the kitchen and filled a glass dish with potato crisps. 'Would you like a sherry, Grace?' she said. She was standing at the sink, peeling potatoes, back to normal. She had a philosophy too, evidently.

'No, I never touch it, thanks. Beetroot wine's ma

limit.' She heaved a lugubrious sigh. 'Ah well, life must go on.' Somebody had to say that, Van thought, going back to the sitting room with her glass dish. She took a crisp. It made a comforting noise.

The two sisters came into the room with identical smiles firmly in place.

'Good idea, Van,' Anna said. 'Isn't it, Jean?'

'I can think of worse.' She took the glass of sherry Van offered her. 'Thanks. You're a good lass.'

'Ah, well,' Anna said, taking a sip from hers. 'This will do us good. Life must go on.' Wrong, wrong, Van thought, or at least unwise . . .

Jean said in the small silence, 'You'll be justified again, Anna. You always said *I* was the queen of tragedy. Remember?'

'That's no way to talk.' Anna eyed her over her glass.

'Isn't it? I have to talk, to get rid of this bile.' Her voice quickened. 'When Ritchie left you for that woman, you said, "There now, that's us equal," but I *knew* he would come back to you. I always told you you were soul mates. He might have a little flutter out of curiosity, but you're joined at the hip. Wasn't that what you said about you and me once, when Frederick drowned? That's when I learned the phrase, but it's you and Ritchie it applies to, joined at –'

'Shut up, Jean.'

'You two!' Van tried to laugh.

'Well, here I am,' Jean waved her glass, 'away ahead of you again. A period of happiness with my husband and family, and then Roderick taken away from me because of that bugger Logan's filthy accusations.' Van got up.

'Sit down!' Anna lifted her hand. 'You have to hear

this, the lengths she will go to.' Van subsided in her chair. 'They were justified,' Anna said to Jean. 'He could have raped his daughter.'

Van watched as Jean rose to her feet. Her eyes were wide. 'Did you say raped? Raped!'

'It could have come to that. You know it in your heart, that's what's screwing you up. Now you're trying to get at me through your dead son. Give it up.'

'My dead son!' Jean leaned on the arm of her chair as if Anna had struck her. 'Trust you to say it. The words. Taken away from me, my only chance to get rid of my guilt as long as he was living. *Dead.*'

Anna shot a quick glance at Van as if to say, 'See what I mean?'

'Stop being dramatic, Jean.' Her voice changed, became tender. 'You'll have to face up to it. He wouldn't have had a long life. John warned you often. His heart was weak at birth. He always said you had to enjoy him, the two of you, because he wouldn't be with you for long.'

Jean had sat down again as if exhausted. Her voice was toneless. 'Listen to the prophet of gloom.' She addressed Van. 'The one who knows everything. She's been like that since I've first known her. Always knows better. Superior Anna, watching me making a muck-up of things, calling me the queen of tragedy, the downright cheek of it . . .'

Anna got up and slapped her face. Van winced. She opened her mouth to say something to protest, and then she saw that Anna was kneeling beside Jean, cradling her in her arms, speaking softly to her while Jean sobbed, broken, bitter sobbing.

'Yes, he's dead. It's another terrible blow, but you can take it.' She seemed to giggle, or at least snort.

'You've had plenty of practice. Think of the good things. Roderick gave you joy, the wee Chink, while you had him. You have a loving husband, a fine daughter, two beautiful grandchildren.' She turned her eyes to Van. 'We're upsides. I have a fine daughter and son, a great little grandson and a peach of a husband. And he's a peach of a painter into the bargain. Cry away, Jean, you poor soul.' She rocked her in her arms. 'You always take a devil of a time to get started . . .'

The door opened and John came in. He took a look at the two women and came over to them. 'I'm here, Jean,' he said, kneeling down beside Anna.

Anna got up and beckoned to Van. They both went out of the room.

Seven

They were back to the status quo at Clevedon Crescent. Anna and Ritchie worked most of the day in their studios; Van's day was punctuated by her morning trip with Sam to school and her shopping in the afternoon before she collected him and brought him home.

She knew better than to interrupt her parents when they were working. That wasn't strictly true. Anna quite liked chatting while she hammered, but it only reinforced Van's awareness of her own maladroitness. However, one day in that dead period after lunch when it was cleared away and Bessie was having her daily 'sidoon', she ventured upstairs.

Even in her voluminous smock Anna looked smart. Her straight black hair was shiny and controlled in its expensive bob, her face delicately painted for daytime. The deep sky-blue colour of her smock emphasized her china-like complexion which made such a dramatic contrast with her dark hair. Van knew from Bessie that she now hennaed it – 'They towels.' She wondered if Ritchie would start doing the same. Already he had a few threads of grey amongst his curls.

'I'm having no luck in finding a job, Mother,' she said when she was sitting on a high stool watching her. 'Miss Clewes offered me helping with the children, but I don't think it would be fair to Sam. I want him to be independent of me.'

'You're right there.' Anna went on hammering, skilful little taps, rather, round the motif. 'What is it you really want to do?' She was shaping a Scottish rose on the brass clockface on her bench. It seemed incredibly intricate work to Van, and she marvelled that she could talk while she worked.

'You know me. Well, you ought to. Some kind of caring job. I thought of writing to the Glasgow Corporation to see if I could find anything in one of the new housing schemes. I read that they've started up advice bureaus.'

'Oh, that would be too complicated for words. Endless leaflets you would have to understand. Beyond you.'

'Thanks very much.'

Anna looked up and laughed. 'Sorry, but you know yourself you're better at the practical stuff. And you've always disliked the thought of sitting at a desk.'

'I could learn. No, that's not the difficulty. They're all out of the city, and I have to be there for Sam and to put him to bed. You and father are out a lot in the evenings and I couldn't ask Bessie to do it. She's getting on.'

'What age do you think she is?'

'Around sixty? Or a bit older?'

'She's seventy-eight. She'd kill me if she knew I'd told you.'

'Seventy-eight! And still working?'

'She wants to. Of course Mrs McKenzie does all the real work every morning and you do the shopping. But if I took away the cooking from her she'd die. That's one of the reasons Ritchie and I eat out a lot, to spare her. We aren't always at official functions or meetings.'

'I'm flabbergasted, although I should have realized that she would be the same age as Granny Rose, if she were living.'

'I wanted her to retire when we came here, but she wouldn't hear of it, although her friend Mary Pollock was keen for her to share a house with her in Helensburgh. That was Nancy's housekeeper. I thought she would be horrified when I told her you were pregnant and she surprised me by saying it was high time we had some "wee yins runnin' roon the hoose again."'

'She's a surprise packet!'

'Scots women are tough. She wants to die with us. And if that's what she wants . . . But don't let on to her that you know her age. It's her one vanity.'

'No, I wouldn't dream . . . anyhow, Sam's my responsibility. Now he hasn't even got a father.'

'He was never much good to him or you when he was alive, let's face it.'

'It wasn't for want of you telling me.'

'I've finished with that now. I've learned my lesson. It was just . . .' she tapped delicately round a leaf, 'I thought you were worth a lot more, still do.'

'As long as you're not dreaming of a white wedding.' Van laughed, then sobered. 'Mother, I feel so dependent on you and Father. It makes me feel guilty.'

'Does it ever occur to you that I'm not very proud of myself either? Always wanting things my way. Mother used to tell me about it because she was the same. I've had to get rid of my jealousy of Ritchie, realize that he's not my property. I'd still draw the line, of course, if he –' she smiled. 'But the thing I disliked about Eb was that he *took* all the time. But then I've never suffered from polio. Now I realize I should have had more compassion. He was black in a white society, he couldn't work because of his disability. But in the end I should have realized it was none of my business. I wouldn't care now if you took up with a Hottentot. Everybody needs a man.'

'I need first of all to be independent. Sam and me.'

'Get it straight, Van. The money side isn't worth even talking about. We have more than we can spend. We'd like you to take more than you do. Besides, think of the joy that lad gives us.'

'Oh, Mother . . .' She looked down at her hands.

'For God's sake don't feel grateful. You're our daughter. But, most of all, we want you to be happy. I know you turned down going to university when we were at Renton, but why not go and be trained in social work? There are colleges, courses. Arrange something to suit your time.'

'It means more money.'

'Look, Van, don't expect me to be sloppy – I'm only that with Ritchie,' she laughed, 'but we would consider it a favour. Don't get obsessed by Sam. It puts a burden on him. That's where I went wrong with you. And look at your Aunt Jean over that poor soul Roderick. She's back painting now, thank God. It's her salvation.'

'Well, I'll do what you say, make enquiries, enrol for a course. Thanks, Mother.'

'Don't thank me.' Her eyes sparkled. 'Who knows? You might meet a bobby-dazzler there!'

'Me?' She shrugged.

'You've grown into yourself, Van. I'm quite jealous of your looks.'

Van went out smiling. That was the biggest compliment Mother had ever paid her.

She looked in her mirror when she was getting ready to go out to meet Sam. Black frizz, but making an interesting halo round her face. Good eyes. Not bad mouth. People said she had a smile they remembered. And maybe the black-rimmed spectacles gave her a young professor look, a woman who knew her own mind, who could accept responsibility. She would buy earrings, big important ones, start looking like Aunt Jean.

Anna and Van were in the kitchen helping Bessie to prepare dinner. Nancy and James had been invited – 'It's high time we had them,' Anna had said a week ago. 'Nancy will know it's my "turn", as she calls it.' Gordon and Wendy had also been included, 'as light entertainment' Ritchie had said wickedly.

Ritchie, who could be outrageous when they were there, was fortunately too subtle for the Pettigrews – Nancy, James, her husband, Gordon, their son, and Wendy, his wife – to understand. At least this was a commonly held belief in the Laidlaw household. But as Anna had said, darkly, warning him of any excesses, 'Maybe they're not as green as they're cabbage-looking.'

Van loved him when he was on form, finding him inexpressibly funny. She called it his Jimmy Logan act.

Wendy was a golden, bosomy young woman, a few years older than Van. She seemed to take herself seriously and her role as a rising young architect's wife. 'It's very good of you to have us for dinner with Mummy and Daddy,' she said to Anna. This is what she called Gordon's parents. Her own she called

'Ma and Pa', which was supposed to denote an upper-class informality.

'Sit there, Wendy,' Anna said, pointing to the sofa. Wendy subsided, her fat hips made her short skirt ride up and show a pair of plump knees, and was there just a fraction of something more intimate, a brief flash of white? Van would ask Ritchie later at the postmortem. He never missed a thing.

'Luckily you chose a night we *could* come, Aunt Anna. Gordon's swept off his feet!'

It would take a Force Ten gale to do that, Van thought. Her thoughts became as wicked as Ritchie's. The slim golden Adonis whom she had worshipped as a girl of fourteen was lost in the portly young man in the dinner suit sipping his gin and orange beside his father. The contrast between them was striking, Uncle James looked dessicated, Gordon was oozing with over-ripe good health and too many wine-washed official dinners in the Malmaison or the Grosvenor.

Ritchie must have had the same thought. 'Swept off your feet, eh?' He nodded gravely, as if it was a new conception requiring consideration.

'You artist chappies –' 'chappies' and 'blokes' were favourite words of Gordon's. Perhaps he picked them up on his occasional visits to London. The average Scot would have died rather than use them – 'you don't know what it's like with board meetings and conferences and inspections at sites and all that. And then Wendy keeps a very heavy engagement diary going for us. White tie affairs often.' He glanced across at her, his eyes lingering briefly on her cleavage.

Ritchie had followed his glance. 'You're looking

lovely tonight, Wendy,' he said, raising his glass of whisky to her.

'Don't listen to a single word that wicked uncle of yours tells you,' Nancy trilled. Her voice had lately developed this quality, as a result of taking singing lessons. 'He's well-known as a breaker of women's hearts.' Van wondered if this was a sly dig.

'But yours has remained impervious, Nancy, try as I might.'

'There's never been anyone for me but my James.' She beamed across the room at him and he looked vague for a moment before he smiled. Uncle James, in his sixties, sometimes looked as if he had embarked on a slow slide into senility. Anna said he put it on to avoid having to answer Nancy all the time.

Ritchie was back on the attack. 'You wouldn't consider modelling for me, would you, Wendy?'

She shook her finger at him. 'Would it be in the nude? I know you artists.' She rolled her eyes at Anna. 'What a time you must have with him! All those young things queuing up to drape themselves on his couch.'

'They only do it once,' Anna said. 'They don't like the result, a nose where their ear should be and hands the size of a Brechin's pie.'

'You mean, like Picasso?' Wendy was proud of her artistic nous.

'I was thinking more of Matisse or Magritte.' Ritchie looked serious.

'Or Renoir,' Anna said, equally straight-faced, passing round cigarettes so that she could smoke herself.

'Gordon would put his foot down,' Wendy said coyly, getting out of the impasse.

'Who says?' Gordon smirked. 'I'm quite well up

in those nude jobs, you know. You should see the calendars they stick up in the office. The typists have complained to me. But some are quite arty. Who was the bloke who did that woman on a couch with a black ribbon round her neck and a flower in her hair?'

'Manet's *Olympia*?' Ritchie pursed his lips considering, 'Not quite Wendy's style, Gordon.'

'And there's a black servant there.' Gordon was carried away with his own expertise. 'We could get Sam to stand in for her.'

'I don't think that's quite nice,' Nancy said, 'offending Van. She can't help it if she has a little boy who's not quite . . . but Van is *family*.' She drew herself up. 'That's what I always say, Vanessa is family.' Her voice trilled and soared. 'I've got a soft side for her.' She smiled at Van, beatifically. 'I tried to do everything for her when she was a girl because I knew you were worried about her, weren't you, Anna? Remember I fixed up for Gordon to take her to the tennis club, and then the Saturday hop there?'

'And he forgot and went off with you, Wendy,' Van said.

Wendy looked reflective. 'We went to Helensburgh, yes, that's right, to see Pa's new yacht. We got becalmed. But he didn't tell *me* you'd be waiting, Vanessa. I wouldn't have dreamed of it if I'd known. We girls must stick together.'

'Oh, I didn't *mind*. I was relieved, as a matter of fact.'

Ritchie looked apologetically at Van and then got up with the decanter and went to James. 'Another tot, James?'

'Fill up the gin drinkers' glasses too, Ritchie,' Anna said. The teasing had gone off at half-cock tonight.

70

Now she was admitting defeat. 'Tell me about your latest cruise, Nancy. You go to such interesting places.' Van heard her begin on a detailed description of the ship, the food, the guests at the captain's table, the presents they had brought back. Never anything about the ports of call.

At the dinner table Gordon was sitting beside Van. He was affable and condescending. 'You've changed these days, Vanessa. You used to be such a quiet little thing.'

'I still am.'

'Still waters run deep.' He searched for a sexual flicker in her eyes. He almost sighed. 'You're stuck with your parents too much. I'll get Wendy to ask you over to one of our dos. See if we can't get you matched up with one of our business friends.'

'Would you really, Gordon?' Ritchie and Anna were having a bad influence on her, but she recognized in herself the ignoble wish to have something to retail afterwards. 'And I said, "Would you really, Gordon?"' Out of the past she remembered Anna telling her of Nancy talking of getting her and Jean 'matched up'. 'Like a pair of Liberty curtains,' Aunt Jean had said.

Gordon had mistaken her silence. 'Don't worry about me,' he said. He dropped his voice, looking round the table as if looking for Russian spies. 'I'm broad-minded. About Sam.' He even touched the side of his nose. 'The things I hear at the Conservative Club . . . well, I wouldn't soil your ears.'

'It's not infectious, Gordon,' she said, 'being an unmarried mother of a coloured child.' She turned to her Uncle James who was sitting on her right in a grey silence.

* * *

Ritchie came and sat beside her after dinner. Gordon had gone back to Wendy, summoned by a glance. Ritchie was intuitive. 'What's a nice girl like you doing in a place like this?' He put an arm round her. There was always Ritchie's affection, she thought, it had been there all her life, steady, uncritical, undemanding.

'I've nowhere else to go,' she said.

'Would you like to meet a man?'

'Oh, Dad!' She laughed at him. 'You and mother are dying to get me married.'

'Well, it wouldn't be natural if you didn't. You're free, white and over twenty-one. You should have someone. You're a smasher to look at.'

'And don't pull my leg. I look like a frump compared with Mother.'

'You have a look of Jean, and she's the beauty of that pair. It's something that men go for, believe me.'

She smiled at him. At fifty-six he was still very handsome. Was it that there was a feminine streak in him which made him so sympathetic and understanding of women? And did all painters have that, *need* that? He had an enveloping kind of charm, yet it wasn't assumed. No wonder Mother got jealous.

'The only man I meet with any regularity these days is the janitor at Sam's school.'

'That's because you won't come upstairs when we give one of our studio parties.'

'Maybe I've been stupid, but I think I'm coming to my senses now. I don't regret my life with Eb. I had a very special kind of feeling for him.'

'No love's wasted. But he took too much from you without giving anything back. You have to learn the hard way. Mish is different. He seems to have been born with all the answers, but then those level-

72

headed people never know the heights nor the depths. Anyhow, you come up to my next party.'

'The best thing for me would be to find a job. Mother's persuaded me to take a course in Social Sciences. She's always right.'

Bessie put her head round the door without knocking. 'Will youse yins be wanting any more coffee before I go to ma bed?'

'No thanks, Bessie,' Anna said. 'And if we do, I can make it. Off you go.'

'It was a lovely dinner, Bessie,' Nancy said. 'You're a marvel.' Nancy had said to Anna that she should 'check' Bessie's familiarity, advice which Anna studiously ignored.

'It would have been better if they two,' she included Anna and Van in her glance, 'had kept oot o' ma kitchen.'

'Good night, Bessie,' Wendy said, as one who knew how to deal with old family retainers.

'Oh, it's you, Mrs Pettigrew. I didny notice you,' Bessie said, putting Wendy firmly in her place. 'Aye, well, good night.'

'There goes the ruler of our roost,' Ritchie said, when the door had closed behind her.

Eight

Van enrolled at the Commercial College in Pitt Street right away. She would be older than the other students, the Principal told her, but against that, she had worked in various institutions 'in the south' and that was in her favour.

'At least you should have a maturity which the younger pupils lack,' he said. 'You say you've worked in the less favoured parts of London?'

'Yes, Clerkenwell. Renton, which was our home near Aylesbury, was half-suburban, half-country.'

'I don't think you'll have come across the poverty and overcrowding you'll see in Glasgow. Sometimes I feel it is our only claim to fame.' He smiled. 'Some of the old people you'll have to interview in their homes or in hospital will have brought up large families in a single-end . . . Where do you live, Miss Laidlaw?'

'In Clevedon Crescent, off Great Western Road.'

He looked at her as if she had told him a joke. 'When you see the single room where these families were brought up, only a cold water tap at the jawbox – that's a stone sink – no toilet or bath, you'll find it a world away from Clevedon Crescent.'

'It's my parents' house, not mine.'

'Even so. It may be a rude shock for you but it will certainly open your eyes.'

'They were opened a long time ago,' she said. 'London isn't paved with gold. I found that out.'

He grinned, looking younger. 'I imagine you're quite like your father. I'm a great admirer of his work. He can paint ugliness too. That's what makes him so good. You'll see plenty of ugliness in this course, but you'll be constantly amazed at the spirit of the people and how they can make anything of themselves at all.'

'My father's the product of a background like that.'

'Ah!' he said. 'He's the one that got away.' He laughed, then sobered. 'Lack of jobs. Lack of decent housing. That's the great bugbear of Glasgow. It leads to despair, humiliation, drunkenness and violence.'

'You're not trying to put me off, are you?' If she had been straight from school she couldn't have spoken like that.

He grinned again. 'I think you can cope with it. Now, let me tell you about the course. You'll have mostly tutorials to begin with, general lectures on housing, hygiene, slum clearance, social benefits, generally preparing the ground before you go out. It leads to a worthwhile job, I think, even if it's not too well paid.'

'As long as I earn enough to keep my son and myself. I want a place of my own.'

'That's wise. Just remember, common sense is the best attribute. Don't get too involved. That's *not* wise.' She thought of Eb. 'Good luck.' He half rose to dismiss her.

She left his office fired with enthusiasm. She would put her back into it. Ritchie and Anna had at least set her a good example there.

She found the course hard at first. She was a born

listener and quickly absorbed the lectures, but collating her thoughts and committing them to paper was more difficult. She longed to be done with the theory and out in that world which the Principal had said would give her a rude shock.

Anna gave her valuable advice. 'Your father absorbs everything through his pores, but he's one of the lucky ones. Lesser mortals like you and me have to get their heads down and study. It means sitting down at a desk when you've put Sam to bed, opening your books and cutting yourself off.'

'I'm going to be hopeless.'

'No, you aren't, and don't denigrate yourself. You've had ten times more practical experience than the others, and you've had a richly varied life, God knows. I haven't ever lived in a single-end so I can't help you there. Your father was the slum dweller. Speak to him.'

She was certainly different from the majority of the pupils, girls who had just taken their Highers, others who were working in offices but were doing a part-time course. Sometimes she looked around and wondered what a mother of a boy of five was doing there at all, and yet at other times she felt they accepted her. She quickly found out that where there is a common interest and a common goal, the rest didn't matter.

She could giggle when necessary like a girl of eighteen, admire clothes which the students bought on their Saturday sorties to Argyle Street – Sauchiehall Street was considered 'too pricey'. For most of them, her own clothes, she knew, were thought to be 'toney', upper-class, frumpish. She listened to their tales of their 'boys', and thought in retrospect that she had missed out on a lot.

But her depth of experience enabled her to get more out of the course in other ways. She knew the poverty she had seen in Renton when she had visited Adelaide's home was not on a par with Glasgow's, but she had a broader view than the average pupil who had never left the city.

She knew London. She understood and could drive on the new motorways which were beginning to desecrate the old Glasgow, and could admire how they made transport easier and faster. She knew and recognized how they had destroyed the close-knit communities like the Gorbals and the inner city, and how many of the people incarcerated in their new housing estates on the fringes felt lost and longed to be back.

What they had left became a dream to them where everyone had jobs and they had lived in cosy squalor together, where the pub was round the corner and the betting shop and the pawn shop and the 'steamie'. A bathroom in the new housing scheme if you had no day's toil to wash off was better suited for keeping coal in.

When Van looked back on the children's home where she had worked, it wasn't the eternal toileting of incontinent children she remembered, the messes of food and faeces, it was the children themselves, their character shining through their eyes, their dependency, their laughter. It would be the same in Glasgow, because human nature was the same everywhere.

And she was fortunate that Anna and Ritchie were different from the ordinary run of parents. They kept abreast with the world outside Glasgow, discussed Vietnam, the students' revolution in Paris, they recognized that it was the joblessness in Easterhouse and Castlemilk and similar peripheral estates which led to vandalism and worse. They had long conversations at night over the dinner table, they showed a lively interest in her studies.

But, unlike Van they had never felt the need to expiate their guilt. They contributed time and money to worthy causes, and worked towards the bringing of art to the people. They couldn't alter their place in society, and didn't crave a 'feeling experience' with the deprived. Their approach was intellectual.

'However much you want to be involved,' Ritchie told her, 'the poor will recognize you as being different. You hold your body differently, you may look anxious at times but never defeated. Your clothes and hair and hands are well cared for, you look middle-class. You're a toff. I think that's what Eb resented in you more than you getting pregnant. It went deeper than that. He felt you patronized him.'

She swallowed that and bought some Beatles records so that she would be *au fait* with John Lennon. Sometimes she hummed their songs in the corridors of the college.

Her attendance there, strangely enough, formed an extra bond with Sam. He was intrigued that Mummy had gone back to school. He gave her one of his spare notebooks, and allowed her to select a coloured pencil from his pencil-box with its motley collection of tractors, compasses, india rubbers, white, green and brown. The pencil sharpener was an especial joy.

He asked the names of the other students, and wanted to know if any of them were like him, coloured brown. Interestingly enough, there were one or two from Uganda. Glasgow had always been more cosmopolitan than its sister city, Edinburgh. Van learned to like the writing out of précis – her gift for language asserted itself and sometimes her essays were praised. 'Don't regret Eb,' Ritchie told her. 'Nothing is wasted. You can bring something to your work that the other students can't.'

They went to Kirkcudbright to spend Christmas with Jean. John couldn't get off to come to Glasgow, and neither sister could imagine spending Christmas without the other. Also, Anna wanted to see for herself how Jean was coping with the loss of Roderick.

They found her cheerful, a little brittle, but enthusiastic about her painting. Ritchie, who was taken out to the studio to see the one she was working on, declared that there was a greater depth and richness there, that she was making him jealous.

They went to have tea with Sarah, and she listened to her mother with her wise, quiet eyes as if to a child as she passed round her home-baked scones. 'Painting has saved my sanity,' Jean told them, 'but no more than Sarah's two little lads, especially that one.' The baby was lying in his carrycot on two chairs beside them. Van saw her aunt's face soften as she looked at the small hands waving, pink in the glow of the fire.

As usual, Van thought, Sarah has done the right thing without even being aware that she was doing it, providing a substitute, a surrogate for Roderick, and a perfect one as it happened. 'Your mother's looking happy,' she said to her later, and Sarah nodded.

'And Aunt Anna completes it.' She understood the bond.

They were staying on that evening as the Campbells always kept open house on Boxing Day. There had been a family Christmas dinner with Jean and John in their house, and they had toasted 'Absent friends' and opened the presents from Karin and

79

Mish in New York, who had promised to join them in Arenys de Mar next summer. Mish had quite a few connections with gallery curators in Barcelona, and it would be a case of combining business with pleasure.

'I wish they'd take time off to get married.' Anna made the usual complaint, and Jean teased her and said she was beginning to sound quite like their mother.

Van came back to the subject of Mish and Karin when they were upstairs dressing for the party. 'That can't surely be the hold-up – I mean, Mrs Gottleib not liking a Gentile for a son-in-law?'

'It might be that Karin has to get used to the idea too. It certainly can't be money. Wait till you see their flat, I mean, apartment. And they're so suited! Come to think of it,' she turned to Van, 'you never talked about marrying Eb, before Sam.'

'He never asked me. It wasn't his thing.' She thought of Eb in his wheelchair, the trousers in folds round his wasted limbs and her eyes filled with tears. She felt Anna's hand on her shoulder.

'I don't know what made me say that. Stupid. In any case, marriages aren't always the be-all and end-all of people's existence. You know me, of course – one-man woman. I think I'd die if I lost Ritchie – those euphemisms – if *he* died.' Her voice shook a little. She looked young and beautiful in her white satin slip, as neat as a ballet dancer. Van smiled at her with love. Sloppy, she thought, the cardinal sin.

Sam was happy too, accepted into two loving families. His worries about his colour seemed to have disappeared. He said to Van one day, 'I'm not the only one. Some boys have brown spots all over them.'

'They're called freckles. Yes, you're quite right, just broken spots of brown.'

'Maybe it's just that my spots of brown have joined up.'

'That's an interesting thought,' she said, keeping her face straight.

Before they went downstairs for the party, she and Anna went into the nursery where Sarah had two single beds and a cradle for little Jamie, Alastair's own cradle which had been sent from his home when Sandy had arrived. Van held up her finger to Sam – she had seen his bright eyes. The two Campbell children were asleep.

'Your dress hasn't any sleeves, Mummy,' he whispered. 'Will you not be cold?'

'It's an evening dress. Same as Granny.' Anna bent down and patted his cheek.

'I don't think *grannies* should wear them.' He frowned.

'Christmas is special. But grannies can tuck in big boys, can't they?' She bent over the bed, and Van admired her slim waist in the white dress, the jet earrings swinging. Barcelona had given her an extra flair. Perhaps it was the thought of Maria Roig somewhere in the background.

The party was lively because Alastair was a lively host. He put the same energy into entertaining as he did to his work. He kept refilling glasses with jovial good humour.

Sarah's buffet complemented his generosity. She was the picture of a fulfilled woman, Van thought, as she watched her pressing people to eat – 'Alastair doesn't like vol-au-vents for breakfast.' Plates were emptied and rapidly replenished. Everyone ate and drank as if Christmas dinner had never been.

In between there was Scottish dancing with Alastair's yellow-checked kilt leading the way through the reels. He brought up a youngish man to meet Van. 'Your next partner, Van. Alan McAlpine. He's one of the pillars of the town. A well-known solicitor.'

Alan McAlpine looked like a man of substance in his dinner suit. He was good-looking in an unobtrusive way, a slight air of shyness well concealed, possibly just with women. His hair was well brushed, well cut, plentiful. Van felt he had checked himself in his mirror before he left, everything was just jeco . . . what a useful word it was. She guessed he might be in his early thirties.

He danced confidently with a straight back, neat-footed, well taught. That had also been taken care of. She wondered why she was so analytical, but decided she liked him. He led her to a seat and sat down beside her when they had finished the eightsome reel.

'You must be dancing reels every day, Mr McAlpine,' Van said, fanning herself with her hand. 'You're very expert.'

'No longer. But when I was a wee boy I was sent to Miss MacLellan's Dancing Academy, and I've never forgotten the steps. You haven't seen my Flowers of Edinburgh yet.' He smiled at her.

'I can believe you're just as expert at that.' He shrugged. 'I think I met you at my Aunt Jean's house a long time ago.'

'You did.' He was confident. 'I was still at school and you'd come on a visit from down south.'

'Yes, we lived down there.' Her mouth quirked.

'Why I remember you was because of your voice. Very la-de-da.'

'Oh my!' she said, amused.

'I left Kirkcudbright to go to Glasgow University, and then worked there. I only came back when my father died and I took over his practice. I had to.'

'Didn't you want to leave Glasgow?'

'Not really. There was the possibility of a partnership in the large firm I was in, and other . . . ties, but things fell through, so I came back. I'm glad I did. I like it here.'

'I've only been in Glasgow for five years. My parents came back, and they asked us to come too.'

'"Us"? Oh, yes, someone said you had a son. Is . . . his father here with you?'

'He died.' And that'll do you to be going on with, she thought in Bessie's phraseology. He was the typical lawyer, naturally curious.

He stayed with her for the rest of the evening. Once she deflected a quizzical look from Ritchie who was being the life and soul of the party. He liked Alastair.

'My father surprises me,' she said to Alan McAlpine. 'I don't think he has a thing in common with most of the people here, but just look at him!'

'Do I detect a slight condescension in that remark?'

'Oh, goodness no! He'd be at home in a dustmen's convention!' She put a hand to her mouth, laughing. 'Have I made matters worse?'

'Don't apologize.' He was stiff. 'I understand what you *aren't* saying. Your father's a famous painter, he hobnobs with famous people all over the world, and here he is, able to enjoy himself with a group of people whose only interests are small-town ones.'

He doesn't want to be classed along with the inhabitants of this little town, Van thought. She smiled at him, and his smile was stiff. No sense of humour? 'I'm getting into deep water. I suppose I'm envious of my father's capacity for enjoying the moment. I've always been awkward and shy.

83

Perhaps that's why I've worked with people who have disadvantages.'

'To assert your superiority?' He was astute, even if he didn't laugh easily.

'Not consciously. I felt for them, deeply, the way my father feels for what he's painting. He gets right inside and looks outwards. Maybe I was doing the same with people.'

'And have you lost this capacity?'

'Oh, I hope not. But I think I was misdirecting my energy. I'm now a student at the Glasgow Commercial College. I want to become an almoner, or something like that. And I want to be independent. But that's enough about me. What about you? Is there a Mrs McAlpine?'

'I thought there was going to be, in Glasgow, but it didn't work out. She married the man who got the partnership.' He was being frank.

'That was sad.'

'Better in the long run. It's better to be a bigger fish in a smaller pond. My mother was still in the family house after father died, so I moved in with her. And that's the story of my life. So far.' His smile was a quick gleam, but friendly.

The Laidlaws left the following day. Anna and Ritchie had too many commitments, and Van had to prepare for going back to the college, as Sam had for going back to school. Van had a talk with Jean on her own when her mother was out shopping for some 'Kirkcudbright goodies' to take back with her.

'Are you beginning to get over Roderick, Jean?' she asked her. 'That was badly put. I know he'll always be very special to you.'

'Very special. Anna and I have had some heart-to-

84

hearts. She breathes new life into me, that mother of yours.'

'Especially when you go hammer and tongs at each other?' Van smiled.

'That's even more proof. And we're both lucky with our men. I saw young McAlpine paying you a lot of attention at Sarah's. Did you know it was his father who was Tim Logan's lawyer? If I were vindictive I could say that he was instrumental in getting my Roderick locked up. But I'm not any longer, and the man was only doing what he was told to do by Logan.'

'I never thought . . . and he didn't say . . .'

'I'm not accusing *you* of anything, Van. They say he's quite well liked. Mistake, him staying with his old mother, though. Everybody should be independent, married or not.'

'That's what I want to be too, independent. That's a surprise about Mr McAlpine. Alan. He never said.'

'Why should he? Have you fallen for him?'

'Have a heart, Jean. He has no sense of humour . . . but he's a good dancer.' They both laughed.

Nine

Alan McAlpine didn't let the grass grow under his feet. He drove to Glasgow most weekends, sometimes with the excuse that he had legal business to attend to. He took her for dinner, booked seats for shows, was generous with chocolates and flowers. Sam was in bed by the time he called for her.

The pantomime season was still in full swing – they generally went on until the summer shows started with the advent of *Half-past Eight* at the King's. Alan suggested taking Sam to see *Puss in Boots*.

'It won't do any harm,' Ritchie commented when she told him, 'it shows he has a kindly streak.' Both parents seemed amused at her being 'courted', as Anna put it, but were noncommittal.

Sam was naturally delighted, and on the evening of his visit he went running into the hall, then stopped short out of shyness. Alan was standing there.

'Is *this* your son?' he said.

'Yes.' She tried to ignore the emphasis. 'Sam, shake hands with Mr McAlpine.' The boy held out his hand. She saw the tightening round Alan's mouth as he took it. She was aware that Bessie was standing at the kitchen door, watching, and she said, sharply, 'Is there anything you want, Bessie?'

'Just to see he has a clean hankie.'

Sam felt in his pocket. 'I've got one.' And, his shyness going, 'This is Mummy's friend, Bessie. He's taking me to *Puss in Boots*.'

'Well, you watch that cat.' Bessie was not at all discomfited. 'It'll have you off to a giant's castle, or up a beanstalk before you know it.' Van shot an amused look at Alan but he was straight-faced. Sam giggled.

'I'll tell you when I get back. I'm ready!' He was in a high state of excitement. Surely no one could fail to respond to it, Van thought, as they went out to the car.

Alan put Sam in the back seat for the short trip to the theatre. Ritchie always allowed him to sit in the front. Van answered dutifully as Alan, rather deliberately, gave her news of Kirkcudbright and what he knew of the Whitbreads. Her aunt was having a local exhibition at Easter. It was said there were some dealers coming from London.

It was obvious what had upset him. Whether it was Sam's colour or the fact that it had been kept from him, or both, was scarcely important. Her guilt at her own secrecy made her feel aggressive, but there was no way of bringing up the subject while Sam was there.

He sat between them in the orchestra stalls, and his genuine enjoyment was infectious. Van met Alan's eyes over Sam's head and they reflected his laughter. He was getting used to the situation. She should have told him. She was to blame.

He was taking her out for a late supper afterwards. Anna, who was going to be at home that evening, had said she would put Sam to bed, and when the pantomime was over a happy little boy with his balloon, his programme and his bag of sweets was delivered into her arms, with Bessie hovering in the background.

'So Dame Hanky Panky didny catch ye after all?' she said, her mind a welter of bygone pantomimes. A flood of happiness swept over Van as she kissed Sam good night, and admired his good manners when he said, 'Thank you for my treat, Mr McAlpine.' Anna sped them on their way, smiling, assured.

Van's mood carried her throughout their meal in the Central Hotel and afterwards when they were sitting in the lounge having coffee. 'It was very kind of you to take Sam, Alan,' she said. 'He'll "fair deafen" Mother and Bessie telling them all about it.'

'I'm glad he enjoyed himself.' He seemed to sit straighter. 'Cigarette?'

'You know I don't smoke.'

He lit his own, slowly, deliberately. 'I'm a man of the world, Vanessa. I'm wondering why you were so secretive with me, and why you didn't tell me that your son's father was . . .'

'West African?' she said, the happiness vanishing, and because she had drunk several glasses of wine during supper, 'Almost as black as coal. Sam's skin is a few shades lighter . . . a judicious mix, I expect.'

He drew back at this. 'Were your parents surprised at you marrying him?'

'We weren't married. Eb didn't want the responsibility of a child. He was a child himself in many ways. And he was disabled.'

Alan frowned, then nodded, like a lawyer. 'I see. So you met him when you were do-gooding?' The remark pricked her into quick anger. He seemed a picture of moral rectitude sitting across from her in his correct city suit with his well-groomed hair. His hands were lawyer's hands, she thought, dry, chalky.

'I wasn't do-gooding, Alan, as you put it. It was far more than that. I've always been painfully aware of people who had not the same advantages as me. I was guilty, I felt I had to do something about it. My parents understood – at least Father did. I think Mother does now. They're paying for my course at the Commercial College.'

'You wouldn't need any of that if you had someone who could take care of you.'

She felt her cheeks burn. 'I'm not looking for someone to take care of me! I want to take care of myself! And my son. My parents are taking care of us just now and although I know they do it out of love, it doesn't make it any easier. Mother understands. So does Aunt Jean.'

'Perhaps I've been unfair.' He dowsed his cigarette, seemingly mollified. 'It was a shock to me at first, your son. I don't mind admitting it. But he's quite a decent little lad in spite of . . .'

She breathed deeply. 'In spite of his skin?'

'I'm putting it badly. Perhaps in London unmarried girls with a child are more plentiful. Of course I'm not ignorant of the situation, and that one comes across it more and more in these times. Hippies . . .' his voice trailed away. 'And, of course, there are sad cases in my practice . . .'

'I'm not one of your sad cases, Alan, I'm making a determined effort to do something with my life, and I don't intend to go around apologizing for past mistakes, if mistakes they were. The man I loved is dead. Maybe it was a mistake loving him, but it happened. And Sam happened. I'm hoping it will make me a little more understanding when I start working.'

'You'd be able to give up all that if you were married.'

Her anger flared. 'Since there's no possibility of that I don't see how it comes into the conversation.'

'I had been hoping, in our case –'

'And you've changed your mind?'

'No, no, we just need a little longer. I was immediately drawn to you, Vanessa, when we first met.'

'How generous!' He gave her a reproachful look.

'We would have to discuss things, give ourselves time . . .'

She didn't know whether to laugh or weep. She got up from her chair. 'It's hopeless, this conversation. I'm going home.' He half rose, alarm in his face. 'No, stay where you are. Thanks for the meal, and taking Sam out. I'm sorry you see him as a skeleton in the cupboard . . .'

'Sit down, Vanessa.' He looked around, fearfully, she thought. 'It isn't that. It's the surprise . . . of your past. I'll take you home. We could talk.'

'No, thanks! We've talked enough. I can get a taxi at the rank in the station.' She went swiftly, her head down.

She had to tell the driver to wait at the door of Clevedon Crescent so that she could run in and borrow a pound from Anna. She had forgotten to take her purse.

'Thanks, Mum.' She followed her upstairs to the drawing room. Anna was keeping her surprise at bay.

'What happened to Alan?' Ritchie said, looking up from his book.

'I've had enough of him.' She threw herself down on a chair. 'He was annoyed I didn't tell him about Sam being a bastard if you want to know, a coloured bastard.'

'That's a bit strong, Van,' Anna said.

'As a matter of interest, why didn't you?' Ritchie laid down his book, his eyes bright with interest.

'Well, it was none of his business was it, at the beginning, but then . . .'

'Maybe you haven't been very understanding with lawyer McAlpine. They tend to live in a straitjacket. Prejudices stick to them like barnacles.'

'My, my!' Anna said.

'Shush . . .' he said, waving his arm. Van remembered he had been going out to dinner. He was always voluble afterwards. 'What I'm trying to say is that Van has to be tolerant with that fraternity. Artists wear coats of many colours. We can move about in them more easily. No straitjackets for us. He's all right, lawyer McAlpine, sound as a bell, not a crack in him.'

Van laughed. 'You're being carried away by your own erudition. Anyhow, Mother was never very enthusiastic about him, were you?' She was disappointed they hadn't shown more sympathy. 'But then you weren't very enthusiastic about Eb either. It's difficult to please you.'

'Don't take your ire out on me,' Anna said. 'Of course you're upset, but put yourself in his place. He thought he was meeting an ordinary daughter of middle-class parents, eminently suited to be his wife. He would see you as a young widow with a child, and then he finds out your background is not what he thought. He's parochial, but I think he's fundamentally kind-hearted.'

'I'm not apologizing for my past, or Sam, to him! I was quite happy doing what I was doing, working to make myself independent, with your help. I don't need this.'

91

'But you must admit it's nice to be courted,' Ritchie said.

'Who wouldn't?'

'Let it cool, then. See how the wind blows. Eh, Anna?'

She nodded.

Van looked at them, sitting together on the sofa, perfectly suited, having reached still waters in their lives with so far no tragedies. Mother had had no worries, except her, she supposed, and Maria Roig.

'Work hard and play harder,' Ritchie said, and broke into song, singing rumbustiously in his cracked voice, '"Hi-ho, hi-ho . . ."'

Van got up, shaking her head at him. 'I'm off to bed.'

In a few days a letter came from Alan. He had been very upset about her leaving him so abruptly. They needed to talk, to be perfectly frank with each other. She had been looking tired – he thought she was working too hard at that college – but he'd had it in his mind for some time to invite her to spend the Easter weekend with him at the Portpatrick Hotel. Would she consider it? He would try to be understanding.

He didn't mention Sam. Sam's the flaw, Van thought grimly, but if that's the case, so am I.

She voiced her doubts to Anna, who thought she should go. 'Give him another chance,' she said, 'get to know his views. We'd love to look after Sam for the weekend. Ritchie's been dying to take him to Edinburgh Zoo for ages.' She reminisced about the hotel.

'Your grandfather used to take us girls there, with Mother. I think they both thought we should be

taught how to behave in hotels. Mother rigged us out
in dresses we hated, Nancy's all frills, Jean and I in
chartreuse green – I bet you've never heard of that –
complete with silver shoes and silver evening bags to
match. And nobody asked us to dance! We were far
too gauche, so Father took us round the floor one by
one, with Mother looking on with her gimlet eyes!
What a pantomime! That finished Jean and I for anything matching. She started concocting her own
dresses, and I saved like mad to get only the best . . .'

Van wrote back to Alan and said she would be
pleased to go to Portpatrick with him at Easter. Her
parents would take care of Sam, she added pointedly.
As Mother had said, although she didn't put that in
the letter, spending the weekend with him would be
a 'fair test'. When Van asked what she meant, Anna
said she would find out when she was there.

Ten

The schools and colleges in Glasgow were coming up
to their Easter break, and Ritchie was holding his
end-of-term shindig, as he called it. He was a visiting
luminary in the Art School, and liked to entertain
some of the staff around this time, and any other
people he had come across during the course of his
work.

Van's college was also closing down for Easter. Her
end-of-term examinations had been promising, and
she was beginning to see her way ahead. Hospital
work appealed to her. She hoped to be sent to one
of the city ones for some practical experience. She felt
she was able to slacken off. Her only recreation had
been her fortnightly outings with Alan, and Saturday
afternoons spent shopping or taking walks with Sam.
Clevedon Crescent, Anna commented, had become
a hive of industry.

Up until now Van had refused any of Ritchie's invitations to the informal get-togethers he held in his
studio. She wasn't convivial, as he was, but felt justified in accepting this one. Her world was sharply
divided between that of a student and a mother, and
her friendship with Alan. She didn't want to read
any more into the relationship than that. Since their
quarrel in the Central Hotel he had been extremely
circumspect.

When she went upstairs about nine o'clock the party was in full swing. The volume of conversation was deafening, compared with the quietness downstairs. Sam and Bessie were in bed. Van had persuaded her to have an early night, seeing her into the little room off the kitchen which had once been their breakfast room when Anna and her sisters had all been at home.

'Changed days, Bessie,' she said as she helped her to fold back the coverlet.

'Aye, changed days.' She sat down at the side of the bed to take off her shoes. 'Look at the swelling on them feet.' She pressed a finger into the puffy ankles. 'I'm gettin' too old for a' this.' And then added, looking into Van's face, 'But I want to see how you get on before I kick the bucket, and that wee black lad o' yours. Yon's a fine strappin' gentleman that takes you oot. No' like your mither's choice, howthery sort of creature, her man, but he could charm the birds aff a tree.' Van laughed, thinking how Bessie could cut them down to size. 'Aw the same, they two canna see past each ither. At their age they should know better.'

Ritchie and Anna could certainly run a party, Van thought, when she was absorbed into the crowd and a glass of something or other thrust into her hand. She had better watch out. It could be lethal. Ritchie was beside her, having apparently seen her arrival out of the back of his head since he'd been the centre of a group of laughing men. 'You'll know some of the folks here, Van?'

'I think so, yes.' She looked around. 'Mostly your Art School friends, aren't they? Don't worry about me. I'll mingle, isn't that the word?'

'You learned that in Renton.' He grinned. 'I don't

95

know what they say up here. Probably "barge in".'

'Am *I* barging in, Ritchie?' A young man was at his elbow.

Ritchie turned round. 'Oh, it's you, Purvis!' He smiled. 'No, you're a mingler, I'd say.' He introduced him to Van. 'He's forever chasing me. Harold Purvis, he's employed by my publisher. I bet you've come up to see how the wild Scots live, isn't that it?'

'To get you to write an introduction to your book.' He included Van in his smile. 'What a man! Don't forget I've an appointment tomorrow morning with you.'

'Sure, sure . . .' Someone called his name and Ritchie vanished.

'Are you a painter too?' Harold Purvis asked her.

She shook her head. 'I hardly know one painting from another. Father's given me up.'

'You must have other attributes.' Beguiling, she thought, seeing the smiling eyes. 'Ritchie's charm, for a start. They're mad about him in London. Especially the women.'

'Don't tell my mother that.'

'She's no cause for worry. That is *chic* and I mean *chic*! You're not at all like her.'

'Thanks very much.'

'Hey, is my face red?'

'Don't worry. I'm used to it. Mish, my brother, has the looks and artistic ability. Everything that a son and a daughter should have, rolled into one.'

'Do you always put yourself down like this? You need another drink.' He took her by the elbow and steered her to a table with two large punch bowls on it. Already her head was light. She had seen her father making the mixture, being reckless with bottles of rum, whisky and various other alcoholic beverages. 'I'm called Hal, by the way, to my friends. Harry's my Scottish name as in Harry Lauder.' And when they had their drinks in their hands, 'You haven't a Scottish accent.' He steered her to a window seat when they had helped themselves to plates of food.

'No. We lived near London until my mother inherited this house and they decided to make the move.'

'It's got great character. You'd pay the earth for the same thing in Mayfair. You don't find it provincial in Glasgow?'

'I don't make judgements like that.' First Alan being shaken by her past, now this one being condescending. Men were the limit.

'And that's called being put in my place.' He laughed, looking at her over his glass. 'You're a serious girl. Different from your father.'

'You only see him at play. He works like a beaver. We all do. There's a strong work ethic at Clevedon Crescent.'

He nodded. 'What's your territory?'

'Territory? Oh, I've gone back to school. I'm hoping to be trained in hospital social work. It's a two-year course.'

'An almoner? Very worthy women. My mother has a friend –'

'Do you like *your* work?'

'Love it. I'm a failed art student. Just didn't have it. Our firm produces art books. I'm tickled pink at having landed your father. He's the biggest fish so far, but the devil to pin down. I get to travel about a bit – Paris, Barcelona, New York. My series is called *Painters at Work*. I'm not so interested in retrospectives.'

'We have a house in Barcelona. Arenys de Mar.'

'Yes, Ritchie told me. I like the Spanish. What took him there?'

'He fought in the Spanish Civil War, and always had a soft side for the people. Then a dealer there, Manuel Folguera got interested in him.'

'I know Folguera. Quite a type, a kind of Spanish grandee. I'm more aware of a kind of aristocracy in Spain than in England. Better-looking for a start . . . Do *you* like it?'

'I used to, before my father became so well known. I made a little nest for myself in our house and was very happy while he and Mish, my brother, toured the galleries. I feel decidedly disadvantaged when the three of them are together, Mother, Mish and Father.'

'I can see that.' He nodded. She was disappointed he didn't dismiss the idea. 'So, what does it matter? If you want to make nests, go ahead and make one.'

'Oh, I think I've grown out of that. I was fourteen at the time.' She boasted a little. 'It's pretty lively here. Pretty international, I mean if you're in Father's orbit. But he doesn't pressurize me. He's very understanding. I've always been able to go to him with any problem . . .' She looked down at her plate, feeling years older than this young man beside her. Would he be *her* age? Did he have a wife? Or children?

'There's something bugging you,' he said. 'I've been watching it in those big eyes of yours. Or is it that your lenses magnify them?'

'I don't know.' She took off her glasses and saw him in soft focus. 'Tell me.' She had never been coquettish in her life.

'Still big, and deep, deep blue, like a Spanish sky. Great short lashes, long ones only get in the way. Yes, definitely good eyes, with or without glasses.

Put them on, you're peering. I'm beginning to think I've got a spot on my nose. So your father's all right, and their life-style is all right, but what else? I sense reservations. Are there prejudices up here?' His mind seemed to dart about as if he were wielding a butterfly net to catch anything that passed.

She said, without volition, 'I've a son of five and a half whose father is West African – was, because he died. I feel different. People, a man I met, think I'm different once they know.'

'Aren't you lucky?' He looked genuinely envious. 'Damned lucky. Here am I, just run-of-the-mill, ordinary family, ordinary parents, living amongst other people living like me. I'd give anything to be different. So, go on, tell me about the other prejudices, apart from racism. That's endemic. Tell me about particularly Scottish prejudices. I want to compare them with English ones.'

'Well, apart from Sam's "lick of the tarbrush", as Bessie, our housekeeper calls it, more than a lick, there's the moral prejudices. I was never married to his father. That seems to worry people. Maybe it's not just Scottish.'

Hal looked disappointed of all things. 'So that's the big deal, is it? I thought you were going to tell me you had known Martin Luther King. Now that would have been *really* something.'

She didn't like his facetiousness. 'Eb had polio. He spent most of his life in a wheelchair.' She had a sudden memory of helping him to make difficult love, of lifting his limbs . . . A flood of red swept over her face.

'Here!' Hal Purvis's eyes were like gimlets. 'Are you too hot? You look as if you've just burst a blood vessel.'

'No.' She touched her cheek. 'I've drunk too much. But since I've gone this far, *if* I'd told you all about my son, and *if* you'd been seeing me, taking me out, would you then have been shocked, surprised, disappointed?'

'Oh dear, you're as clear as glass, love.' She felt her face stiffen. 'All right, a serious answer to a serious question which isn't worth putting. You're you. Keep telling yourself that. In any case, in twenty years we'll all be like liquorice allsorts, and marriage will be a thing of the past. Tell yourself you're avant-garde. In London these things are ceasing to matter much. You're in the vanguard. So that's that! So should we talk about me now?' She felt cheated because there had been no reaction from him, nor answer to her question.

'Let me guess. You're married with two beautiful children and a beautiful wife. You live in Surrey in a mock-Tudor residence.'

'Now you've really insulted me. And got it wrong. I'm twenty-eight and I'm in no hurry. I haven't any children, as far as I know. I'm a beaver for work too, and I've angled for half a year to tie your father down to this book. I think he's a superb painter. I'm lost in admiration. His spontaneity is out of this world – or is it planned spontaneity?'

'That's right!' She was pleased. 'Planned spontaneity. He lies for hours on his couch cogitating, then springs at his canvas like a hungry wolf.'

'You've got it! Except that he's *joyous* in execution. By God, you're lucky!'

Two people who knew Hal joined them, and then Anna, looking as chic as he had said, and he was carried away.

He came the next morning but was closeted with

Ritchie for a couple of hours, and then went away. Van was disappointed. She didn't know what she had expected, but she knew she had hoped they might meet. She had an absurd desire to let him see Sam.

Ritchie said at lunchtime, 'That man Purvis is dynamite! He got some sort of preface to this book out of me without me even realizing it, and he's fixed up very advantageous terms.'

'How did you like him?' Van said, looking cool.

'He's a hustler, almost as if he were American, and yet relaxed at the same time. I never met anyone who could go so fast and yet look as if he was lying in a haystack, a sort of "Lazybones, sleeping in the sun," act. Convincing. Sends his regards to you, Van. Said to tell you to remember what he said. What was that?'

'Oh, nothing personal. We were talking about prejudices up here.'

'They're all the same. Think they're going to find us living in bothies with the sheep.'

Eleven

Van drove to Portpatrick in Anna's car, which she had loaned to her. She had promised that if possible she would call in and see Jean if there was time. She didn't want to leave Sam too long.

On Ritchie's advice she took the road running south from Ayr in order to enjoy the coastal run and the view of Arran and Kintyre. 'Renton could never offer us scenery like that,' he said. 'You'll agree when you see it.' She kept a lookout for Ailsa Craig, better known as Paddy's Milestone, he'd said, so that she could tell Sam she had seen it, and that indeed it looked like an inverted plum pudding. She had pointed out to him in his picture book puffins and kittiwakes which could be found there.

Ritchie's memories of it were more mundane. He had been taken as a little boy on a never-to-be-forgotten trip by his parents. They had sailed from the mainland. As they neared the island, the underground shelf of rock caused the eponymous little paddle boat to pitch and toss, and everyone was sick. They disembarked, whey-faced, ate a huge tea of home-baked scones and pancakes made with goat's milk, served by the islanders, had a walk round, embarked again and were sick all the way back. 'A great day,' he said reminiscently.

Van stopped at Turnberry Hotel for tea, on Anna's instructions, and was suitably impressed. Anna had been taken there by her father, especially in the later years of his life when he had become addicted to golf. Her memories were not so plebeian as Ritchie's, Van thought, sitting in solitary splendour on the vast terrace of the hotel looking at the emerald turf.

She reflected that she had no grandparents now. She had been especially fond of Ritchie's mother and father who had died within a year of each other. She remembered sitting fascinated as a girl, watching Walter, his father, inching a tiny sailing ship into a glass bottle, his fingers, now unsullied by work, holding the pliers neat. He had been on the dole as long as she remembered him, a quiet, self-effacing little man in direct contrast to his wife, Lizzie, with her thin face lit by those large intelligent eyes, Ritchie's inheritance from her. He always said she was a woman with great talent who had never been given the opportunity to develop it. She knew the book that was being written about his work was to be dedicated to her.

Van thought of the young man, Hal Purvis, whom she had met at the party, and how she had unburdened herself so easily to him. Was it that he had invited confidences by his open manner, the impression that nothing would shock him, unlike Alan.

By now, she thought, Alan had had time to get used to Sam and her unmarried state. This invitation was by way of an apology. She would be more open and relaxed with him this weekend. There was a steadfastness in him which she liked. He could be a bulwark . . . but then, she reminded herself, she was studying at the college to equip herself so that she would have no need for bulwarks. You had to be your own person, find your own identity, not look for support from others. She had a son. She would think of Lizzie Laidlaw and how she had worked hard all her life to give Ritchie the chance he deserved, and supported her husband as well.

In the car again, driving through the clear, fresh air, Van found herself still raking about in her past. She remembered her boyfriend, William, at Renton, her effort to conform to convention by allowing herself to think of him as a possible husband until Dottie, 'tricksy Dottie', had come along and ensnared him, also his well-meaning parents. Now she saw Dottie with her short shorts and her giggle as her saviour from a fate worse than death.

She went from William to Eb, with his Afro plaits and his wide white smile, and his capacity for making her compassion turn into love. 'Vanny', he had called her. And how she had discovered that underneath his charm there was a self-pitying creature who had a perpetual grudge against society.

She remembered Anna's dismay, so carefully concealed, as she had thought, on the day she had come to visit them at the flat in Clerkenwell. Now she saw that the dismay her mother had felt was in direct relation to her love, the aspirations she had held for her daughter. She would be careful that she didn't put such a load on Sam.

That night, when Anna had gone, Eb had made cruel and violent love to Van. Even his wasted limbs had been imbued with short-lived strength. 'I'll show you, and her, I'm a man,' he had said. He had meant Anna. Van remembered the wide white smile seen in the darkness, and the sudden fear she had felt for this black stranger before she reminded herself this was Eb, who needed her, whom she loved.

She felt salt on her tongue, and realized the tears

were coursing down her face. She had to pull in at a lay-by because she couldn't see to drive. And when she started up again, there, lying at the foot of the road was the shining sheet of Loch Ryan and beyond that she knew were the Rhins of Galloway, her destination, Portpatrick, Alan.

She was there in time for drinks with him on the hotel terrace after she had been shown to her room to freshen up.

'Did you like the harbour view from your room?' Alan asked her as if he had designed it himself. She assured him she had, and had spent more time watching the fishing boats than 'freshening up'. He laughed, looking relaxed. She thought he looked like a handsome naval captain in his blazer and white open-necked shirt and the tanned complexion of a keen golfer.

She looked around, thinking that the position of the hotel was like an eyrie on the cliff top, giving a bird's-eye view of the sky. Maybe this is my fate, she thought, a bird tethered to a safe keeper, allowed to look but never to escape. An upright keeper, a bulwark for her and Sam, who would take her on occasional weekends to let her imagine what freedom would be like.

Sam would need someone like that as he grew older, who would give him a sense of security, who would take him to football matches – no, Alan would prefer rugby – who would answer his questions in a man-to-man fashion and teach him how to hold a cricket bat. It might not be too bad.

'I'm happy here already, Alan,' she said. 'I feel I'm floating on a cloud, looking down . . .' He looked pleased, as if he had raised the curtain himself on such a pleasant outlook.

He wasn't going to take advantage of the excellent hotel golf course, he told her, and was excited to know that she had stopped at Turnberry. 'Marvellous course,' he said. 'Did your father ever play there?'

'Gosh no!' she laughed. 'He thinks golf is one of the most comical spectacles of all time.' She was joking, but his eyebrows shot up in surprise.

'Meaning?' he said, as if she was being questioned in court.

'Oh, it's his usual attitude to games in general. With golf he can't understand anyone hitting a little ball for miles when it could be picked up and taken to the next hole.' And seeing Alan's face, 'He's too busy for games which monopolize your time.'

'I'm busy too, but I think everyone should take a regular exercise, especially in a sedentary job like mine.'

'I'm sure you're right.' Oh, he's precise, she thought, sitting behind the glass windows like a fish in a tank.

They went for a walk along the cliffs, and she forgot him as her eyes swept around and down to the whitewashed cottages clustering at the foot round the harbour, across the wide expanse of sea to the Irish coast. 'I can see the mountains,' she said.

'Yes, the mountains of Mourne. I'm not mad about Ireland.' He drew her to his side, dismissing Ireland. 'It was good of you to come, Vanessa. I felt we had got off on the wrong foot. I wanted to rectify that.'

'Don't apologize.' The feeling of release on this Scottish clifftop had opened her heart, and perhaps the weeping she had done for Eb. She felt cleansed and renewed. 'I can understand that you were surprised . . . Look at that bird, soaring. Isn't it wonderful?'

106

The small waves were frolicking beyond the boat spars, the sunlight caught in their spume, the wind was soft on her face. It was spring and she was only twenty-six, Eb was no more but she had his child who was surrounded with love. 'I feel I could fly,' she said, raising her free arm, 'sail away like a bird. Do you ever get a wonderful, light and airy feeling as if you could soar away if you lifted your arms?' Roderick thought he could fly, she remembered.

He smiled indulgently, tightening his arm round her waist. 'I don't think men feel that way. They have their feet on the ground. You're a brave girl considering all you've been through, probably through no fault of your own. Young people can be led astray. And now you're alone, with your . . . responsibilities.'

'Oh, I'm not alone,' she said, deflated, 'I have Sam. And my parents. I don't think anyone should feel sorry for me. You see,' she felt she should try to explain, 'there was a time in my life when I had this overwhelming feeling of compassion, undirected. I had to do something about it, like a balancing act for my own good fortune. Oh, I was intense! I wasn't brought up in a sanctimonious manner, nor guarded from life, but I suppose it was a kind of guilt – no, it was more than that, it was a pain, in my heart.' She stopped because of his bemused expression, then felt she had to go on. 'But my parents didn't smother me, they lived their own lives, worked hard, played hard. My God, you should see some of the parties they give! I went to one last week, I don't usually, although the house *shakes* when they get going up there, especially when my father's punch starts to work!' She met his eyes and he was smiling uneasily.

'Well, arty people,' he said, 'we see them at Kirkcudbright . . .'

'Oh, don't think it's a den of iniquity! It's just that they know how to let their hair down. They're quite . . . moral.' Except for Father's one fall from grace, at least one she knew about.

'Did you bring your tennis racket?' Alan said in a reprimanding kind of voice.

She swallowed. 'I did, but I don't mind if we don't play. I was never any good.' Shades of Gordon Pettigrew.

'We'll see. I'll be quite happy with you, just talking, and walking. As I told you, I purposely left my clubs at home. I might have deserted you.' The smile he now turned on her was boyish.

'You know I'm twenty-six, Alan,' she said, which was as big a *non sequitur* as the tennis racket.

'Not afraid to give away your age, eh? I'm thirty-one. I don't feel it with you. By the way, I said to Mother we might run over to Kirkcudbright tomorrow. She would like to meet you.'

'Well, if you like. And I should see my aunt and uncle.'

'Right. That's fine. I like making plans. Dinner here tonight, or maybe a run to Port Logan if you like gardens, to Kirkcudbright after lunch, perhaps go down the cliff steps for an aperitif at the Harbour Inn before dinner?' Living it up. There was another Van inside her, a naughty one, whom perhaps Hal Purvis would like.

'That sounds nice,' she said. 'But I shall have to leave on Monday morning. I promised Sam.' She felt she was dangling Sam before his eyes, but he refused to comment.

'Whatever you say.'

She excused herself and went up to dress for dinner and the dance which followed. She had bought new shoes, high-heeled, and sheer stockings. She had one evening dress, a Christmas present from Anna, which the assistant had told her was the same blue as her eyes. It was plain. She thought anything frilly looked ludicrous on a girl who wore glasses. She tried doing without them after she'd had her bath, but it was no good. Everything had a furry edge. Ritchie thought that from a painter's point of view myopia might give one a unique vision.

Silly happiness flooded through her again when they were in the dining room amongst the chattering guests. It had no basis, except that of a child being given a treat. The wide pale-coloured walls and large windows made her feel as if she were inside a peach, a peach with cream because of the peach-toned wallpaper and snowy tablecloths.

'Lovely and comfortable here,' she said, looking around at the elderly guests bent over their plates.

'Yes, it's very civilized,' Alan said. 'It's well worth paying the extra to stay in a decent hotel.'

She nodded, wondering how she would feel about him if they were in a sleazy one. He was a man who needed what he considered his rightful ambience, she decided.

At the end of the dinner she said she would go and telephone home to say good night to Sam, and Alan looked surprised. 'If you think it necessary,' and, as she got up to go, 'Put it on my bill.'

Sam was excited. They had seen gorillas and flamingoes and a striped horse.

'A zebra.'

'. . . and penguins which marched one after the other.'

'I'll be back soon, Sam.'

'Don't rush,' he said grandly. 'Granny's looking after me very adequately.' He had recently begun to borrow their vocabulary, which made them button up their smiles.

'That's good. I'm going now, Sam.' She was mindful of the telephone bill.

Alan welcomed her back. 'The band's starting up.' He didn't ask about Sam.

'He's having a wonderful time with my mother and father.'

'Good. Shall we go?' And as they walked to the ballroom, he said, putting on a man-of-the-world expression, 'They're quite . . . ?'

'Quite what?'

'I mean, about you . . . not being married . . . that sort of thing? And the other . . . business?'

She looked at him. 'They're the last people . . .' She was swept into his arms. 'You should talk to them.'

'It's you I want to talk to. The object of this exercise.' Dancing seemed to give him a kind of superiority. He smiled magnanimously. 'But tonight we'll just enjoy ourselves. We'll have plenty of time tomorrow.'

He did a comical dance step which tied her feet in knots and she apologized. 'But don't patronize me,' she mumbled. She didn't think he heard her.

She had already discovered that he was a good dancer, straight-backed but adroit, handsome in his dinner jacket. He held her closely and there was the expensive smell from him, strong, masculine, perfumed. It was heady. She thought again of Hal Purvis and imagined that in comparison his bow tie might be askew and that his hair might be rumpled. And he would have sung along with the crooner.

Like Ritchie. Was that why she was attracted to him?

They danced until the band stopped playing, until the last waltz, when the lights were lowered and people danced closely. Sometimes she saw a couple kiss. She looked up at Alan and found him gazing down at her. She thought he appeared tense for some reason, and smiled reassuringly at him. He was really very good to her. In spite of his sophisticated appearance, could he be shy? That she could understand.

At the door to her room he said, 'I have a terrible thirst. Have you a drinks refrigerator? The best rooms do.'

'Yes, I think so.' She hadn't noticed. 'Would you like to come in and see?' He followed her.

'This is nice.' He glanced around like a hotel manager. 'I told them they were to give you a sea view. And lots of hanging space. Girls travel with so much luggage.'

'I don't.' She laughed. 'I'm not like my mother. She's so meticulous. Everything must have the right accessories.'

'She's very smart.' 'Chic,' Hal Purvis had said.

He had unlocked the table refrigerator and had two glasses in his hand. 'What would you like, Vanessa?' She wished he would call her Van.

'Oh, a bitter lemon or something like that.' She had a slight headache with the claret they had drunk at dinner.

'I see they have Johnny Walker here. I'll have a nightcap.' He poured out the drinks. 'I always have one with Mother. She says it's better than a sleeping pill.' She had a picture of him sitting with a grey-haired woman in a pink flannel dressing gown and furry slippers.

'Do you get on well with her?' she said, accepting the glass. He sat down on the bed beside her.

'Oh, yes. Like most mothers she's a bit autocratic. Her dream is to see me settled. She would keep in the background, she says. It's a big house.'

'Is it?' She was alerted.

'Vanessa,' his voice had changed, 'when you meet her tomorrow, would you mind not telling her too much about . . . your past?'

'Like what?'

'Well, I've more or less said you're a widow.'

She breathed in, felt her mouth tighten. 'I wasn't married. I told you.'

'I'll tell her that . . . afterwards. And your son – don't . . . elaborate. I thought if you agreed to . . . think of me in a . . . certain way, we could . . . introduce her to the circumstances bit by bit. And then he'd . . .' he evidently couldn't use Sam's name, 'he'd be going off to school, maybe boarding school and . . .'

She sat up straight. 'Are you saying you want me to *hide* Sam?'

'No, it isn't that. It's just not . . . to rush everything, give Mother time to get to know you, and . . . and the boy.' She moved impatiently but he went on, 'She's what one might call a good-living woman, she knows young girls make mistakes –'

'Will you please stop this!' she said. Her voice sounded odd in her ears. 'I don't want to listen to any more. I've no intention of wearing a hair shirt for the rest of my life. I have Sam. His father is dead, but I have his son, Sam, and I love him very much, more than anyone else in the world.'

He put his glass down on the side table. 'Don't forget, Vanessa, I'm a lawyer. It's not the first family problem I've had to sort out.'

'But there's no *problem*!'

'Not to you. But the world . . .' She saw he was trembling, 'Vanessa, I've fallen in love with you. I don't know why. I always thought it would be one of the girls I know in Kirkcudbright, but when I met you, something about you, the difference in you, stabbed at my heart. I thought it would go away. It hasn't.' To her surprise he leaned forward and took off her glasses, put his arms round her so that his weight made them fall back on the bed.

She struggled. 'What do you think you're doing?' She struggled more fiercely, but his weight bore her backwards again. She felt his mouth on her neck.

'We can't stay at arm's length.' He was muttering, his lips moving, downwards. She felt acutely embarrassed. She shouldn't have sat here.

'Let me up!' She tried to sound stern, wanted to giggle.

'I thought you of all people wouldn't . . .' His body was strong, his perfumed smell seemed to increase, filling her nostrils. She opened her mouth to speak as the impact of his words struck her, but she was silenced by his kissing her fiercely, a sucking kind of kiss which imprisoned her bottom lip and hurt. It hurt very much.

The kiss went on. It was as if it were some kind of release to him, words he couldn't say. There was a kind of steady desperation in his kissing, and in the equally steady machine-like massaging of her left breast. She struggled, choked violently so that he had to release her. She sat up and he sat up beside her. She smoothed her clothes.

'That was ridiculous,' she said, 'ridiculous.' She knew her voice was shaking. 'Hand me my glasses, please.' He did, and she put them on, feeling she was restoring her sanity.

'I can't apologize enough.' She couldn't look at him. 'I don't know what . . .' She got up and went to the window while he stammered, stood with her back to him. How sad the sea was now, black, lifeless, no moon. '. . . what came over me.' His voice had steadied. 'That's a stupid thing to say. I find you so appealing, so different –'

'And quite prepared because of "my past" to be amenable.' She turned round to face him. 'I feel terrible, cheap, as if you'd brought me here, paid for me, in order to . . . for a specific reason.' She couldn't use words like 'seduce' or 'rape'.

He got up, came over to the window and stood beside her. She could feel the tension in him. His arm against hers was shaking, and her anger turned to pity. My undoing, she thought. She remembered Eb telling her how he had thought of her all day, was on tenterhooks for her to come home, 'and it wasn't so that you could cook dinner for me,' he had said with his wide melon grin, his eyes hot and moist.

What would Ritchie say if he could see this pantomime? she thought. She often treated him in her mind as a yardstick. 'What's wrong with a little roll in the hay?' Or 'Poor chap'? It wasn't all that important, really. She felt she could be objective, because even with Eb she had never known this overpowering sexual drive. There had been too much compassion in her feelings for him.

'It's not important, Alan,' she said, slipping her hand through his arm. 'I should feel flattered that you find me attractive. I'm not exactly a *femme fatale*.'

'You are to me. I don't know why. I wouldn't have

chosen you, to be honest, it would have been so much easier with a local girl, like Cissie Crichton – you won't know her, but Mother likes her. God knows, there are plenty to choose from, pretty, competent, known in the town. You're just . . . different.'

'Well, I don't suppose any of them are unmarried mothers.'

'I don't think of that,' he said quickly.

'It's there.'

'I suppose you want to leave tomorrow morning now?'

'Should I?' She smiled at him. 'Goodness no, Ritchie and Anna would laugh themselves silly.'

'Is that the only reason?'

'Well, I promised to see my Aunt Jean.'

'Nothing more?' He looked young. The stiffness had gone out of his posture, indeed there seemed still to be a faint tremor in his features, in his eyelids. She remembered the battered wives she had looked after saying that it was all they wanted, men, and wondered if it were true. She hadn't much experience – William Armstrong, the embryonic bank manager who had been so easily taken from her by tricksy Dottie; and Eb. Both takers. And now Alan.

'I like you, Alan.' She liked him more in his present state of doubt than the self-possessed man she had first met at Kirkcudbright. That had been the public persona. 'I don't have many friends. I wouldn't like to stop being friends with you over a paltry incident.'

'Are you saying it's a pity I didn't go further?' he said, surprising her.

'No. Did it sound like that? Sorry. I think you should go now.' She held up her face, and his lips were cool and didn't linger.

*   *   *

When she entered Alan's sitting room from a large hall gleaming with a brass display of knick-knacks, which existed, Van thought, to keep some poor domestic busy, she was greeted to her nervous surprise, by two pairs of eyes, those of a well-preserved matron, who would be a few years older than her own mother but seemed to belong to a different era, and those of a large striped cat, which looked steadily and disconcertingly at her. Van smiled uncertainly as Mrs McAlpine held out her hand.

'Come away in, Vanessa! Alan hasn't told me your other name so you'll have to excuse me. Sit down there. Don't mind Tom. He seems to have taken quite a fancy to you.'

She sat down gingerly, one eye on the cat. 'He's very big, isn't he?' As if to show how big it was the cat rose, stretched like a boxer flexing his muscles, and sat down again. Its eyes returned to Van again. She thought it had a human face.

She made herself concentrate on Mrs McAlpine who was telling her about the many happy weekends she had had with her late husband at the Portpatrick Hotel. 'Ah, happy days,' she sighed, 'perched up there in our love nest.' She looked, with her large masculine features, an unlikely inhabitant of a love nest. 'There is nothing like a good marriage. That is my dearest wish for Alan.'

'Oh, come off it, Mother,' Alan said boyishly. They proceeded to engage in a bantering match, to Van's surprise, coy and even flirtatious, an attitude which was belied by Mrs McAlpine's appearance, the safe, good clothes which would be stylish ten years hence because they had no style, the pearl button earrings and necklace, which were discreet enough to be real, and the hair permed and styled in the neat shingle which was how hairdressers thought women of her age should have it dressed.

Van surreptitiously smoothed her own wiry hair which refused to lie down and be sleek. She had a hatred of going to hairdressers and chopped bits off whenever it seemed necessary. Its frizziness concealed any untidy ends.

'I have to let you into a little secret.' Mrs McAlpine returned her attention to Van. 'Alan's never *done* talking about you. I think he's smitten.' She was smiling. She had horsy teeth. Alan must resemble his dead father.

He sat down on the arm of Van's chair, still being boyish. 'You're embarrassing Vanessa, Mother.' She wasn't embarrassed, only when she looked down at the cat and found it looking up at her. Had the soul of Alan's father, she thought wildly for a second, transmigrated into this huge beast?

'Of course I've heard of your mother,' Mrs McAlpine said. 'A twin of Mrs Doctor Whitbread, isn't she?' She shook her head slowly, lowered her eyes, as if the thought stirred up memories. 'I believe they're quite different?' She looked up again.

'In appearance, but very alike in temperament. They're really close.'

'You'll know about my late husband's involvement concerning that son of theirs.' Mrs McAlpine's chest swelled. 'It's best to be frank. A terrible business, but Mr Logan only did his duty. My late husband assured him on that count.' She shook her head. 'I often think it drove my poor Dick to his grave. The worry.'

'You probably heard Roderick died,' Van said. 'Shortly after he ran away from the home.' She emphasized the last word.

Mrs McAlpine, rather surprisingly to her, nodded

117

approvingly. 'The best thing. Your aunt will now be able to devote more time to the doctor, and cut down on her art work.' Van looked away in case she would reply angrily, and met again the cat's gaze. Its eyes were cold and disapproving.

'Well, enough of sad things,' Mrs McAlpine said. 'You have a little boy, Alan tells me. You look so young.' She tut-tutted in disbelief.

'Yes.' Van felt her inside coiling in a tight knot. This was not going well.

'And his father died?'

'Yes.'

'What was his name, if I may ask?'

'Eb.' Mrs McAlpine looked uncomprehending. 'Ebenezer Carradine.'

'Well!' She smiled, as if to show how broad-minded she was. 'Well, I know what to call you *now*, but I think Vanessa is friendlier, so we'll stick to that, eh? I'm going to be quite frank although I see Alan looking at me. Those sons!'

'Those mothers!' Alan said in the bantering tone he seemed to use with her.

'Although he's my son and I shouldn't boast, I think you would find him very understanding. "After all," I said to him, "you would be getting a ready-made family. It would get you used to having some of your own."'

'What did I tell you?' Alan said to Van, shaking his head like a comedian. 'But you know what mothers are like.'

'Mine isn't.' She looked coldly at him.

Mrs McAlpine was sweeping on. 'I think as you get to know Alan you'll find what a treasure he is. Well respected in the community. Everyone in the town wants to see him married.'

118

'That will do, Mother,' Alan said with an amused look. 'You'll be putting Vanessa off.'

The knot inside Van was tighter than ever. How much had he told his mother about her? Had she said, 'Leave it to me, son, I know how to deal with young women of her kind'? Anger flooded her. It was the rectitude she minded. Her parents were volatile, tolerant, quick to anger, quick to forgive. She should have realized they were exceptional.

'I think I should be getting on to my aunt's, Alan,' she said.

'But you haven't had any tea!' His mother was horrified.

'I really haven't the time. I'm sorry.' Van got up. So did Mrs McAlpine. So did the cat.

'I'm sorry your visit was so short. Anyhow, enjoy yourself at the hotel for the rest of your stay,' Mrs McAlpine said. 'Ah me, to be young again!' She looked sadly at the huge cat standing at her side. 'Eh, Tom? Still, I'm glad we met, Mrs . . . Carradine, was it?'

Van felt ice-cold. 'No. *Miss* Laidlaw. Thank you for having me.'

Alan's mother didn't answer. She stood like Lot's wife, face blank.

Alan drove the short distance to Jean's house in silence. Van sat beside him, equally silent. Let him speak first, she thought. But when he stopped at the gate she said, 'Are you coming in with me?'

He was staring through the windscreen, his face grim. 'You should have left it to *me* to tell her you weren't married.'

'Well, why didn't you?' She was suddenly tired of him. '*Are* you coming in?'

'No, I'll go back home. Ring me when you want me to come back for you.'

119

'I suppose you're going back to discuss me with your mother?'

His face reddened. 'That's unfair. It would be a bit of a blow for her the way you blurted it out, but she would have come round. She's really very kind. And well thought of.'

'Is she?' She looked at him and saw that he was distressed. And, strangely, still boyish. It was as if contact with his mother had taken away some of his maturity.

'You've lived in London,' he said. 'Your parents are cosmopolitan. I'm considered in Kirkcudbright,' he laughed, 'quite a man of the world, but I've never been away from the place except when I was in Glasgow and on occasional holidays. Your family make me feel . . . provincial. But I've never met anyone who touched my heart like you – oh, plenty of suitable girls but there was never this feeling. You're like a strange bird, exotic.'

'Oh, Alan!' She had to laugh. 'I'm a frump!'

'Not to me. It's your . . . ambience.'

Her heart softened, was suffused with pity, her bugbear. It would have been much better to say that the weekend was over, that she should go back to Glasgow from Jean's house. Instead she touched his hand and said, 'I'll ring you when I'm ready,' and got out of the car.

Jean welcomed her in her studio with a warm hug. 'Hello! Your mother told me you were living it up at Portpatrick.' Her glance strayed to her easel. 'This is tearing my guts out.'

'What's wrong?' Van sat down on a nearby stool.

'It's just not coming right.' She bent forward and touched the canvas with the paintbrush she was holding. 'Don't mind me if I go on doodling. Have you had tea with Lady McAlpine? Anna and I thought you'd be taken there for inspection.'

'No, I refused it. Do you like her, Jean?'

'Hate her. You know why. She's tainted as far as I'm concerned. Oh, bugger!' She poked her head forward. 'Pass me that rag.' She stretched out a hand. 'And don't hang over me like an avenging angel.' Van had got up. 'Sit down.'

'Sorry.'

'Don't say sorry.'

'Sorry.' She laughed. 'Alan wasn't in the firm when –'

'No, he took it over when his father died. But when the old man *was* alive, I bet he and his wife discussed Roderick endlessly. You could call her the sleeping partner of that firm. The town divided into two camps, for and against. I was so miserable that I felt like clearing out completely, but John told me not to be cowardly, so I stayed. And found true friends. And life went on. You can't stop it.' She was painting rapidly. 'And then Roderick ran away from the home, and you know the rest. Anna always says she envies me my tragic life.' She bent forward with her nose almost against the canvas and painted a minute section of landscape so carefully that it looked as if she were dissecting it. At least Van thought it might be landscape. To her it was an amorphous mess.

'Are you making that better or worse?' she asked.

'That's a moot point. I'm simply waiting for the pain to go when my mind dwells on Roderick. Do you feel like that too about your black man? Most of the time all right, then a *burying* kind of wave of pain?'

'Regret more than pain. I could have done so much more for him, should have.'

'You were always a bleeding heart. Don't. You

121

have Sam, and Anna and Ritchie, and you could have Alan McAlpine if you liked. Anyone who gets through the portals guarded by his mother is home and dry.'

'I don't know if I want to be home and dry. He made a pass at me at Portpatrick.'

Jean looked round, the grief disappearing from her face and replaced by amusement. 'Did he? Well, he's human after all! I often wondered if she had made him impotent as well.'

'Oh, Jean!' She laughed. 'It didn't get that far. Do you like him? He's very stiff and proper, isn't he?'

'That's his mother. And the local dancing classes. John said he was sent too, when he was a boy. I have thought, though, about Alan, that if the right woman took him in hand he might become like my John, reliable, straight, a bulwark.'

'But his wife would have to live in that house with his mother.'

'Oh, put your foot down about that! She would ruin any marriage. This is flowing now. Lovely. What were we talking about?'

'Alan. I honestly don't think of him *vis-à-vis* marriage. The most important thing in my life is my studies. I want to work in a hospital, be an almoner. That's coming first with me. I'd only marry anyone who would let me work, like Father and John.'

'You're showing sense. Well, you have the rest of the weekend to lay down your conditions if . . . get it in writing.'

'And there's Sam. He can't quite reconcile himself to Sam. But he would have to realize that where I go Sam goes too.' She stopped abruptly.

'What's wrong?' Jean said. 'Your face changed.'

'The prospect suddenly seemed inexpressibly bleak. I realize I'm happy as I am until . . .'

Jean had turned and was looking at her, her brush poised. 'You're not a child, Van. You've been through a lot. I think you've come to the stage we all reach that no one can help you. You have to make up your own mind. But be your own person first and foremost. Even two people as close as Anna and I are came to that stage. I think it may be a sign of maturity – if we ever *do* grow up. Look at us, in our fifties, and we're still pretty silly at times.'

'You're both too beautiful to be in your fifties.'

'You mean Anna is. She's glamorous. Chic. How is she?'

'Being glamorous and chic and sensible at the same time, but then she has my father. If Alan were like Ritchie I'd jump at him. There aren't many couples with that . . . specialness.'

'It doesn't come often. I had it once, long ago . . .' She was painting as she spoke with a concentration which was frightening. 'I really think . . . this is coming right at last . . .'

It was no longer even vaguely like a landscape. It was a hotchpotch of colour that made Van's eyes ache as she stared at it.

'One thing,' she said, 'I'll never marry a painter.'

'Neither did I.' Jean went on painting.

Twelve

Van went back and fell into the Clevedon Crescent pattern, taking Sam to school each morning, then catching the bus to Sauchiehall Street and walking along to Pitt Street and the college. She liked Glasgow, the busy shops, the Glasgow voices, the kindliness. She liked the view uphill from Pitt Street to Garnethill where her mother and father had attended the Art School and fallen in love. She felt part of the pattern.

Her examinations would be in June, and she wanted to do well. It would mean independence, if she succeeded, whether she married or not. She didn't think of that. Her visit to Portpatrick and then to see Alan's mother had been like a cautionary finger. She would be careful.

She realized that what she was now studying formally was the logical conclusion to her earlier amateurish sorties into social work. Now she was learning when she went with her tutors to the Royal or Western Infirmaries how to be objective, and that ill-informed and misdirected pity was a hindrance and an insult to the person she was trying to help. She was being taught to use her talents in a positive way. And she was seeing what another side of life was like in the huge Glasgow hospitals where the old people, particularly women from the East End of Glasgow, had known nothing but a life of unremitting poverty and hardship.

Once more she was made painfully aware of the difference in class. In Renton she had lived in a house with a large garden bounded by a protective stone wall; here in Glasgow she lived in a spacious terrace designed by a famous architect to house in comfort members of a privileged society. Even with her father and mother, Bessie, Sam and herself, there was privacy for three separate units.

Her first case, Mary Cafferty, was seventy-eight, looked eighty-seven at least, and had long since given up any pride in her appearance. Her bottom false teeth had been 'that sore' that she had stopped wearing them; her hair, a thin grey plait, was pinned up in a pathetic little bun. She had brought up seven children in a single-end. 'They hippens were the worst when the weans were wee,' she told Van, 'wi' only cauld water to wash them in, and a closet on the landing. I couldny have done withoot a po under the bed. They're a' away and mairrit noo. Only Tam writes regular like.'

'And when you got ill,' Van asked her, 'you wouldn't be able to go downstairs to the . . . closet?'

'Ach naw. I kept a pail below the bed and a neebour would empty it fur me when she was passing. Neebors are often better than families when it comes to the bit. It wis a neebour that found me when I fell gettin' oot o' the bed in the middle of the night. The Social got me a hame help then, a nice wee soul, then I got this.' She wheezed. She had bronchial pneumonia.

'Well, you're in good hands now, Mrs Cafferty,' Van assured her. 'When you're better we'll get you into a nice home where you'll be well looked after.'

The old lady's mouth shut like a clamp. 'There wull be nae hames fur me. I want back tae ma single-end and ma neebours. *That*'s hame.'

It's high time, Van told herself, that you stopped wearing that hair shirt. It's getting threadbare. Your spacious terrace house is no better a home to you than Mary Cafferty's single-end is to her. Your mother doesn't feel privileged. She's comfortable with the position she finds herself in.

She recognized that it was Sam's birth which had changed Anna's impatience with her. This she could deal with, a *fait accompli*. Mother also had had some ditching to do, she thought now. Granny Rose had been the nigger in the woodpile – she smiled at that, thinking of Eb – with her snobbism. Anna had rejected all her teaching by deciding to marry Ritchie Laidlaw, a poor boy from the other side of the tracks, a near-slum tenement on the outskirts of Glasgow.

Van said to Anna that night when they were having dinner, 'I went to see one of those one-roomed tenement flats today, on a project, cold water tap, no bathroom or lavatory.'

'A single-end?' she said, looking up from her plate. 'Ritchie would say, "You're out of your league there!" ' She laughed. 'I can just hear him pontificating: "Ma mither an' faither," he always adopts the vernacular, "started life in yin. They thought they were goin' up in the world when they got a room and kitchen. I slept a' the time I wis at hame in a fold-up bed in the parlour." ' Her imitation was good. 'Talk about inverted snobbery!'

Van laughed too. 'If he could hear you! But it was the lack of privacy that must have been awful. Five

126

girls, a woman I saw today, *five*. Just think, if they were, you know . . .'

'Menstruating? It's a thought. And how about the mother and father making love under the blankets when he came stotting home from the pub, and some of the kids sleeping in the same room?'

'It's funny that I should have to come back to Glasgow to feel my middle-classness so acutely.'

'They have their pride, don't forget. Didn't you see all the photographs in the single-end you visited? Most of the children scattered to the new estates, or further afield to America or Australia?'

'You're right. I did. The tutor said that in spite of all the advantages of the new houses on the outskirts they were queuing to get back into the city.'

'They miss the warmth, the friendliness, even the bedbugs . . .' She looked up. Ritchie had just arrived home from London. He came and kissed her, looking into her eyes for a moment as he always did.

'Hi, Van.' He put a hand on her hair as he passed.

'We're talking about the friendliness of the slums, Dad.'

'Friendliness? That's an "outside" word. Warmth. That's what it is. A giant tea cosy over the Gorbals. Here all I get is a polite good morning from our neighbours.'

'That's because they think this is a Bohemian household,' Anna said, 'bringing down the tone.'

'Toulouse-Lautrec?' He got down on his knees and waddled towards them, making them giggle.

'Well, your parties do go on for a long time,' Van said, still giggling. 'Bessie thinks you're all mad, the noise you kick up. "Whit ur they laughin' at a' the time?"' She could use the vernacular too.

'Listen to Miss Prim!' Anna said. 'I didn't exactly

127

see you rushing away from the last one. Let yourself go, didn't you? Discovered there are more things in life than the history of the British working classes?'

'Don't tease the girl,' Ritchie said. 'So what's the *Daily Worker* saying today, Van?'

'You're a pair.' She smiled at him. He had seen her blush. 'Down with the white-collar workers?' She liked his general untidiness, she thought – and he couldn't sit in a chair properly, his legs got in the way, he nearly forced the back off. Perhaps she was noticing more acutely after her weekend with Alan whose general demeanour left nothing to be desired, except for his lapse in her bedroom.

'Did you sleep in that shirt?' Anna asked him.

'No, in my birthday suit, as you well know. Besides ma gensy covers it up.' He pulled his grey jersey straight.

'And your hair looks like a fireside rug,' Van said.

'God, why do I come home? Was Portpatrick very *comme il faut*?'

'Most of the time. But nothing compared with his mother. She didn't approve of me at all. Nor did her cat.'

'*Formidable* was she?' He gave the word a French whirl. 'Well, you'll have an antidote at Arenys de Mar when you come with us.'

'Was London tiring, Ritchie?' Anna said.

'Exciting.' He leered at her, grimacing horribly.

'Have you eaten?' She raised her chin.

'I was fed like a fighting cock. Lauded as a representative of the Scottish School. Heady stuff. The book's coming out next spring. By the way, Van, I met Harry Purvis.'

'He prefers Hal.'

'You're further on than I am. Suits him, though,

good King Hal. He was telling me he's just back from the States. I'd given him Mish's address and Karin invited him to dinner. They had a lot in common. He's raving about Mish's expertise and Karin's charm.'

'Did he say anything about me?' His presence was strongly in her mind at the mention of his name, his easiness, the feeling of sympathy and rapport behind the breeziness. So different from Alan. She had the niggling feeling, not new, that she had gone down the wrong path there. Gordon Pettigrew, William Armstrong, Eb and now Alan. She was a poor judge.

'Just asked if you were still so serious. If he could see your face now he wouldn't have to ask.'

'I was just thinking.'

'You're in a permanent brown study.' Ritchie scratched his curls. 'I've often wondered about that. Why a *brown* study?'

'Aren't they all, velvet brown? But do you *think* I look serious?' She appealed to both of them.

'I like a bit of seriousness,' Anna said.

'As long as it's not disapproving,' Ritchie said.

'Oh, you! You're making me out to be a prig!'

'No, you're a sweetie. Just prickly. The man who gets you – and I don't think you've really been "got" yet, in spite of Sam's father – will discover how sweet you are.'

'What else did Hal Purvis say?' she asked. It hurt to think of Eb dead, but her father was right.

'Let me think . . .' She saw the swift look between them and thought, I'm in the way here. They should be on their own. So should I. 'Oh, he asked about Sam. "Tell her to hang in there," he said. I don't know what he was talking about, but then he talks all the time. A firebrand. But he's put together a good book. Made me blush.'

She felt stirred, it was a new, tender feeling. Not all tenderness, there was excitement too. She felt her cheeks hot again at the thought of him. 'I'll go and make you some coffee.'

She stayed in the kitchen talking to Bessie for a long time. Bessie was sitting at the Aga with the little oven door open and her feet half in it. She felt the cold now in spite of the comfort of the house.

'She'll be happy noo,' she said.

'Who?'

'Your mither. Have you ever seen her face when he comes in? You'd think Leerie had come along with his lighter and lit a lamp in it. By gum, it's lasted a long time.'

'What has lasted a long time, Bessie?' She wanted her to say the word.

'It's a kind o' . . . saftness. They kin' o' melt when they clap eyes on each ither. Aye, by gum, it's lasted a long time.' Van looked at her. The old face was wistful, perhaps at the thought of pleasures she had never known.

'Would you like to pop into bed and I'll bring you a wee tray?'

'Aw right.' She nodded grudgingly, but her mouth quirked upwards. 'But no' any o' that coffee you're makin'. Bitter stuff.'

'What would you say to a nice cup of tea and a Jacob's chocolate biscuit?'

'Aye.' She nodded judiciously. 'Ur they ony o' they sandwich yins left? Wi' the icing in between. I'm partial to banana, or apricot.'

'I'll have a look while you're getting ready, Your Highness.' She bowed.

'Nane o' your daft stuff here, a big lass like you! Aye, but you're bonny aw the same, even wi' they specs.' Van knocked them down to the end of her nose and was rewarded by Bessie's chuckle as she rose stiffly from her chair.

She went upstairs to bed after she had given Anna and Ritchie their coffee. They were deep in a discussion of Ritchie's book. She looked in on Sam in the room next to hers, to tuck him in. In the light from the lamp outside he looked like Eb asleep, the dark face, the frizzy hair, the high brow, and the same sweetness about the mouth in repose. She kissed the brow, as if she were kissing Eb, whose discontent with life had always been ironed out in sleep.

But it was Hal Purvis she thought of in her own bed later, not Eb, nor even Alan. 'Tell her to hang in there,' he had said to Ritchie in London. The words brought him back so clearly to her, the feeling of energy which emanated from him, that you might get an electric shock if you touched him. It had been so strong that now she set herself deliberately to reconstruct his image in her mind, his slight figure, the general spareness of him, except for the thicker waist, the swift smile, the quick movements, a Puck, a firebrand, Ritchie had said, a firebrand. He wouldn't make any demands on her, unlike Alan, or Eb. He would always be his own man and allow her space to be herself. She was sure he would have thin arms and legs and a fat belly, like Humpty Dumpty, she thought, and found herself giggling. She pulled the sheet over her head like a child and went to sleep.

Van had a talk with Miss Clewes when she was collecting Sam from school on the last day of term. She was aware that he had a quick bright brain, but there had been complaints from Miss Clewes about his naughtiness.

'He feels different, of course,' the teacher said. 'Children are cruel. They probably taunt him about his skin. I can't stop that. But I would like him to channel his talents into work, not mischief. He'll thrive better when he's older and goes to a school where the discipline is stricter.'

'What do you think of boarding school for him?' Van asked, thinking about Alan's remark.

'It could be a great success or a terrible failure. Personally I'd keep him at home. He's sure of *you*.'

That at least was true. He always came to her with his problems. 'When I go to Grandpa's house in Spain,' he said to her one day, 'I'm not going to hold up my face to the sun the way the other boys do. I'm going to stay inside.'

'But you go to Spain for the sun,' she reminded him.

'Oh, I'll come out! I'll wait till they're all the same colour as me, *then* come out.'

She hugged him. 'Don't wait too long.'

Alan still came fortnightly to Glasgow, 'on business,' he said, and although she protested half-heartedly, he still took her out. He had apologized for not telling his mother she wasn't married.

'She's never come across it before, you see, I mean . . . your situation . . . except for a maid we once had. She's really a good, kind person. Ask anyone in the town. Once she gets used to the idea she'll be all right.'

'It doesn't matter, Alan, really.' It was difficult to protest too vigorously over a delicious meal in Danny Brown's excellent fish restaurant.

132

'She liked you, and she's fond of children. Look how she showed you all those photographs.'

'But they were of you!'

'Yes, I know, but still . . .'

Van thought very little of herself for going on seeing him, except that she liked him. He was in some ways like a well-dressed Eb, deserving of her pity. He solved other people's problems every day and yet could not solve his own. And he loved her. He trembled when he kissed her – only on meeting and departing, certainly, but he wrote her passionate love letters until she told him that they embarrassed her too much. The hurt on his face made her squirm.

She needed him too, in a strange sort of way, to reassure her about her femininity, as a reward for her hard work at the college, needed him for the ordinary pleasures of being able to dress up and be wined and dined.

She did well in her examinations. Her teachers congratulated her on her application and her understanding, Ritchie and Anna congratulated her but not with any surprise. Anyone who wanted to do well worked hard and got results, it went without saying.

Alan was pleased and proud, he said, that she was a clever girl, as if she had completed a piece of embroidery or made a quilt. There was no point in asking him what his views would be of a working wife when it was obvious that he regarded her course as a hobby to be dropped on marriage to a well-known lawyer.

The last day of term for both of them, Van suggested to Sam that they should get off the bus and walk the rest of the way home.

'It's too far to Granny's,' he said, pouting.

'And you're too lucky,' she said sharply, 'collected

by Granny or me all the time. Riding home in cars or buses. Some children have to *walk* to school.' She saw his hurt face. 'We'll buy an ice cream at Byres Road, and by the time you've finished it, you'll find we're at Clevedon Crescent.

'That will balance the books,' he nodded, lips pursed. 'Could I have a McCallum?' She laughed as they got up and jumped off the bus at the Botanic Gardens. 'A McCallum' was Ritchie's name for an ice cream topped with raspberry cordial.

The McCallum was entirely to Sam's satisfaction, and together they crossed the road to the Gardens side and began their walk. The trees beyond the railings were deep green, the glass of Kibble Palace reflected the bright blue of the summer sky.

The 'scheme' she had been visiting in that afternoon had only a narrow slit of sky above the towering flats, and the bright splashes of rose beds they were passing had been matched only by the bright clothes of the children. Here there was only the noise of the traffic, in Castlemilk voices had shouted, screamed, laughed, cried, women stood on the pavements gossiping, men kicked a ball about, boys joined in or rode madly about on bicycles. The place teemed with life lived on the streets.

She looked around her. Even the traffic seemed to purr after it left Queen Margaret Drive and to proceed in a stately fashion between the gracious terraces of Great Western Road. She thought of the young man she had been visiting that morning, an applicant for additional benefit. He'd had an anxious face, was severely disabled with a back injury, and his wife had been fat with uncombed hair and a trio of dirty children around her skirts.

'You're too saft, Geordie.' She constantly

134

interrupted. 'Tell her aboot the awful pain, how you can't even struggle oot for a pint when I want you to cheer us up. He wulny speak up for hisself, miss, that's his trouble.'

He answered Van's questions in a low monotone. Sometimes his wife punched him in the back to get him to speak up, but although he winced, he didn't reprimand her. He looked cowed. But when Van questioned him about his last employment, she saw a different man. His back straightened in the wheel-chair, his eyes lit up.

'Aye, I miss it all right, see, it's the camaraderie. Hard work but jokin' and that, and cairyin' the rid-hot pots owr tae the mould, and seein' they faces aw roon it, lit up wi' the glare, and the . . . pride, aye, pride. An' then, breakin' it oot o' the mould when it was cauld and the feelin' that you had *made* some-thin'. Aye, it was a good life. You came hame good and tired but it was worth it.'

'It's the wee lassie in the office he misses, sure it is, Geordie.' The woman leered at Van. 'Aye, he's no' tellin' you aboot that!'

'It was a happy working place?' Van smiled at him.

'Aye, a big happy family, the boss used to say, and this wee lassie Maggie's tellin' you aboot, she used to cam roon every Friday wi' oor wages and we had a bit o' a joke. When she was getting married us yins aw clubbed thegether an' gied her a chimin' clock for a present. She brought in a bottle o' whisky an' we aw had a dram thegether. We had great tares sure enough.'

'Aye, he can go on an' on about her, but whit aboot me, oot on a cleaning job every day in a dirty factory in Parkheed?' His wife had her hands on her fat hips, her face sour.

135

'Well, I look efter the weans, don't I? No' much fun that for a grown man.' Van noticed his wife was pregnant, and remembered one of the almoner's comments, 'Making babies is the only fun they have.'

What a difference here, she thought, as they walked along the well-kept road, no children, few passers-by. Sam was cheerfully licking his 'pokey-hat', as Bessie called it. He's habituated already to decorum and lack of noise, she thought, a privileged child. It was strange that Ritchie, who had known a rough upbringing, should have supported Anna in her desire to send Sam to her own school. Was it his Achilles heel, a liking for privilege? But it shouldn't be right that Sam didn't know what went on in other areas less privileged than this.

'My best friend at school, Ludovic, said "bugger" today,' he said. He had emptied the cone and was now sucking the remainder of the ice cream through a hole in the bottom. All children did that, regardless of class, and all children took a delight in saying 'bad' words.

They turned into Clevedon Drive and a dog ran towards them. It wasn't a stray, judging by its well-tended coat, but it was a dog, nevertheless, which had escaped.

Thirteen

The journey to Spain in Ritchie's capacious Rover had
the appearance of an Eastern caravan, loaded as it
was to the roof and beyond that with suitcases, satch-
els, easels, paint boxes, a typewriter, Van's economic
and social history tomes, Sam's favourite picture
books and toys, manuscripts and galley proofs, which
Ritchie had to read. Sam was tucked into one corner
wearing a panama hat which Van had bought him so
that the sun wouldn't 'get at him'.

The voyage across the Channel was choppy and
made him sick. It was a windy day, cold for the end
of June, and his face became a dirty yellow. He had
inherited his father's dislike of the cold, and although
he still had to realize it, his body craved the sun.

But all was forgotten as they trundled rather than
sped through France towards Toulouse and across
the Pyrenees. The journey so far hadn't been ardu-
ous. The three of them had shared the driving, and
they had stopped each night in a comfortable hotel
and during the day for picnic meals which Sam loved,
although he was always careful to wear his panama
hat.

'Where do we get to when we cross the mountain, Grandpa?' asked Sam as they descended the
Pyrenees into Spain.

'Barcelona. I thought it was smashing the first time I set eyes on it. Wait till you see it. There are fountains –'

'Kelvingrove Park has a fountain. And a man on a big horse. Bronze, it's called.'

'It's *made* of bronze. It's Lord Roberts, who was a fine old soldier. But wait till you see the fountain in the middle of the Plaça Reial. And the market, *La Boquería* –'

'*We* have one, we have one! Paddy's Market. Mummy says you can buy anything at Paddy's Market.'

'Aye, even a chanty . . .'

'Shush,' Anna said, laughing. 'You have a very vulgar grandpa, Sam. But I'll tell you what. In Barcelona and where our house is, you can sit outside in cafés and get the sun, lots of it.'

'Oh, I'm not going to do that! I'm going to stay inside till the other boys are the same colour as me.'

'Do you know what I'm going to tell you?' Anna said, turning round to him. 'I *prefer* brown boys. I have *always* preferred brown boys.' Changed days – Van hid a smile, remembering her mother's tight face when she had first met Eb. 'And another thing,' Anna was saying, 'you don't have to stay inside in Spain because the boys aren't pink and white like Scottish boys. They're more like you.'

'Is that a fact?' Sam said, speaking with Bessie's voice.

'Indeed it is.'

'Well, I'm going to stay in Spain for ever and ever and ever. Who cares about dirty old school and fat old Miss Clewes?'

'Sam!' Van said, and then to her parents, 'Don't laugh at him you two. He's being naughty.'

' "Naughty's" a word you brought with you from Renton,' Ritchie said. 'Tell him he's a wee rascal.'

'I'm a wee rascal.' Sam sounded pleased. Van noticed he had taken off his panama hat.

Van had always liked the house at Arenys de Mar, and her room on the top floor. Here she had made a nest for herself, so she had told Hal Purvis, she remembered, in her 'difficult days', while Mish and Ritchie toured the galleries in Barcelona, or went to the old warehouse on the harbour where Ritchie had a studio. She had felt more disadvantaged than ever in comparison with Mish, with his knowledge of paintings and his urbanity even at nineteen.

Once she had said to him, 'Do you always feel at ease, Mish? Those Spanish people – they're so smart and worldly. Don't you feel inferior?'

He hadn't really known what she was talking about. ' "Inferior"? I don't understand. You're far too introspective. You're always going inside yourself and asking "How do I feel about this, or that? Do I like this person, that one? Do they like me?" I've seen you when Dad brings some of his friends home. Your brows draw together as if they were going to bite you.'

'I'm frightened,' she had said.

'Does it never occur to you that they may be frightened too? They're visiting a famous painter and his family.'

'But they're not. I know by their confident look. They talk and laugh, they move about easily in their skin.'

'They could be better actors than you.'

'I'm all right with people I *like*,' she had protested.

'You mean people who are no threat to you – even

139

better, where you can be Lady Bountiful to all those beatniks you pick up? Maybe you know that you make *them* inferior.'

'That's rubbish,' she had said, because truth always hurt.

It was the only time she remembered having that kind of conversation with Mish. And then he had gone to New York and she had missed him badly. She hadn't realized nor valued the support he gave her by his presence.

Sam was ecstatic about the pool at his grandparents' house, and soon established himself as the chief ladybird catcher, armed with a net attached to a bamboo cane. Ritchie paid him a penny for every one he caught, and together they released them in the garden. 'Grandpa says it's in the interests of *i*cology,' he informed Van.

In no time they fell into a family routine. Ritchie was away all day at his studio, Anna spent most of her time in an attic where she worked out her designs. Sometimes Van heard her car leaving the house and knew she had gone off to wander about Barcelona looking for ideas, completely self-absorbed.

It was left to Van to do the shopping in the town, which was no hardship. Here she could indulge her interest in people. She enjoyed watching them as they strolled on the promenade, or shopped like herself. They were lively, talkative, volatile, the sun opened them up, like flowers, she decided. She would walk slowly up the hill laden with baskets of fruit and vegetables for their evening meal, often a brace of rabbits, or a plump chicken to be plucked by Juanita, the girl in the kitchen. Sam was her porter, his face the colour of a toffee-apple, and as gleaming.

He had no worries now about the sun 'getting at him'.

Anna often joined her and the Catalan girl when she came downstairs, especially if they were entertaining. She had a flair for cooking, but then, Van thought, she had a flair in everything she tackled, quick, efficient, deft, creative.

Manuel Folguera, the old friend who lived nearby, was a frequent visitor. Van had always liked him. She remembered her first visit to his house, and how, perhaps sensing her shyness, he had shown her around, drawing her out, so that she was soon at ease with him.

It was here that she had first met Maria Roig with her beautiful little daughter, Ana. She had thought the child spoiled, but that was perhaps because she had envied her self-confidence even at eight years of age. Or perhaps it had been because she was the daughter of Ritchie's lover, and must often have been a spectator of their intimacy. She had scrutinized Maria fiercely on that occasion, her trim, rounded figure, the blonde hair piled on top of her head with the escaping ringlets, the white swimsuit she wore which was like a second skin on her bronzed body. Anna was taller and less curvaceous, but the Spanish woman couldn't touch her for elegance. The image of her father and Maria Roig both naked between silken sheets was a strange one.

A week after the Laidlaws arrived at Arenys de Mar Karin and Mish came, and the tenor of their life was changed. They were married now much to Anna's secret delight. She had been proud of herself for not commenting on their sharing an apartment when she had stayed with them. She had soon become convinced that they were made for each other. As yet they hadn't any children. Anna said that probably Karin had had enough trouble persuading her mother to accept a goy without adding any offspring to the problem. Maybe Mish would have something to say about 'cutting a little boy's willie'. Besides, Karin worked with children as a psychologist. Perhaps she wanted peace and quiet when she got home.

Mish was an American now in voice and attitude. He made Ritchie look more Bohemian than ever with his spare figure and spare lean suit. He hugged Van fondly. 'You look different. Getting tanned suits you.'

'Great face for earrings,' Karin said as they kissed. 'Luckily I've got just the pair for you in my valise.'

'Oh thanks, Karin.' She liked the look of her sister-in-law, the dark compactness of her, the bright eyes. 'You're brown too.'

'It's an expensive tan, this. Sun bed stuff. New York makes you wan.' Van felt a tug at her skirt and turned to find Sam, suddenly shy, at her side.

'Come and say hello to your aunt and uncle.' She drew him forward.

'Hi, Sam!' Karin kneeled down to be at his level. 'My, you're cute.'

'Miss Clewes says I'm naughty.'

'Does she now? Well, you tell Miss Clewes that's a sure sign of genius.'

'What's genius?'

'It's being smarter than anyone else but not too smart to be a pain in the neck.'

'Well, look who's here!' Anna had appeared from upstairs. It was typical of her, Van thought, that she should become completely absorbed in what she was doing although Karin and Mish had been expected. 'I didn't hear the car!' She embraced them both. 'Good to see you. You look great, Karin.'

142

Van, watching her mother's glowing face, saw the rapport between the two women. She remembered Anna and Ritchie had been living apart when Mish was home from New York, and how she had decided to go back with him. And how she had come back a different person, the misery gone from her face and able to get on with her own life. She had been enthusiastic about Karin.

They had a family meal after a long happy drinks session round the pool. Karin, in contrast to Van's memory of Maria Roig's slenderness, filled her jazzy swimsuit. Van, never proud of her own appearance had submerged herself in a white robe.

The talk round the dinner table was serious. Karin was deeply distressed about the state of the children in Biafra and said she would like to go out and work there. Mish wouldn't stand in her way. 'I don't take sides any more,' she said. 'Politics get you nowhere. Look at Vietnam and the misery that has caused.'

'I wouldn't mind going with you,' Van said. She had been haunted by a newspaper picture of an Ibo refugee carrying her dead child over her shoulder. 'But there's Sam.'

'Your hostage to fortune?' Karin smiled. She seemed wistful.

'Then you have proper qualifications. I wasted a lot of time when I was younger dissipating my energy here and there. Sam's the witness.'

'So what? Take it from me, there will always be plenty of causes coming along. Finish your course. The poor and sick are always with us.' She cocked her head towards Ritchie and Mish who were talking animatedly about civil rights.

'I met James Baldwin once,' Mish was telling him. 'Tiny, but a great figure in the battle, a great

143

enthusiast. Martin Luther King was a peacemaker, Baldwin was a flame, a focus. You have to be black to really understand the anger, or have a background where there has been deprivation. I never had that. Karin did, being from a Jewish immigrant family. That's what makes her feel for the plight of the Biafran children.'

'She has a large heart.' Anna was listening with her chin in her hands.

'Sure. I'm white and privileged in New York. Any Britisher gets the full treatment. The blacks, no matter when they arrived, or wherever they come from, even if it was from the South, have to fight every step of the way. When we left, there was a three-day occupation of Cornell by black students because of segregation. So it goes.'

'Sam suffers from some of that at school,' Van chimed in. 'Do you think it would be as bad for him in America?'

'I don't know. It's a class thing too. If you live in Upper East Side and have a rich Momma and Poppa, things are different. His father was West African, wasn't he? There's a sub-division there also, between them and the American negro.'

'So, do you shut all that out of your mind when you work there, Mish?' Ritchie asked.

'Yes, I do. I compartmentalize. I don't come out of the crowd and declare myself like Karin. I'm a poor white compared with her.' Van saw the look he and Karin exchanged, and it struck her that they had a marriage like her parents. If she married Alan, would that grow in the same way? He was steadfast, highly moral. Why didn't he excite her?

Anna rallied them all at one in the morning when they were still sitting over coffee. 'Mish and Karin must be dead tired, and jet-lagged. Tomorrow evening we're having a party so we've got to show you two off. Not bug-eyed.'

Van got up. 'I'll take the stuff to the kitchen, Mum. Off you go with Dad. Go on, Karin, you look dead.'

She wasn't really odd man out she told herself as she went into Sam's room later to tuck him up.

Fourteen

It was a typical Anna and Ritchie party. During the years of owning a Spanish house, they had acquired a coterie of friends, artists, architects and various working colleagues of Manuel Folguera from government departments, the Institute of Art and so on, whom he had brought along with him from time to time. It was clear to Van, joining the party when it was in full swing, that her parents had gathered around them the same kind of people they knew in Glasgow. If you put them in the Isle of Skye it would be the same. To be an artist in whatever discipline gave you a passport into their kind of world.

Anna saw her hesitating at the doorway. 'Come along and help me,' she called, and when Van was at her side: 'You look great. White suits you.'

'Karin suggested it to set off the earrings she gave me.' She touched the silver rings. 'And I made up my face, like you.'

'Like Jean and me. "The Painted Ladies" we used to call ourselves. Nancy and Mother too. You look like Jean tonight. She always wears earrings.'

'Doesn't she ever come here?'

'Not often. She doesn't like leaving John now that they're alone together, but I think it's partly an excuse. She has an uninterrupted day of painting before he comes home at night.'

'She'd like this crowd,' Van said, looking around at the people. Like butterflies, she thought. She was pleased by her mother's compliment about her appearance. Perhaps she should start using her full name, Vanessa, to suit her new image, the Painted Lady. She remembered her father telling her of the origin of her name from a butterfly collection they had.

They were in the large salon – it had been two rooms when they bought the house – with its wide glass doors opening on to the patio. Some of the guests had spilled out to occupy the chairs and tables round the pool. Ritchie had put some covered candles amongst the orange trees, and in the bougainvillaea which climbed over arches and clung to walls. There was music coming from somewhere. The air was soft, seeming to hold and trap the sound of voices and laughter.

'What do you want me to do?' she asked Anna.

'On second thoughts, nothing. They won't eat for ages yet. Just mingle and enjoy yourself. Tell them there's loads of fruit cup here and to help themselves. They're like birds. They make swooping sorties on food when they feel like it.'

'Have they bird-like appetites?'

'The women have. They're always fighting their natural tendency to plumpness, and they like to please their men.'

'The men too?'

'More or less. They don't gorge like the Scots, but in any case they'll wait till after ten . . . Look, Van, you don't have to make conversation with me. Plunge in. Don't you see anyone you know?' Mother always saw through her. There were natural party-goers, and people like her who found it difficult to break into a group. I should wear a name-tag, she thought, 'Vanessa Laidlaw, unfamous daughter of famous painter. Doing her best.'

She searched the room with her eyes and then looked out to the patio. She saw a familiar back, Manuel Folguera's, the hair long and sleek following his skull and tied back in a ponytail. He was talking to Karin and two other people Van didn't know. It seemed to promise an easier entry than some.

'I'll just go and have a word with Manuel Folguera,' she said to her mother, lifting her glass and making her way through the crowd, saying, 'Sorry' and 'Excuse me' as she went towards the tall figure.

'Hello, Manuel!' she said as she reached him, too heartily, and interrupting the man who was speaking. 'I see you've met my sister-in-law.'

He turned round. 'Señorita!' His face broadened in a smile. 'Now my cup of happiness is full. Your sister-in-law is a true breath of the United States, so refreshing to us Europeans.'

Karin smiled at her. 'He really means I'm brash, Van.'

'What is this "brash"?' Manuel said, 'Brush? To sweep the floor?' The girls laughed and he looked in puzzlement at the two young men who made up the group. 'Vincente? Pablo? But I forget, I must introduce you. Señor Vincente Losas, and Señor Pablo Valino. And this is the daughter of our host, Señorita Vanessa Laidlaw.' They both bowed. 'These are two very well-read gentlemen, you know. They study butterflies, Vanessa – well, Vincente is an expert, you know, a . . . ?' He looked enquiringly at the young man.

'A lepidopterist, Manuel.' He smoothed his already smooth quiff. 'You have the name of a butterfly, señorita. It is beautiful, Van-ess-a.' He held up a hand, as if to listen.

'And so is she,' Manuel said. 'Once, long ago, she was a shy little creature in her chrysalis and now she has emerged.'

'Imago!' Vincente Losas pronounced. 'You see, Manuel, you are also a lepidopterist.'

'Do not confound me with science, dear Vincente. Speak simply. You must work for your supper, you know.'

'Task master!' The two young men exchanged laughing glances. 'It is simple. In the butterfly world it applies to a sexually mature insect after metamorphosis. See, imago!'

'And not only in the butterfly world?' The two young men laughed again and looked down. They both had long eyelashes. Van caught Karin's eye and they joined in the laughter. Ritchie's lethal fruit cup was possibly having its effect. Van heard her father's voice behind her. She looked round, still laughing. He was like an elderly Botticelli angel with his mass of greying curls.

'You seem to be enjoying yourselves.'

'Karin and I are being amused by Manuel and . . .'

'. . . my bodyguards, Ritchie, Vincente and Pablo. I don't go anywhere without them nowadays.'

'Quite right too. You may well have secret enemies in the Departamento de Justicia. But you're hogging Karin, my friend. I want to introduce her to the others. And you two,' he shook his finger at the two young men, 'have you kept your promise about bringing some records to play at my party?'

'We have brought you a good selection,' Vincente

149

Losas said. 'Bang on. The latest from England. They are in the foyer. Would you like us to play them now?'

'Would you? I think we'd better get the dancing going before we eat. *Gracias.*'

'We go.' They went off, looking pleased with their commission.

'Dear boys,' Manuel said, 'so willing at all times.'

'I'm sure. You don't mind leaving this charmer, Karin? I must show you off while you're here.'

'On you go.' Manuel smiled at them. 'I'm very happy with the daughter you have left me.'

'That was a nice compliment,' Van said to him when Ritchie and Karin had gone away. She was feeling elated, and at ease.

'Oh, my dear Vanessa, it wasn't a compliment. It was a matter of fact. I don't see you very often. Every time you come here there is a little change, but now there is a big one. You have a lamp inside. Perhaps Vincente was right. Imago. Maybe it is simply a matter of being *maduro*, mature? And yet, you have the air of waiting in the wings of El Liceu for something to happen.'

'You're making me feel good. I'm older, at least. Sam is six now.' He shrugged. Manuel had no time for children, she remembered.

'Perhaps there is a difference in your life-style since you live with your parents in Scotland now.'

'I'm studying. I want to become an almoner . . .' he wouldn't know that word, 'a person who discusses the affairs of patients in hospital who need help, a kind of link between doctor and patient.'

'Very worthy. Anyhow, you are different from the young girl I led up to my tower. So reticent and shy. Do you remember?'

'Yes. I was very unsure of myself. Some people

have the art of living. I'm learning it. I'm still no expert.'

The music struck up, an old tune, 'Rock Around the Clock'. Its rhythm made people begin to clap, pleased recognition on their faces.

'Would you like to dance?' Manuel asked her.

'All right.' She smiled at him. 'I warn you, I'm no expert.'

'I shall teach you. Vincente and Pablo demonstrate the steps to me. They says, "You must keep up-to-date, Manuel. Don't become an old man." Of course they pull my leg, but they are dear boys and we have fun. Not like . . .' He stopped, and she remembered he'd had a friend for many years. Had he died, or left him? Perhaps he had decided there was safety in numbers.

'Do you ever do the *sardana* at parties like this?' she asked him. They were moving slowly together, hardly dancing, as they talked.

'Oh, no. Perhaps on a special occasion if the guests are all Spanish. Franco might not like it. Now, we must stop walking round the room like two old people.' He released her with a spin away from him, still holding her hand. 'Now, watch my feet, as the boys say.'

She laughed at him, and as the rhythm seemed to enter her bloodstream, it seemed also to do wonders to her feet. She copied Manuel with far more dexterity than she had thought herself capable of, feeling light-hearted, and, as he had said, on the brink of some-thing. They sang the words as they whirled around each other. His long limbs were flexible, his skull-shaped face was split in a grin. Now they were too busy to sing, as her hands, body and feet followed his with confidence and even abandon. Once when

151

he spun her around she bumped into Karin dancing with Mish.

'Look at you!' Karin called, surprise on her face, and before Van realized it she was with Mish and Manuel had whirled Karin away.

'How to lose a wife,' Mish said, weaving in front of her. 'This is a new Van.'

'Manuel's been teaching me.'

'He's certainly brought you out of your shell.' His footwork was even more accomplished than Manuel's, with a few American innovations.

'Maybe it's the Spanish atmosphere. I feel happy, happy . . . as . . . give me a break, Mish!' They slowed down, breathless.

'We'll both have a heart attack if we keep that up. As if what?' He held her in a brotherly embrace.

'This will sound silly to you.' She felt her heart quieten. 'As if my worries were over.' He didn't reply. 'Or going to be over.'

'Good. Karin and I admire you.' He spoke softly. 'Did you know that?'

'Whatever for?'

'Chiefly for being Van, I expect. You've ploughed your own furrow, taken the knocks as they came along without –' They were halted by someone.

'Change partners, Buddy!' Her heart leaped. It was Hal Purvis beside them, smiling at them, tanned, in a white shirt open at the neck. Her throat went dry.

'Well, for God's sake, Hal!' Mish said. 'Where did you spring from?'

'London, actually, old fruit.' He drawled the words, laughing. 'Ritchie said I'd be welcome if I dropped in here. We're holding up the traffic. See you.' Mish seemed to fall away, Hal was facing Van, taking her hands, drawing her to him, the thrill she

152

felt lasted as he drew her closer, closer, looking down at her, smiling. She thought she might die of it. 'How are you, honey?' he said, and, as if he knew she couldn't bear it any longer, drew away from her, still holding her hands.

'Fine.' She looked at him. He drew her against him again, curved over her, the thrill began and it was unbearable. Imago. What Vincente Losas had said. IT. She would have to be sensible. 'I'd *no* idea you'd be in Arenys. It's taken . . . I'm surprised.'

'I didn't just drop in. I came to see a serious girl and then I saw her dancing like a dervish and I said to myself this I have to be involved in.' The thrill had made a steady progression through her body. Now it seemed to burst like a firecracker at the top of her head.

'Wow!' she said, and shivered.

'What's wrong?' They parted again and she saw his face, the quirk at the side of his mouth, the smiling eyes. She was so sure that he was *it*.

'Nothing. I just felt . . . happy. I keep on wanting to say that word, happy, happy, happy.'

He was saying it too.

'That makes two of us.' He had put his cheek against hers.

The feeling persisted as they danced, an entirely new feeling. Although she had slept with Eb, made love with him, had his child, it didn't seem, in retrospect, as intimate as this. She wanted to stay like this for ever, preserve it like a Tiffany egg. It was only when she realized the music had stopped and they were still dancing, that she drew out of his arms.

There was laughter and some clapping. She caught the amused looks on familiar faces, Ritchie, Anna, Mish and Karin, who were seated at a table. She was confused. 'Oh God,' she said to Hal, 'we've been making an exhibition of ourselves. Dancing as close as clams.'

'Who cares?' He was unabashed. He bowed, grinning, put his arm round her shoulders and steered her off the patio. 'Let's go and eat after that. And maybe we could both do with a drink. Van?' He tightened his arm and she nodded. He said as they stood at the buffet, 'I haven't asked you yet how your chap's getting on? Is he still hanging in there?'

Fifteen

Happy, happy. The word kept reverberating in her mind. Happy . . .

Hal could only stay for a few days and they were constantly together. 'Bring your chap,' he said, and most of the time Sam went with them, delighted to have a surrogate father figure. They took him to the fair in the Ciutadella Park, and finished up with ice creams in one of the many cafés in Catalunya Square; they swam in the pool because Hal had an open invitation to the house. He stayed in a hotel nearby although Anna said they had a spare room.

Van was bewitched, possessed, obsessed, she tried to find a name for this new state of never having Hal's face nor his voice out of her head. If he touched her when they were together her skin burned. She was totally in love.

Anna said to her one morning, 'So what's the programme today?'

She tried to look nonchalant, to take the constant smile off her face. 'We're going to the Ciutadella Park again. Sam adores the roundabouts because Hal goes on everything with him. I'm too scared. He's so good with him, Mother.'

'I believe you. But that's not the only reason for

the change in you. Go on,' she teased, 'let the smile out. I felt like that once.'

'Did you? Somehow you think your feeling is quite unique. It's so quick, so consuming, and yet it's got a steady quality, a sureness that it will last. Did you feel like that about Father from the very first day?'

'Oh, yes. That's our way. I couldn't take my eyes off him. Poor Jean, listening to me. But we had to wait. There had been no Swinging Sixties. John Knox was still casting a canny eye over us from his pedestal in the Necropolis.'

'Hal's going back to London tomorrow.'

'How does he feel about you?'

'The same as me.'

'He's said it?'

'He's said everything. Except, "Will you marry me?"'

Anna laughed. 'You're a real old-fashioned girl nowadays. Did William Armstrong?'

'Oh yes, we had it all planned. Both working in the bank until the babies came, then me ruling over them in a semi-detached in Aylesbury. But then, if you remember, one flick of tricksy Dottie's skirt wrecked all that.'

'Good thing. You would have looked stupid working in a bank and living in a semi-detached.'

'Oh, I'm not decrying that.'

'Nor am I, but you would still have looked stupid. And then Eb. He never –?'

'You know that. Not even when I told him I was pregnant.'

'That was a blessing. I mean, that you didn't marry him. It wouldn't have worked. Your idea of being an almoner is much better. It will be there. Women need something to be there, whether they're married or not.'

'That's your theme song.' She smiled. 'But I'm greedy. I want Hal as well.'

'Have you spoken to Ritchie?'

'No, but I know you tell each other everything.'

'There's no need to with you going around with a face like a harvest moon.' She suddenly leaned forward and kissed Van's cheek. When she drew back Van saw her eyes were wet. 'I would have been furious,' she said, 'if you'd never known what Ritchie and I have known. You deserve it.' She waved her hand, 'Away you go and sort things out for yourself. I've got work to do.' When she opened the door to go out Sam rushed in.

'The sun's burning a hole in me, Mummy!' Bessie. The panama hat had long since been forgotten. 'You were going to show me that new stroke.'

'Is that the crawl?' Anna asked.

'Yes, I think so, Grandma.' Van nodded.

'I do it better than your mummy. Better in fact than your Uncle Mish or Aunt Karin.'

'His right name is Uncle Hamish. He told me.'

'That's only when he's in Scotland. Would you like me to teach you the crawl and then we'll go to Sitges and have lunch and ice cream, then have a look round the shops to see what they have? For boys?'

Sam frowned, his lips disappeared as he bit them in concentration, and concealed greed. He nodded. 'Yes, I wouldn't mind a bit of shopping in Sitges.'

'Well, that's settled.' She looked at Van. 'Okay, Mummy?'

'You're a temptress.'

'What's a temptress, Grandma?' Sam was saying as they went out.

When Hal called for her an hour later she said to him, 'We have a whole day together.'

'Without Sam?'

'My mother tempted him with goodies in the Sitges shops.'

'Well, good on her. Maybe I can tempt you with goodies too?' He gave her an exaggerated leer.

They drove first of all to the Barri Gòtic in Barcelona for her special present. She remembered Maria Roig lived here, remembered one Christmas when she and Mish had been taken to see her by Ritchie, and her little daughter, Ana, had said, 'I go in Ricardo and Mama's bed in the morning.' And how sheepish her father had looked.

She chose a marquise ring, heavy in the Spanish mode, and he put it on her right hand. They had lunch in the Santa Anna district because it was such a good mix, Hal said, and sat over it for a long time.

'You know I'm dying of love,' Hal said.

'Yes,' their eyes met, 'I thought you must be. I couldn't have this feeling on my own.' The busy chatter of the Spanish voices round them seemed to isolate them further, the swift waiters glided past her as if in a dream.

'On fire?'

'Yes, but sure.'

'Sure it will last?'

'As sure as I can be. It's a unique feeling.'

'I'll be honest.' He leaned forward, his eyes held her. 'I thought I'd been in love before, but now that there's us I know they were just passing fancies, sometimes even for an ulterior motive like being seen with the right girl at the right time. But there's no ulterior motive with you. In fact there are snags.' She heard the sudden insistent twanging of a guitar behind her. The throbbing was in her head, prophetic.

'Snags?'

'Only practical ones. Your blue eyes went black. We live hundreds of miles apart. I've got a contract which will take me even further away, to New York, and you have to finish your course.'

'I have to have something *there*,' she said, remembering her mother's words.

'I'm with you. But once you get your Diploma, you can work anywhere?'

'I expect so.'

'I know they're desperate for almoners in the London hospitals. And Scottish girls are at a premium.'

She looked at him, smiling. 'You're making that up.'

'It's obvious, isn't it? Serious girls like you, the salt of the earth . . .'

'It isn't a problem, where I work. But if . . .' he didn't jump in, '. . . you wouldn't object to me working?'

'I'm counting on it. I've never thought it was a good idea for a girl to hole up waiting for her man to come home.'

'But if there are children?'

'Well, of course, that justifies the situation.'

She gave up. 'What an academic discussion this is!'

'I'm not feeling academic.' He lifted his glass. She saw his hand was trembling.

'What about Sam?'

'I'm depending on Sam.' His smile made her swallow and blink. Sometime, when they were having another academic talk, she would discuss with him the physical symptoms of love, how her throat went dry, how her hands trembled, how her tear ducts became active, how the back of her knees went weak

. . . John Whitbread could explain it for her. 'Who else would waken us up in the morning? Sam I love. He's a great guy. Sam's a part of you. I want the whole package.'

Her eyelids fell with delight. 'He's happy with you. You fulfil a need.' He nodded and put down his glass as if fortified.

'Look, Van, there's an air of unreality about this. But I'm telling myself it's true, it's happening. I never thought I'd be sitting in a Barcelona restaurant vowing eternal love, and meaning it. I'd meant to mosey around like a butterfly from girl to girl. Now, to my surprise, horror, even,' he grinned at her, 'I find myself needing you, wanting you, permanently.' This time the physical sensation was like a swoon. A part of her floated away. She closed her eyes, and opened them, to clear her vision.

'Let's get out of here and have a walk. Or drive up to Monjuïc and look down on the city. I need air.'

'Right.' He stood up, then sat down again. 'God, my senses are leaving me! I haven't paid.' He waved to the waiter and she saw the man gliding swan-like towards them, protruding chest, white dickie.

'You enjoyed your meal, señor?' he enquired as he wrote the bill and handed it over with the grace of the aforesaid swan dipping its beak.

'We enjoyed it. And how. *Muchas gracias*.' The waiter swivelled his long neck and bowed to Van as if he were paying silent homage.

'He thought you were beautiful too,' Hal said as she floated beside him.

'I *nearly* feel it, except that I feel invisible, incandescent. Did you know I have a butterfly's name? Vanessa?'

He turned to look at her. 'It's pretty. You never use it.'

'I might start. The Painted Lady. One of Manuel Folguero's young men explained the whole thing to me.' She felt her legs trembling. 'It's in a chrysalis, and then when it's ready it bursts out and that's called imago. I feel like that. Like a tethered balloon.' She wouldn't tell him the rest.

'Imago,' he repeated. 'Never heard that word. I like it.'

They walked along the Rambla to Catalunya Square and sat in a café drinking sangria because the air was stifling. And her legs were still trembling.

They didn't speak much. She was afraid to look at him. She felt she might explode into fragments of Van Laidlaw. She sat, wearing a calm look, waiting until she couldn't sit any more. 'Let's walk,' she said.

They got up and strolled along the Rambla again, stopping to worry about the finches fluttering behind bars – at least she did – stopping at the flower stalls so that Hal could buy her roses which were wilting in the heat. Her body soaked up their smell.

When they were coming near the Liceu, he said, 'This is my hotel, next door. I have the room until tomorrow morning. It's got air-conditioning.'

She stopped and looked at him. 'You're flying back tomorrow?' Her equilibrium had returned.

'Yes, very early.'

'We still haven't talked, really talked.'

'No, not really talked.'

She looked at his face, now serious, the face she would like to live with, to sleep with, the face which would give her life meaning. Who cared about any more talking, or that the words hadn't been said, 'Will you marry me?'

'All right, then,' she said, 'the roses could do with some water.'

The room was cool and dark and without thinking she lay down on the bed and stretched herself. 'Lovely,' she said, 'to escape from the sun. Sam was afraid it would make him browner.'

'I hope you disabused him.'

'He forgot. I have a feeling he will adapt better in hot countries than cold. It's more natural for him.'

He lay down beside her and took her hand. 'This is the same as strolling along the Rambla, only in a horizontal position. And much cooler.'

'Much nicer.'

She wasn't in a hurry. It was the feeling of rightness which was so right, not a question of seizing the moment because it might not occur again, so different from being with Eb who sometimes had been sullen and grudging about all the ablebodied, even herself.

'Can you contemplate being with me for always?' Hal said.

'Oh, yes. That's the easy part, once I get the decks cleared for action.' She hesitated. 'I haven't really spoken to you about Alan, Alan McAlpine. I've been seeing him for quite a time. I met him at my aunt's in Kirkcudbright, and he comes to Glasgow every fortnight. He's a lawyer.'

'A lawyer?' He was cool. 'Not a solicitor?'

'Tomaytoes, tomatoes . . . He's coming to depend on me, you see.'

'He's coming to depend on you. In what way?'

'He wants to escape from his mother, and he thinks he can do it through me.'

'He can't use you.' He was stating a fact.

162

'No, he can't use me.' She suddenly giggled. 'Why have I become so irresistible? Me?'

'It's the imago thing.' He propped himself up on his elbow and looked down on her. 'You're . . . ready. Aren't you?' He said it slowly, 'Sexually ready.'

With the phrase her whole body seemed to thrum, to quiver and become tense and yet open to receive him. She sat up and pulled her dress over her head, then discarded the rest of her clothes like encumbrances. She knew by the small movements beside her Hal was doing the same thing.

'With one bound he was free,' he said, turning to her.

He took her in his arms and they laughed against each other. She drew away. 'No shame,' she said. 'Look at you. Comical. No shame.'

'No shame at all. That's how it should be.'

There was no pity in this love, as there had been with Eb, it was an equal giving and taking, demanding and receiving. She was full of passion, she ran with sweat, her hair was limp with it. Tears gagged her throat when they lay beside each other again.

Hal said, 'We have a lot to live up to with that.'

'For a simple stroll along the Rambla?' She turned towards him. 'We're born-again lovers. I feel I know for the first time why I'm here, I mean, on this planet.' He took her face in his hands.

'I love you, Van.'

'I love you, Hal.'

'I love Vanessa.'

'I love Harold.'

'We'll go on loving?'

'For ever and ever.'

'Wherever we are?'

'Wherever we are.'

There was nothing more to say except the one thing he didn't say. They lay in the cool darkened room until she began to shiver and she said she must get back to Sam. They were cold against each other now. There was no time for more loving, she said, and he said perhaps it was just as well. Who wanted to have a heart attack at such an early age?

Ritchie and Anna gave her covert glances at the dinner table after she had gone to Sam's room to say good night. She couldn't stand it any longer. 'All right,' she said, 'I know I'm smiling all over my silly face.'

'Didn't say a word,' Ritchie said.

'I once sat in the Tube facing a girl who did the same thing. Sometimes she laughed out loud. With my training I thought she must be a schizophrenic.'

'Or in love?'

'Or in love. Funny, I never thought of that . . . at the time.'

She relived their passion in bed that night, and from that thought of the one omission. It couldn't have just been an episode? Early morning was doubting time. Hal wasn't like Alan, solid, respectable, staying in the one place all the time. His job necessitated him travelling about the world.

Did he realize this, and wanted her, therefore, to make her own choice without being influenced? And if she freely chose him, would he then want to live with her in a new kind of marriage, an avant-garde kind of marriage where he wouldn't tie her down with children unless she wanted to, where they trusted each other implicitly and where she would be free to pursue her own career? Or hadn't he really *thought*?

They had been too busy loving. As the sky became gilded with the promise of another hot day, she got up and pulled on her swimsuit, feeling positive. First things first. She would have to tell Alan she should never be able to marry him, that she had met someone else. And she would have to say to Sam, because that was very important, 'How would you like to live in London with Mummy and Mr Purvis?'

The pool was gilt-edged, and cold as she dived in. The shock formed the words on her lips. 'It's up to you, Hal.' She used the purposeful crawl her mother had taught her, trying to be like Anna, who always knew her own mind.

Sixteen

'I had coffee yesterday morning with Mrs Crichton,' Mrs McAlpine said to her son as she handed him his usual breakfast of bacon and eggs – no sausage. Alan had struck against the sausage last year. And the potato scone. His father had been very partial to a potato scone fried in the bacon fat.

'Oh, yes?' He unfolded the starched napkin, put it across his knee. He was alerted.

'Cissie Crichton's mother.'

'I know.'

'She said Cissie was wondering why you hadn't been in touch recently. Didn't you usually take her to the Golf Club dance?'

'I was at Portpatrick that weekend, if you remember, Mother.' The 'best Ayrshire bacon to be had' was suddenly stringy and indigestible in his mouth.

'Oh, yes. With that girl. Don't you like your bacon, Alan? There's someone here who's got his eyes on it.' She put her hand down to the huge cat sitting at her side. It swivelled its head in a small ecstasy.

'*That girl* is Vanessa Laidlaw, Mother. I've told you her name hundreds of times.'

'*Miss* Laidlaw, she informed me. I've heard many things, but the arrogance when she said that . . . it left me speechless.'

'Vanessa couldn't be arrogant if she tried. She was stating a simple fact.'

'So an unmarried girl with a child is a simple fact? I'm not easily shocked, but that takes the biscuit.' She breathed in, as if to control herself. 'Mrs Crichton was telling me this morning of Brenda in the bakers who had to leave suddenly. "Well," I said, "anyone looking as *she* did, bleached hair and with a name like Brenda, *makes* you suspicious." What's wrong with your breakfast, Alan? All you've done is mess up that lovely egg with your fork. "You'll not find many eggs like those, Mrs McAlpine," Tommy said to me only this morning when he delivered them. "Best farm eggs." And they always pick out the brown ones especially for you.'

'I'm not hungry this morning, Mother.'

'Well, push it to the side.' She waved her hand impatiently, 'I'm the last one to force anyone to eat when they don't want to. I wonder what Miss Laidlaw's *parents* think of her and her child,' she was reflective now. 'I hear he's famous, Mr Laidlaw. Mrs Crichton says Cissie saw an exhibition of his work in Glasgow when she was up. She was quite interested because I had told her you were friendly with his daughter.'

'Why did you tell Cissie that?'

'You sound as if you were ashamed of it. I wasn't *telling* her. I was simply mentioning it in passing. "Is that why he wasn't at the Golf Club dance?" she said, just jokingly, but, of course, I didn't tell her you were at Portpatrick Hotel with Miss Laidlaw.' She raised her chin. 'I'm very fond of Cissie, always have been. She looked so smart and pretty that morning. I told her: "You really look so smart and pretty this morning, Cissie," and she said, "I'm glad *you* think so, Mrs

167

McAlpine." I thought her face became quite sad –'

Alan interrupted her. 'I have to go, Mother. I'll be late for the office.'

'I don't see how you expect to do any decent work on an empty stomach. If I made you some scrambled eggs would you prefer that? Some are even double-yoked. It would take no time at all.'

'No, thanks. I've got to go.'

He rose, and the cat rose also and followed him to the door, stood aside like a butler as he opened it, then padded slowly back to the dining room. It didn't sit down, but moved restlessly round and round Mrs McAlpine's chair, rubbing against the legs.

'I know what you want, Tom,' she said, wiping her lips on her napkin, 'Alan's breakfast. Come on, then.'

She rose and lifted his plate and went towards the door. She held the plate aloft. 'Follow me, my beauty. We don't want to waste good food . . .'

The cat stalked behind her, long-legged, big-bodied yet graceful, its tail stiffly in the air.

Hal telephoned Van the evening of the day they arrived back at Clevedon Crescent. She heard the familiar voice, 'Hello, Van!' and then him whispering in her ear, '"Was it a dream?"'

She giggled. 'No, it wasn't a dream. Does it feel like that to you?'

'A dream come true. I'm walking on air. Everybody tells me how well I'm looking. I'm doing the best work I've ever done. What about you?'

'Day-dreaming as well as night-dreaming. In constant fear of bursting out of my skin. But I've got to be practical now. There's heaps to do, shop for Bessie who says it's high time we're back, get my books ready for college tomorrow, first of all take Sam back to school.'

'How's my best pal?'

'He tried to rub off some of the brownness in his bath tonight. He said they'd call him "darkie" again.'

'Tell him to biff them one.'

'No, no. I tell him to ignore it.'

'You're a better Christian than I am. Well, he can try both, ignore them, and if they go on saying it, biff them.' His voice became tender. 'And how about my own girl?'

She sat down on the hall seat because her knees suddenly became weak. 'Missing you.' It was affecting her voice as well. They had never discussed the physical symptoms of love after all. 'But I'm going to work very hard at the college. I'll *swing* into Pitt Street from Sauchiehall Street every morning full of endeavour. Then I'll telephone my Aunt Jean to see if it's suitable for me to stay with her for a night or so. I have to get up there.'

He didn't ask why. 'Let me know when you'll be away. I intend to come up on business to Glasgow very soon. It's absolutely essential that I see your father. I'm completely held up otherwise.'

'You had lots of chances at Arenys de Mar.'

'Ah, but it's something that's cropped up *since*. And I'll see you too, of course.'

'How generous!' She laughed.

'Actually the book's going swimmingly, but only frequent sightings of you is going to keep me sane.'

'Hal . . . !' She sighed. 'This is ridiculous. Hang up. Ritchie will be complaining about me monopolizing the phone.'

'I must keep on his right side. I'll ring you every night, though, to fan the flame.'

'My parents will tease me.'

'So what? There's nothing wrong with being in love, is there?'

'It feels all right.'

'Give my regards to them, my best to your chap, and cuddle yourself for me.'

'I promise.'

'See you soon.'

'See you soon.'

She replaced the receiver on its cradle and sat back. Ridiculous, she thought. Her body was thrumming again. It was the only word to describe the sensation, something less than a tremor, a fine tuning, making her feel acutely alive, making her yearn for him.

She got up suddenly and went upstairs. Granny Rose had thought that the only place for a drawing room was upstairs. Her parents were still drinking their coffee. 'That was Hal,' she said, having difficulty with her ridiculous face.

'Oh, yes?' Anna looked up, amusement in her eyes. So did Ritchie. If only they weren't so smart.

'How is he?' Ritchie asked.

'Fine. He's coming up to see you soon. Some trouble with the book.'

'Such attention.' He rolled his eyes. 'I thought everything was settled.'

'Apparently not.' She poured herself some coffee. Give yourself a break, Van. Keep off the subject of Hal. Your body hasn't got used to being in love. You've lost control. She turned, with a new face on, a practical one. 'Mother, I have to go to Kirkcudbright. I have to tell Alan that it's all over. It would be too cruel to write or telephone.'

'Because of Hal?' He was back in the picture again.

'Oh yes,' she said, 'because of Hal. But I still feel terrible.'

'Has he laid down conditions? Off with the old first?'

'Hal? No, he hasn't . . . just . . .' she saw their eyes on her, 'a mutual commitment. It's Alan who lays down conditions.'

There was a quirk at the side of Anna's mouth. She was going to sit on the fence. No one spoke.

Van said, 'You're both falling over backwards not to influence me, aren't you?'

'Isn't that what Hal's doing?' Ritchie said. 'No moral blackmail?'

'Yes, I suppose so. He thinks everybody should be a free agent. It seems he's always been . . . sure like that.'

'Some reach that stage quicker than others,' Anna said. 'You've been a slow learner. Supposing you go and phone Jean and ask her when it's convenient, then give me a shout? I want to have a word with her.'

'Right. About Sam: it would be easier if I don't take him. Are you free next weekend if this suits Aunt Jean?'

'We'll make it free.' Anna smiled at her. 'It's nice to see you looking so happy.'

'It's feeling sure that does it. With the others – God, that makes me sound like Emma Bovary – there was always an ulterior motive, trying to be conventional with William, feeling so heart-felt sorry for Eb . . . you don't want to hear this. One thing, whatever happens I'm going to finish my course, get my Diploma, if you'll put up with me here.'

'We asked you to come, don't forget. And I should have been disappointed if you'd given up the course.'

171

'You're luckier than your mother,' Ritchie said. 'In her day she was supposed to stay at home and be kept by me. If only they'd realized how we could have done with the extra money!'

Van laughed. 'You're easier to live with than *some* men. Look at Gordon Pettigrew, for instance.'

'Oh, Wendy's happy at home. She's a breeder.'

'They're looking in tonight to welcome us back,' Anna said. 'What's the betting she's pregnant again? I thought so before we went to Spain but Nancy didn't say anything.'

I would like Hal's child, Van thought. 'Good luck to her. You know, sometimes I look up to Garnethill when I'm going to the college and think of you two when you were students at the Art School. Meeting on the steps, going to the Regal Café . . .'

'Paradise to me, then,' Ritchie said, 'the carpeted staircase, the foyer, the gilded pillars, the soft music. Elegance. There for all the people to enjoy. The thirties knew what glamour meant.'

'And yet you were quite emancipated compared with *the* Glasgow Girls. Aunt Jean told me they weren't even allowed into the Life Drawing class.'

'Nor the men's club in Blythswood Square,' Anna said, 'so they formed one of their own, the Lady Artists. Great-aunt Jessie was a member of that. When you think of it, it would be a good idea for women to divide their lives into two parts, the first for rearing children, the second for their own thing.'

'And two husbands?' Ritchie eyed her.

'You're treading on dangerous ground, Laidlaw.'

'Am I?' His eyes were dancing. 'Am I, ma wee chookie burdie.'

Van looked at her mother and saw the love in her

eyes. 'I'm getting out of this.' She got up, laughing too. 'I'll give you a shout when I've finished phoning, Mother.' Alan first, she told herself, going slowly downstairs.

It was his mother who answered. 'This is Mrs McAlpine, Thornton Lodge, speaking,' she said. Van could visualize her, the straight back, the busty front, like Alastair Sim as the headmistress in that film, she thought.

'This is Vanessa Laidlaw, Mrs McAlpine,' she said. 'How are you?'

'I'm fine, thank you very much.' Her voice was almost as deep as a man's. 'Can I help you?'

'I just wondered . . .' she despised the begging note which had crept into her voice, 'if I could speak to Alan?'

'Alan?' she said, as if she had never heard the name before. 'I'll *see* if he's at home.' There was a long pause, voices in the background, and then Alan, sounding hurried, embarrassed.

'Vanessa! Sorry to keep you. Mother wasn't quite sure.'

'Oh . . . Alan, I'm coming to Kirkcudbright. Could we meet?'

'Meet?' He laughed. 'Well, I should hope so. I was in Glasgow, the day before you came home, I think, but I couldn't wait. I'll be back in a fortnight, but if you're coming here earlier, that's splendid. I'll be pleased to help.'

'It's not a question of . . .' She realized his remark was subterfuge. His mother would be listening.

'Anything at all.' He was still speciously formal. 'Did you have a good time in Spain?'

'Oh, yes, lovely. Alan, something has happened. I have to see you.'

173

'I quite understand.' He was sifting everything he said.

'I hope you wi – You see . . .' But, no, the cruelty of saying, 'I'm in love with someone else,' without seeing him . . . He was decent. He deserved to be told face to face.

'I'll come this weekend,' she made up her mind, 'whether or not it's suitable for my aunt. I can always stay somewhere else.'

'I would ask you to stay here, but . . .' she could imagine the exchange of looks, '. . . it's rather short notice. Mother likes –'

'Oh, I wouldn't dream of it. Jean will give me an address if by any chance . . . but it's a remote possibility.'

'I tell you what. I'll meet you at the Selkirk Arms at six thirty, and we can discuss the matter there.' He sounded more confident. 'Which day will you be travelling?'

'Saturday. I'm at the college all week.'

'Are you still going on with that?' He sounded playful.

'I told you, Alan, I'm studying to be an almoner. I can't afford to miss any lectures.'

'Yes, you told me. So you did. Well, I'll be at the Selkirk Arms at six thirty, then. I'll wait till you come.' His voice dropped. 'I can't tell you how glad I am at the thought of seeing you. You've made me quite . . . hopeful.'

'No,' she wanted to say, 'there isn't any hope,' but she was a coward and hung up after saying goodbye.

Jean was more definite when she telephoned her. 'Great! I'll meet you off the Dumfries bus and we'll have time for a natter before you meet Alan. I'll drive you to the Selkirk Arms.' She was making no comment. How alike she and Anna were!

'Thanks, Jean.' And then, 'Your twin wants to speak to you.'

'My twin? We never think of ourselves like that! We couldn't be more different.'

'Is that a fact?' she said. 'I'll get her.' She went to the foot of the stairs and called, 'Mother! It's Aunt Jean!' And as Anna appeared at the top of the stairs, 'She says you couldn't be more different.'

'Isn't that what I'm always telling you?' She was running down as she spoke, delight in her eyes.

Gordon, Wendy and Nancy were upstairs when Van went into the drawing room. They had tiptoed past her earlier in the hall with exaggerated gestures.

Mother had been right. Wendy was distinctly plumper than she had been before the Laidlaws left for Spain. 'Just a look in,' Nancy said, 'to see if you were all back safe and sound from Spain. Wendy doesn't want to wait too long.'

'Oh, we're safe and sound.' Van smiled at the three of them, Nancy in a blue shirtwaister and large pearl earrings, Gordon looking plumper too, perhaps in sympathy, Wendy in flowery silk, her fat calves and neat ankles ending in white high-heeled shoes.

'Some people have all the luck,' Gordon said. 'Wendy's dying to get away for a little break, but I'm so busy these days flying about here and there. In great demand.' He smiled winningly.

'That's good. How is Uncle James?'

'You can't drag him away from television. This is his third, isn't it, Mother?'

'I think you're right, son. We got one for the Coronation. We were one of the first.'

'He's sat at it ever since,' Gordon laughed.

175

'That's an exaggeration,' Nancy said with the coy look she reserved for her son, 'but at least it keeps him quiet.'

Considering Uncle James scarcely uttered a word, it was a strange remark to make. Van looked at her father but saw he was wearing the usual glazed look which came over his face when the Pettigrews visited. He'd already had half an hour of them.

'These two will talk for hours,' Nancy said, tipping her head towards the door. 'They were always like that, chatter, chatter, chatter, in that big room they shared . . . wasn't it strange?' She appealed to Ritchie, saw he wasn't listening, turned to Van. 'Wasn't it strange when you think of it, in a big house like this and Mother putting them in the same room?'

'Perhaps because they were twins?'

'Yes, it could have been that. She was quite proud of them. I know I always felt left out.'

'Poor Mother!' Gordon said. 'Left out, were you? Was that why you married Dad when you were quite young? To get more attention?'

Nancy simpered. 'Isn't he a terrible boy, Vanessa? He's always pulling my leg.' Her attention turned to Wendy. 'Are you feeling tired, dear?'

'Not really,' she said bravely. 'What did you *do* in Spain, Vanessa?'

Ritchie came to life suddenly. 'She fell in love.'

'Oh, Father!' She felt her cheeks redden.

'She's blushing,' Gordon said. 'You've made her blush, Uncle Ritchie! Whose leg is being pulled now, eh, Vanessa?' He turned his plump face to her, disbelief in its very creases.

'As a matter of fact it's quite true, Gordon. I fell in love.' Gordon drew in his chin, silenced.

'But there's that lawyer who comes to see you!'

176

Wendy looked annoyed. 'I thought you were . . . Gordon and I were quite pleased. Give that poor little boy of yours a name at least.'

'He has mine. And Alan and I are just friends.'

'Well, *someone* is very popular.' She addressed herself to her silent husband. 'Someone, I might say, is coming out of her *shell*.'

'It's the Glasgow air,' Ritchie said. 'It's gone to her head.' His eyes were lively.

Wendy looked from one to the other, an uncertain smile on her face. 'You Laidlaws!' she said.

'Could I get you all a cup of tea?' Van half rose. She saw her aunt's eyes brighten. Scottish hospitality demanded the offer of a cup of tea whatever the hour.

'No, thanks,' Wendy said. 'I *am* feeling a bit tired after all. I think we should go now, Gordon. We've to take your mother home first.'

Gordon got up. 'Yes, well . . . I have a heavy day tomorrow. Ready, Mother?' He helped her to her feet, solicitously.

'I'm not *ancient*, Gordon.' And, addressing the Laidlaws, 'Just to see that you got back all right. And we're off again soon, James and me.'

Ritchie was on his feet too, looking eager. 'Where is it this time, Nancy? The Canaries again?'

'No, it's a new departure for us. We're going to the Greek Islands. Very cultural. There are lectures on the ship. James is quite keen on old ruins.'

'Don't say it,' Ritchie whispered in Van's ear as they followed the visitors to the door. You could understand Mother loving him.

Seventeen

Alan was working in the garden. Had he not been a lawyer, he sometimes thought, he might have made a good nurseryman or market gardener. He liked the feel of soil between his fingers, growing things, each spring meant for him a reawakening and a feeling of affinity with Nature. He had early discovered this enthusiasm, which had the added advantage of offering him a means of escape from his mother, at the same time pleasing her by his prowess and an opportunity to outshine her neighbours.

His enjoyment was genuine. He took pleasure in planning bedding schemes, he grew rare varieties of plants from seed in the greenhouse at the foot of the garden. He exhibited chrysanthemums at local flower shows, and had even gone to Chelsea to look at the different species. He kept his prize blooms under glass, and pinched them out carefully and with love, finding a happy absorption in the task.

Today, as well as attending to his chrysanthemums, he had cut the lawn. The boy who came to help him never achieved the broad parallel stripes which gladdened his heart. And his mother's. He was particularly anxious to please her. He was meeting Vanessa tomorrow, and a spick-and-span garden would soften her heart, he hoped, towards his intention to get married.

He had thought out carefully the problem of Vanessa's son. He would make her see that it would be better if he were sent away to school. He himself had gone to Fettes College in Edinburgh. That way Sam wouldn't be a thorn in his mother's flesh, and in time to come she would get used to him.

If he were honest with himself, he had to admit that Sam was a thorn in his flesh too, but it didn't lessen his obsession with Vanessa. He had never felt this emotion before, with Cissie Crichton nor any other girls in the town. It was her very difference from them, her strangeness, which captivated him.

There was a quality of pathos about her which was almost hidden by her matter-of-factness, an essential sweetness. Her father had the same quality, something childlike inherent in their personality. The malice hidden in innuendo which he was so used to at home was entirely absent from either of them.

He thought often of her level gaze which the glasses seemed if anything to emphasize, the deep blue colour of her eyes, their expressiveness and kindness, almost a holiness, although neither she nor her parents were religious in the common sense of the word, and he understood they were not churchgoers. Still, she might be persuaded . . .

Perhaps it was the feeling of being in a different world when he entered the Laidlaw household which so appealed to him, their broad-minded, tolerant attitudes. It was like going to a far country when he entered that upstairs drawing room with its elegance and good taste, so different from their own with its heavy velvet curtains, its floral cushions, the bulbous sofa and chairs, its worthy landscapes of the surrounding countryside.

But, then, Mother would rather be seen dead than hang any of Vanessa's aunt's daubs which she sold for such high prices.

When Vanessa married him he would find his mother a smaller house. She wasn't old, she was fit and perfectly capable of living her own life. He and Vanessa would go house-hunting for themselves in the country. He would like a garden, and a paddock – he had dreams of a pony for their children – he would allow her to choose the furniture and furnishings although she always said she had no taste, but that smart mother of hers whom he was secretly rather afraid of could perhaps give her a few tips. And her father would certainly advise her about pictures, perhaps even give them one of his to hang above the fireplace – a fine talking-point with the local gentry who would visit them.

They would fix up her son in a good prep school to begin with, and if they soon had children of their own, she would become less involved in him. He had to admit the boy always made him feel uneasy with that steady brown gaze, the almond-shaped eyes, the whites of which were faintly yellow. Maybe when he grew up he would go and live in America beside that clever brother whom she called Mish, short for Hamish. Why did they ruin perfectly good names? They would be calling him 'Al' soon. He smiled at that. It would make him one of them.

It had to be remembered he was a well-known lawyer with certain attributes of his own. Perhaps he would contribute a steadiness to that Bohemianism of the Laidlaw family, which, although it had such an appeal for him, would not be harmed by a little dilution of his steadiness. After all, their life would be spent in Kirkcudbright, not in an arty set in Glasgow.

Then, there was her determination to become a hospital almoner. He didn't deny they did a lot of good, but as his wife she could do voluntary duties in the local hospital, and with the advent of their children she would soon find her life fully occupied.

It was becoming dusk. The roses had lost their colour, the trees were black against the grey smoothness of the lawn, the midges were biting. He looked round the garden and nodded, satisfied.

'I'm going to have a bath, Mother,' he called from the hall. 'When will dinner be ready?' He put his head round the door of the kitchen where she was supervising Mary.

'Half an hour,' she said. 'It's roast beef tonight. It will be ready to carve when you come down.'

'And roast spuds, Mary?' he said to the maid, who was sour-faced. Mother's maids were always sour-faced, and they never stayed long. 'They aren't like the old ones,' she said, 'too slapdash by half.'

'Aye, and caramelized carrots. It's your mother's idea.'

'I got the recipe in *Woman and Home* at the hairdressers,' she said, turning from the stove, 'and thought I'd try it out. Well, away you go, Alan. The water's nice and hot.'

'Right oh, Mother! Have you looked out at the garden?'

'Once or twice. Almost perfect. It's a pity there's not much colour in the rockery now. Maybe you should have made it at the back instead.'

'I'll think of that later on. You might be right.' He went upstairs, feeling slightly deflated after all the hard work. Maybe he should criticize her cooking sometimes, say, 'Isn't this beef a bit overdone?' But, truth to tell, he had never been able to find fault.

He thought when he came down again, as spick-and-span as the garden, and as perfumed, that the heavy oak-panelled walls looked better in the evening when the red shaded wall-lights were on. The white damask tablecloth had a rosy gleam, the candlesticks were silver spears, the roast beef was succulent and crisply brown on its dish waiting for him to carve. Mary was stationed as usual at the sideboard waiting for the first cut which was always hers, the outside slices which had to be removed to reach the best of the joint. The next ones would be smoothly ovoid, rimmed with creamy fat.

'Done to a turn, Mother,' he said, knowing he had missed his opportunity for criticism.

'I thought it would be.'

He sat down at the table, unfolding his napkin. How many times had he done this? Always the slight trepidation, the slight ache in his forehead.

'Yes, I feel good after that gardening!' he said. 'These are the caramelized carrots, are they? Well, I'll try some.'

'Once you get that rockery shifted it should be perfect. You could get Bob to make a start on moving the stones tomorrow. He's due.'

'Yes, Mother.' He plunged. 'Have you remembered I'm going to have dinner in the Selkirk Arms tomorrow night with Vanessa Laidlaw?'

'I hadn't forgotten.' She looked down at the great cat which was in its usual place at the side of her chair, like a courtier. 'We haven't forgotten, have we, Tom?' It looked up at her, green greed in its eyes at the rich smell of meat. 'You know you're never fed at table. You'll get some scraps in the kitchen.' It moved its shoulders.

From where Alan sat the movement had an impatient human quality, like a shrug. I'll be rid of that cat too, he thought. I've always hated it. It looks at me as if it were . . . jealous.

'Things have changed,' his mother was saying. He felt the hair prick at the back of his neck. 'In *my* day no decent girl would have rung up a man and asked to be taken out. It just wasn't done.'

'You're referring to Vanessa?'

'*Miss* Laidlaw.' She started to eat, and Alan did the same. The roast beef no longer appeared succulent, the caramelized carrots seemed to be embedded in toffee which stuck between his teeth. He tried to speak calmly.

'It's a slightly different matter in Vanessa's case. She lives in Glasgow. She's coming to Kirkcudbright. Surely it's natural and not at all forward to let me know if she wants to see me.'

'Wants to see you!' She looked up. 'Are you at her beck and call, may I ask? You, a lawyer, known and respected in this town, and this girl,' her voice was not quite in control now, 'this *unmarried* girl, with a child, what's more, announces she wants to see you!' She looked down at the cat. As if she had passed on her hidden agitation, it got up and stalked to the door, then looked back at Alan, an imperious, offended look.

'Tom doesn't like raised voices,' she said, getting up. 'It disturbs him. Well, on you go.' She opened the door. 'Have your little stroll in the garden. Mary will let you out.'

From one second to the next, Alan made up his mind while her back was turned. He was going to marry Vanessa. He would tell his mother now. The dinner was ruined in any case.

He said when she sat down again, 'I might as well tell you, Mother – you'll have to know in any case – the father of Vanessa's child was a West African.'

'Well, at least that's a little more information,' she said, lifting her napkin. He saw she hadn't understood.

'The boy is coloured. Brown. His father was black, but with Vanessa being the mother . . . well, he's brown.' He was aware that his heart was beating painfully under his ribs, and looking across at his mother, he saw there were two sudden spots of red in her cheeks. Her knuckles were white clutching the knife and fork. Her head came up slowly as if it was heavy.

'What . . . is . . . this . . . you're telling . . . me?'

'Sam, the boy's name is Sam, is coloured. I know it's a shock to you. It was a shock to me, but I've got used to it now, just as I've got used to the fact that Vanessa isn't married. I know it's the last thing you would have wanted . . . it's a fact, and facts have to be accepted, faced, sooner or later. She might not like the idea, but when we're married I'll insist he goes to boarding school until . . . everybody gets . . . used to him, and then I'm hoping we'll have children of our own which will take up her attention.' He saw her half-open mouth, her shocked eyes, but he went on, 'I'm a lawyer, Mother. I haven't told you of every case I have to deal with. I have respected the trust which has been placed in me, but I can assure you that in the best of families, in some that you know, there are skeletons in the –'

She held up her hand, her eyes fixed, her voice hoarse. 'I don't want to hear any more of this.

184

However you dress up this sordid tale, you can't change it. An unmarried girl with a black child! The effrontery of her, thinking she can twist a well-respected figure round her little finger, worm her way into a community such as this, a respectable house such as this, a safe haven, no doubt, with a trail of disreputable friends following her. We'll have a ghetto next!'

It was his turn to hold up his hand. As he did so the door opened and Mary came in.

'Are you ready for the trifle now, Mrs McAlpine? I've put the silver balls on it as you said.'

She waved her hand impatiently. 'Away you go, Mary! I'll ring for you when we're ready. And shut the door after you. I don't like you barging in.' The woman retreated with her tray, her face sullen. 'That'll be it all over Kirkcudbright,' his mother said. Her face was twisted. 'I've never trusted her. Oh, dear, dear . . .' She was suddenly weeping, her napkin to her eyes. 'What am I going to do? My good name ruined! And in a place where your father was a pillar of the town . . .' She sobbed into her napkin.

He could have wept himself. He put down his knife and fork. The sight of the congealed meat on his plate turned his stomach.

'I might have known,' he said. 'I thought this time if I explained to you that I really loved Vanessa, that I feel sorry for the life she's led, that I thought I could show her a different one here, that you would understand. You wouldn't have to live with her when we got married. You could . . .'

Her tears seemed to dry in an instant. She raised her head and looked at him with burning eyes. 'Are you telling me now that I have to be put out of my own house where I've lived all my married life, in quiet . . . gentility, for a little upstart, for a dirty little whore!'

'No, no . . . oh, God!' he said. 'This is terrible!' He put his head in his hands, and in the darkness he knew the truth. If he gave up Vanessa now he would be under his mother's thumb for the rest of his life. He took his hands away from his eyes and met hers. They were burning, yet cold, suffused with hate. It did not matter who the hate was directed at, she was evil. There was no goodness in her. He spoke calmly, feeling deathly tired.

'It's a waste of time having any further discussion.' He imagined himself behind his desk with a client, and some of that authority came back to him. 'I intend to ask Vanessa to marry me. I know her life has been far from ideal, but we can put that behind us. We could be happy. You could be happy. You would have a daughter-in-law, grandchildren . . .'

There was a knock at the door. It was the maid again.

'I told you to wait, Mary!' His mother's voice was harsh.

'I know that. It's just . . . well, I thought I'd better tell you. I let Tom into the garden, and I thought he was a long time doing his business, and that, and I went out and called him, "Tommy . . . Tommy . . . !" but there's no sign of him.'

'You silly woman! You should have told me before!'

'You told me not to come in till you rang.' The woman tossed her head. 'I'll get back to my kitchen.' She banged the door behind her.

'Would you like me to go and see if I can find him?' Alan asked. The thought of a breath of cool air had him half on his feet.

'You!' She turned to look at him. 'After what you've

186

just said to me, your own mother, I wouldn't be beholden to you for ten thousand pounds, not you, of all people!' She got up. Her voice was shaking. 'You don't know what you've done to me this night. You've broken my heart, that's what you've done, broken my heart and ruined my life – ruined it with your stupid fancy for someone who isn't fit to lick your boots.'

He was on his feet too. 'Sit down, Mother. You're upset. I'll go.'

'No, you won't!' Her eyes were blazing. She made for the door and turned before she opened it. 'I never thought I would see a time when I couldn't bear to be in the same room as my own son. You can have that on your conscience, as well as all the rest.'

He heard her opening the front door, and then it shutting. She wouldn't want to go through the kitchen when Mary was there.

He sat, head bowed at the table, in despair. The hate was still palpable in the room, but now it was his own hate of himself as well. Why hadn't he just refused to quarrel with her, why hadn't he just met Vanessa without saying a word? He should have known that he always came out of any altercation with this sick sense of despair, as if their words had stirred up some deep muddy pool which made their life together seem a sham.

She'd been gone a long time. He raised his head. Inconsequentially he wondered if she had taken her stick. She didn't see too well at night. 'Take your stick, Mother,' he would say. 'You don't want to fall . . .' The thought energized him. He got up and went out of the room, opened the front inner door and stopped in the porch for a second to glance at the china cylinder which held a variety of walking

187

sticks, mostly those which had belonged to his father. Hers was still there with the flat ebony head.

His sight was good. She was nowhere in the garden, that was evident. He quickly covered the back and front. There weren't many shadows. She disliked trees. Bushes were kept neatly clipped. He came back to the front drive and saw that the wicket gate was partly open. She was obsessed by that cat. It filled her life.

But wasn't it the same thing as his obsession with Vanessa? Strong feelings should be avoided if one wanted to live a quiet life, he thought, as he went through the gate and began walking swiftly along the pavement away from the town and past the dark laurels of the neighbouring houses, their half-stone walls topped by ornamental ironwork.

How quiet it was, he thought. Occasionally a lit window, the curtains undrawn, gave him a feeling of loneliness, of alienation. In one he saw people round a table talking animatedly together, laughing, their varying postures, bent forward, head thrown back, registering to him untrammelled delight.

That was the word, he thought, 'untrammelled'. He had never known a feeling of ease with his mother. 'I have a very good standing with my neighbours,' she would say, back straight in her chair. Indeed, they always enquired politely after her. Some even murmured, 'What a good woman your mother is,' dutifully.

Dutifully? Would they say it at all if they knew her comments about them when they weren't there? 'I bumped into that old woman at the end of the road, Mrs Caithness – the one who lives alone. What a sight! Stockings round her ankles, skirt squint, hair like a scarecrow. She was picking flowers from the next door's garden through their railings! Such cheek!' Or, 'Mrs Dandy! Mrs High-and-Mighty I call her! "I don't give to charities indiscriminately, Mrs McAlpine, even such worthy ones as the Lifeboat. My son takes care of all that for me. He's a lawyer too, but London-based." A dig at you, Alan. Probably some back street in one of those awful districts teeming with down-and-outs and littered with filth. London-based!'

A long way ahead he saw someone, walking slowly, and as he drew nearer he realized it was her. He could hear her calling in that simpering voice she used only for the cat, 'To . . . om! To . . . om?' quite loudly. She must be out of her mind to do that in this quiet neighbourhood. People would talk, which was to be avoided, normally, at all costs. 'What would people say?' He had grown up with that dictum. It must be their quarrel which had made her forget her own rule about 'keeping up appearances'.

The road was deserted, and poorly lit by occasional overhanging lamps. The trees cast huge shadows across it. Suddenly, or rather sliding into his vision, he saw a darker, steadily moving patch on the other side, a dark shape. It was the cat, seemingly gigantic, padding along. The shape stopped, tensed, listening, a head emerged. It had heard her voice.

She was within hearing distance from him now. He called, 'There's Tom, Mother! On the other side! I'll get –' The words were strangled in his throat. A car was coming round the bend. Fast, he registered, a bit fast, its headlamps dazzled him. He put his hand up to his eyes as he darted forwards. 'Take care, Mother! Mother, don't . . . !'

But it was too late. She had already stepped off the pavement, her body bent forward, her arms outstretched. He thought he heard her shouting, 'Tom . . . !' There was a terrible screech of brakes, a car door banging, a man shouting, and then Alan was in the middle of the road kneeling beside the stranger who was no longer shouting, who had now lowered his voice to a strangled whisper as he realized Alan was there. 'Oh, God . . . I didn't *see* her! A quiet road . . . never anyone about. I swear to God . . . stepped right in front of me . . . you saw it. I didn't have time . . . you saw it.'

'She's my mother,' Alan said, kneeling, looking. He wished he couldn't see, the smashed face, smashed to pulp, the hair streaked across it. In the flattened neck he saw embedded, glittering, small pieces of coal, her black jet beads. She always wore her jet necklace in the evening.

'It's my mother,' he said, turning to the man. The movement made him feel sick and he swayed. The man had taken command of himself now. He stood up and helped Alan to his feet. His voice was level now. It muttered something about getting help.

There were other voices now. He heard one which he recognized, quite close to him. 'Oh, Mr McAlpine. Oh dear, oh dear . . .'

'It's his mother,' the driver said. 'I swear to God . . . Look, could you get an ambulance?'

'Come inside with me, Mr McAlpine.' It was a female voice now, Mrs Dandy's, posh, comes from London. 'Come away in.' He stared at her, son a lawyer, London-based . . .

He shook his head. 'It's all right, Mrs Dandy.' He was pleased he remembered her name.

The ambulance was suddenly there, and then a police car as if someone had waved a wand. He was watching from where he was sitting on a low wall.

Hands had led him there. He knew the inspector. He got to his feet, listened to him making commiserating noises, allowed himself to be helped into the police car. 'Terrible for you . . . Who's your doctor? Dr Whitbread?'

'No, the other practice.' Mother had changed when Father had been involved with the Logan business – 'Take my advice, Tom, and steer clear . . .' He heard her voice in his ears and was suddenly weeping, his face in his hands.

'. . . strong cup of tea . . . terrible . . . statement . . . won't take long . . .' He went on weeping.

Eighteen

Jean met Van off the Dumfries bus (the trains didn't run direct to Kirkcudbright), looking even more exotic in the dingy background of the bus station. Her thick, frizzy hair was tied back, she wore silver earrings with a Rennie Mackinstosh motif, her eyes were heavily made up.

'Mother always says you're the beauty,' Van said, hugging her. 'I don't believe her until I see you again.'

'Rubbish! Anna's the one. And she spends more time on her image than I do. It's a kind of performance with Anna. The car's over here. What time are you meeting Alan?'

'Six thirty. I wanted to have a chat with you. If he comes early he can join us but I hope he doesn't.' They had reached the car.

'In you get. We'll be there in two shakes of a lamb's tail. Granny Rose used to say that. Your heart softens towards your mother once they're dead. No, badly put! I mean they have to be dead before we appreciate their good points. Here we are. The Selkirk Arms.' In a few minutes they were cosily settled in two armchairs at the window looking on to the street.

'How's Uncle John?' Van asked when they had ordered tea.

'He and Alastair are galivanting in Edinburgh! It's a weekend conference and they've got a locum in. Sarah has gone with them so that she can do some shopping for the children. I told her to do some for herself.'

'Didn't you want to go?'

'No, I'm not a shopper. You know me. I never buy clothes. I construct them.' She glanced down smilingly at her multicoloured skirt which looked like a patchwork quilt. 'And I'm in the middle of a big painting. You're about the only one I'd tear myself away for. I'm becoming quite unsociable. I don't even have a Green Gate Close coterie like the Glasgow Girls.'

'Does John mind you being so involved?'

'Mind? He couldn't be more glad that I'm occupied, and happy.'

'Roderick?'

'That's it. The social round would have crucified me. Painting fills the . . . the gap in my heart.' She looked away.

'I can imagine how you miss him, Jean.' She kept on speaking, 'I always *especially* loved him. Do you remember: "And how is everything *down* there?"'

Jean turned back. '"And did you come on the iron horse?"' Her eyes flooded with tears.

'Oh, I'm sorry.' Van put her hand over her aunt's. 'I shouldn't have started that.'

'Yes, you should. I want him *here*. At first I couldn't weep. Guilt's such a big part of grief. "Why did I allow him to go into that home?" "Why did I delude myself for years that he was happy there?" This obsession with paint has been my lifeline. It helped to cover the guilt. Did I ever tell you that the McAlpines had been patients of John's, but after that business with Alice they drew out of the practice? It

193

was that she-devil. Old Mr McAlpine was all right. I never blamed him, nor Alan, who followed his mother's lead when he took over his father's practice. I tried to be friendly because I felt sorry for him.'

Now I've got the guilt, Van thought.

'Here's the tea.' The waitress unloaded an ample tray of scones, butter and jam, slabs of fruit cake and fancies. The teapot and the hot water jug were big enough to slake the thirst of an army. 'I'm supposed to eat dinner after this?' And when the girl had gone away, 'I'd better leave *some* space!'

'Oh, you don't have to demolish it all, just admire it as an example of Scottish baking. So, how's Alan?'

'Alan's all right.' She sipped her tea. 'I like him, Jean. He couldn't quite swallow the idea of Sam, at first – he had his mother on his back all the time, that's the trouble.'

'You're good at creeping into other people's minds and looking out through their eyes.'

'Am I? Sam has got to be part of any . . . relationship I might make.'

'You're the same with Sam as I was with Roderick. Come on,' she held out a plate, 'have a scone.'

'All right. They're fair bursting with fruit.' She laughed.

'There are people who'd travel miles for a Scottish scone. Somehow,' she looked at Van, 'there's a fierceness in the kind of love women feel for their child who hasn't his real father.'

'I was never truly in love with Eb, just naïve, and full of a holy pity which included giving my body to him, not my soul.'

Jean sighed. 'Never pass *that* up if you get a chance. Once Frederick and I went to Rouken Glen, illicitly, as everything was, but the purity of it, the tremulousness of it, with a wee Glasgow keelie, of a conductor acting as Cupid . . . I'm glad I felt like that once.'

'I'm feeling like that about Hal, Hal Purvis. You know?'

'Yes, Anna told me about him.'

She would, Van thought. 'Feeling that this is it. Like your Rouken Glen. I'd just met him when I went to Portpatrick with Alan, and I wasn't quite sure, but after Arenys de Mar I was. That's why I'm here. To tell Alan.'

Jean sat back. 'Well, then! According to Anna he wants to marry you.'

'Yes, he does. And Hal doesn't. At least he hasn't said he does.'

Jean took another scone, buttered it thickly. 'That'll do instead of dinner, then I can work on. It's funny, your experience is the modern version of mine. Frederick *couldn't* marry me because he was already married. Hal could marry you but won't.'

'It's not that exactly. It's the idea of marriage as a bait that he doesn't like. Especially as he knows I'm involved with Alan. He thinks people should sort out their own emotional problems. The idea of him *fighting* Alan for me would be ridiculous to him.'

'He's right. Everybody has to do their own growing up. But you have to have a stick to support you during the growing-up process. Like painting.'

'Or being a hospital almoner. That's mine. It's like a pair of scales. Happiness on one side, being of some use to the community on the other. It's very old-fashioned, I know, to feel that you have to deserve your happiness. I think Karin, Mish's wife, feels the same. She's talking of going to Biafra.'

195

'I admire those strong-minded women who punish themselves.'

'Maybe it is a punishment.'

'Has she no compassion for Mish, leaving him?'

'No, I don't think so. It's a question of the greater good in her case. That's quite like Hal in some ways.'

'Painting is selfish, but maybe just being happy is a help to the community too. Have you thought of that?'

'I'll tell you when I get sorted out. I'm not looking forward to telling Alan it's over.' A man in a dark suit and white tie, dapper, had stopped beside them.

'Good afternoon, Mrs Whitbread,' he said. 'Are they looking after you well?'

'Very well,' Jean said. 'This is my niece, Mr Casson. Mr Casson is the manager, Van.'

Van held out her hand. 'Mother tells me she was brought here as a girl by her father. They used to visit my aunt, Miss Craig?'

'Oh, that was long before my time!' He laughed jovially, professionally. He looked younger than his aplomb, that of a well-trained hotel employee. 'I'm not a native.'

'So you won't be interested in town gossip?' Jean said.

'Well, you hear it in the hotel, of course.' He lowered his voice. 'This isn't gossip, as such. Perhaps you've heard. There was a particularly sad accident last night. The mother of a well-known lawyer was knocked down and killed, by a car. Before his very eyes.'

'Do you know his name?'

Van saw Jean's face change. She herself felt cold. She sat very still.

'Let me see? Yes.' He pursed his mouth, frowned,

'Mac . . . something or other. I've got it, McAlpine. A well-known lawyer.'

'We know him,' Jean said. Her voice was flat. 'Thank you, Mr Casson.'

He looked discomfited. 'I hope I'm not the bearer of bad news . . .' he hesitated. He's giving himself a bad mark, Van thought. Tittle-tattle. Not done. 'I'll . . . I'll see that you get a fresh pot of tea . . .' He seemed to melt away.

They looked at each other. 'Jean,' Van said. She knew her voice was shaking, 'Oh, Jean!'

'Sitting here talking about him. It makes you feel . . . oh God, poor soul. Do you think he'll come here? No, he wouldn't, would he?'

'I don't know.' Van looked at her. 'I don't know. I'm trying to think.'

'You can't just phone. You'll have to go and see him.'

'I know that.' A waitress came with a pot of tea, put it down and lifted the old one. Her look was sympathetic. The manager must have said something. 'Would you like more scones, ladies?' she said.

'No, thanks.' Jean's eyes were on Van as she spoke. 'Thanks all the same.' She waited until the girl had gone away. 'Have another cup of tea while you get used to the idea.' She poured a fresh one for them both.

Van sipped it. The hot liquid lubricated her throat. 'It was going to be difficult enough to tell him about Hal. I can't do it now.'

'No, not immediately. Don't do anything immediately.'

'I'll have to see him. And I'll have to get back tomorrow. Sam . . . they're too busy to look after

197

him, take him to school. And there are my classes
. . . but I have to see him.'

'Would you like me to drive you to his house right
away?'

'Yes, that would be best.' Terrible, she was thinking, terrible. 'But not for you to go in. That's rude –
I mean I'll have to see him alone.'

'Of course. I'll wait in the car while you ring, find
out if he's there, and if he is I'll drive away. It's no
distance for you to walk to our house . . . afterwards.'

'Right.' She got up, fumbled in her bag.

'I'm paying.' Jean took a purse from a quilted patch
on her skirt which was a pocket and laid a five-pound
note on top of the bill the waitress had left. She
pushed them both under a plate.

They didn't talk on the short ride to Alan's house.
Van felt numb, and dumb. Did life never go the way
you wanted it to, or was *that* life? He had been very
attached to his mother. That was a better word than
love. He had never once spoken lovingly of her. His
guilt, then, would be the greater.

Jean drew up at the double-fronted villa. It looked
empty, the curtains were drawn. The front garden
was impeccable, as if it had been prepared for
visitors.

'If he's there, and you see him asking me to go
in . . .' Van said. 'Thanks, Jean.' She got out and
went through large double gates, which were open.
She walked up the gravelled drive. The last time she
had been here was with Alan when they had come
from Portpatrick. She hadn't liked Mrs McAlpine
then, but she had never wished her dead.

Alan opened the door after the third ring. He
looked unusually dishevelled. There was a shirt
button undone under his tie knot. In anyone else it

would scarcely have been noticeable, but he was always so correct. He stared at her for a second, and half smiled. 'Van . . . I remembered. I was thinking of getting ready . . . to go.' He held the door open and she walked in.

Behind her she heard Jean drive away.

She followed him into the sitting room she remembered, so gloomy, so draped with velvet, with its over-stuffed chairs and its bulbous sofa, and yet so unyielding. It was not quite as immaculate as it had been before. The cushions were disturbed on the sofa as if someone had been lying there.

'Mary's gone out,' he said. 'I didn't want any neighbours.'

'Is she looking after you? Mary?' The maid, she remembered.

He shrugged. 'It's the cat that worries her. It lies . . . it lies on . . . her bed . . . all the time. I mean . . . Mother's.'

'That's sad. I was so sorry for you when I heard.' She went towards him in her sorrow, and reluctantly, it seemed, his arms came up and went round her, as if he was afraid of emotion.

'It's the shock, you see,' he said. 'One moment she's here – we were having dinner – and the next minute . . .' His grasp tightened and she felt his body tremble. He was weeping.

'It's so sad. The loss, the emptiness. Oh, I know that.' But she didn't. She hadn't felt empty when she had heard that Eb had died. She'd had Sam. Alan had no one close. She could be that one. She came out of his arms. The room felt stifling. She longed to draw back the curtains, get rid of the gloom. Was . . . *she* . . . still here? But there were mortuaries, places of rest provided by the funeral directors. It was a

199

strange term. 'Would you like to go for a walk, Alan? We could drive to the moors, walk there. Sometimes it helps . . . the fresh air.'

When Eb had told her that he didn't want anything to do with the coming baby, she had walked about Clerkenwell for hours, numb, unable to think. But she'd had someone to turn to, Anna and Ritchie, who had opened their arms to her, and their home. She could be the same to Alan.

'Come and see it,' he said surprisingly. It? She got up fearfully, and they went out of the room, he a step ahead, across the hall and up the stairs close-carpeted in a Turkey red pattern which Jean would have hated.

At the top he turned into a room whose door was partly open. On a wide bed, covered by a plump satin quilt she saw the cat, spread-eagled. Its face was buried in the quilt. The head moved, but it did not turn. The abandon of the animal was shocking.

'It won't eat,' he said. 'I tried to drag it off and . . . it spat at me.'

'Get a vet.' She, who liked cats, in whose own bed once a stray cat had had her kittens, was afraid of this one. 'He would know what to do for the best.'

'That's a good idea.' They stood looking at the cat, prone on the bed. Its tail moved, its paws were rounded in balls as if the claws were digging into the satin quilt. The atmosphere in the room was sinister, pressing in on her, there was a cat smell and she knew she could never live here. It was impregnated with the personality of Mrs McAlpine, this room with its dressing table and its precise layout of silver-backed brushes inset with painted enamel roses, the silver ring-tree, the mirror to match the brushes, the crystal tray. There was a woollen cardigan folded neatly over the back of one chair. She saw a pair of fur-lined slippers placed precisely together at the side of the bed, ready to step into.

They heard the door opening downstairs. 'That will be Mary,' Alan said. 'I'll get her to make you a cup of tea.'

'No, thanks, Alan.' Van wanted to go. 'I had tea with my aunt. It was the manager of the hotel who told us of the . . . accident. I came straight away.' She wondered if she should stroke the cat but was afraid. One paw as she looked was uncurling, slowly, then closing again, as if in an effort to contain its grief.

When they passed the kitchen door it was shut as if the woman didn't want to make any contact. Had it been Bessie, she would have shown herself.

'Are you staying with Dr Whitbread?' Alan asked.

'Only for tonight. I have to get off tomorrow morning. I left Sam with my parents, but he has school on Monday and my parents are too busy to take him there. And I have college on Monday morning.'

'Are you still going on with that?'

'Oh, yes.' She had said this before. 'I have to finish my course.' She wished he would offer her a drink. She had never felt the need of alcohol before.

'I wish you had been staying on here.' He was pale and drawn but dry-eyed.

'I can't, Alan. I really came to tell you . . . no, I can't. But I'll come and see you pretty soon. We have to talk. After the funeral.' She hoped he would not expect her to attend that.

'I don't know when that will be. There will have to be an inquest.'

'Yes, I'd forgotten that. The man involved – have you seen him?'

'Mr Webster? Yes, he called this morning. I think he's in the clear. Funnily enough, our firm looks after his affairs.' He was immediately businesslike. 'I didn't know until he told me. Father was his lawyer, but we've never had any reason to meet . . . until now. We'll have to get someone else to act for him, of course. I'm a witness. I can't honestly say he was driving unreasonably.' He smiled wanly. 'It was the speed of the . . . happening, which was transferred in my mind at the time to the speed of the car. It's unbelievable,' his face twisted, 'one minute here, the next . . .' He put his head in his hands as if he couldn't let her see him.

She went and sat beside him on the sofa and put her arm round him. 'Have you no one who might come and stay?' He shook his head. 'No one who has asked *you* to stay?'

'Yes, the Gilmours.' His voice was muffled behind his hands. 'Friends of mother's. But they'd talk about her all the time. I couldn't bear that. And then there's the cat.'

'Mary would look after it. But if it's not eating, just lying there, you should get –'

'Mary doesn't like it. She feels the same as I do. Uneasy.'

She looked at this man who was a successful lawyer but was afraid of a cat and saw a little boy who had lost his mother. Pity overcame her. She should say, 'Don't worry, Alan, you have me,' and then the image of Eb flashed across her mind, his pouting demands, the constant effort to please him. She hardened her heart. This time there was Hal. 'Do what I suggest. Ask the vet to take it until you get your affairs settled.'

'I've been in touch with the office today.' He sat

up, the lawyer again. 'The head clerk will come round each morning. He appreciates that I can't concentrate on other people's affairs at present. They come in and leave their problems on your shoulders and walk away feeling lighter. That's what being a lawyer means.'

'I understand that.' He caught the sympathy in her voice and turned towards her.

'Vanessa, you wouldn't consider staying up here for a week or so? I know you can't stay in this house, of course, but I'd pay for you in a hotel. I need you . . .'

She met his eyes, and struggled against their pleading. 'I can't, Alan. I came here to tell you –'

'To tell me what?' She saw the fear.

'That I needed some time, that I wasn't ready.'

'But things are different now that I'm alone!'

'Oh, you're not alone!' She tried to be brisk. 'You have plenty of people ready to help you. Let them. The first day people will stay away out of consideration, but they'll rally around. And you have Mary to look after you.'

'That sour-faced bitch,' he said surprisingly. 'No loyalty there, no rapport.' He took her hand. 'If you marry me we'll have a house in the country. I can't stand this place now. Nor her cat. At night I hear it padding about. It scratched at this door, making . . . noises, looking for her . . .'

The door bell rang, saving her, and she withdrew her hand. They could hear voices in the hall, then Mary appeared, unsmiling. 'It's Mr Jameson,' she said. There was a man in police uniform behind her.

'Come in, Inspector,' Alan said, standing up.

'I hope I'm not intruding.' He looked at Van.

'I'm just going.' She got to her feet.

'This is a friend of mine from Glasgow,' Alan said.

'Miss Laidlaw. She happened to be visiting her aunt.'

He shook hands. 'Your aunt?' He had a short hair-cut, and manner.

'Yes, Mrs Whitbread.'

'Oh, the doctor's wife! The painter. She had a show in old High Street not so long ago. A grand doctor, her husband.'

'Would you like a drink, Inspector?' He didn't include Van.

'A nip of malt, if you have it, Mr McAlpine.' He looked at Van. 'A sad business. You would know the deceased?'

'Yes.'

'A glass of sherry, Vanessa?' Alan said over his shoulder.

'No, thanks. I know you'll have a lot to discuss with Inspector Jameson. I'll let myself out.'

'No, no.' He seemed restored by the advent of the Inspector. 'I'll come to the door with you.' In the semi-darkness of the hall he drew near her. 'Shall I see you before you go back to Glasgow?'

'No, really I can't, Alan. I have to get the early bus to Dumfries. I promised. But you'll be coming to Glasgow soon on business.'

'I can't think . . .' He passed his hand over his forehead. 'Yes, I suppose so.'

'I'll ring you. And you know you can get me at Clevedon Crescent any time. You have the number.' She kissed him and he received the kiss without passion.

'Goodbye.'

Even in the gloom of the hall she could see his eyes had the same expression as Sam's when she left him. 'We'll keep in touch,' she said, emulating the Inspector.

Nineteen

Jean and John were sitting at the table having dinner when Van got back to their house.

'Come and have a bite, Van,' Jean said, looking up.

'Here's your chair.' John got up and came towards her to kiss her. She saw the thin face, the hair growing even further back, the sweetness of his expression. He drew out a chair and settled her at the table. 'There now! A glass of wine?'

'Just the thing,' she said, 'but I'm not hungry.'

'It's all on the table, isn't it, Jean?' They were both understanding. 'Help yourself to anything you like. There's a plate in front of you. How did it go?'

'He's very despondent, lost, but with flashes of Alan, the lawyer, when he remembers. But mostly his mother's son.'

'He said he needed you, did he?' John asked quietly.

'Oh, yes.'

'But I gather from Jean there's someone else?'

She nodded. 'It's never perfect, is it? Alan offers marriage, security, and he needs me, or so he thinks, Hal none of those things, but love.'

'Do you mean love, or passion?'

She looked at him. His eyes were on his plate, deliberately, she thought, in case she should read

205

them. 'Yes, passion.' She took a breath. 'Now, that's enough about me. Let's talk about you. Tell me about Edinburgh and Alastair and Sarah, and the children.'

'Oh, Jean will tell you all about that. Edinburgh was . . . windy,' he laughed, 'in more ways than one. But she's finished paintings of the children. They're the best thing she's done.' He looked at her with love. But she had never been able to give him passion, Van thought.

She telephoned Anna later on in the evening and said she would get into Queen Street Station at one o'clock the following day. When she got there Hal and Sam were waiting at the barrier. Her heart surged forward to meet them, her feet were anchored. Sam came running towards her and she bent down to gather him into her arms, dropping her bag, washed over by love of him.

When she stood up Hal was beside her, her bag in his hand, smiling. She was complete.

'Have you one for me?' he asked. She laughed and threw her arms about him. They kissed, and she thought, why did I ever doubt this? Her mouth was trembling.

'Come on, Mummy,' Sam said. 'Stop kissing. Hal's got strict orders from Grandma to get you back home. Bessie's making a clootie dumpling!' He brought out the words triumphantly, his expression comical.

'A clootie dumpling! What is it *for*?'

'It's Hal's birthday! He wanted to buy a cake, but she said that was just his . . . what was it she said, Hal?'

'She said that was just some of my English ways, and she'd make me a clootie dumpling.' His expression was even more comical. The three of them giggled stupidly at each other, until Hal said, 'Come on, then,' and led her to his waiting car where he bundled her in at the front, telling Sam to climb in at the back with his mother's bag. Van was amused at how Sam took orders from Hal with a degree of submissiveness. She remembered in Renton when they'd had a dog and Anna had said, 'We need Daddy's *voice* to control him.' Ritchie had been on one of his numerous trips.

Hal didn't speak much when he was driving through the Glasgow traffic, but occasionally he met Van's eyes to smile at her. She couldn't stop looking at him with delighted pleasure.

'Why are you here, Hal?' she said when they had cleared the busiest part of the city and he was driving along Woodlands Road. 'Is it business?'

'There's always business as far as your father is concerned. It does as an excuse. Your mother rang me to tell me you were away from home, and that a friend's mother had had a fatal accident, and so I thought, that serious girl needs comforting. So here I am.'

Sam was leaning on the back of Van's seat with his elbows, dying to speak. He burst in, 'I weighted out the things for the clootie dumpling!' His tongue lingered round the words. 'Bessie let me.'

'Oh, good!' She leaned back and put her cheek against his. 'Is there lots of fruit, and orange peel, and spices?'

'Oh aye, and dates and sultanas and apricots, "the whole jing bang!" Bessie said. "We'll put in the whole jing bang!"'

'I hope she won't forget the threepenny bits.'

'Those go in *after*, Mummy,' he said with scorn.

'This is going to be one hell of a clootie dumpling!' Hal said.

Sam giggled. 'He said a terrible word, Mummy, didn't he? He said –'

'I heard. Yes, he's a very naughty boy.' She looked at Hal's smug face.

'Yes, I'm a very naughty boy,' he said.

Anna and Ritchie welcomed her upstairs in the drawing room. For once they had descended from their respective studios at the same time, and were washed and brushed up – at least Ritchie more or less was, his greying curls carefully combed – Anna, elegant as usual in a honey-coloured dress unadorned except for a large brooch of Celtic design pinned near her left shoulder.

'How did you manage to tear yourselves away from your work?' she asked them, laughing, being hugged. Good to be home . . .

'Well, it's the Sabbath,' Ritchie said, looking unaccustomedly sleeked down and acting the part. 'It was blackmail on Bessie's part. She said she wouldn't make the birthday dumpling unless we observed the Lord's Day like decent folk. We've promised to take her to evening service at St Columba's.'

'We'll be baby-sitters,' Hal announced. 'I don't want to be saved just yet.'

'We're waiting for the call of the clootie first,' Ritchie said. 'Meantime, anyone for a drink?'

'On the Sabbath?' Hal mocked him. 'I'll have some of your communion wine, if you don't mind.'

'Van?'

'Yes, thanks. I expect Bessie will have the teapot full later.'

'Yes, it's all go in the kitchen. Her assistant's there too.'

Van noticed Sam wasn't in the room. 'I'm becoming a tippler. Jean and John plied me with drink while I was with them.'

'How was Alan?' Anna asked.

'Devastated.'

'I'm not surprised,' Hal said. 'It's generally a strong bond between mother and son, I suppose.' He had never talked much about his parents.

'It was unusual, her death, and cruel.' Van told him. 'She had gone out looking for her cat and she stepped on to the road in front of a car.'

'Killed for a cat,' Ritchie said. 'How about the cat?'

'She never reached it. It was all right. But . . .' she hesitated, 'it's devastated too. It lies on her bed all day.'

'Like the dog that lay on its master's grave in the Edinburgh cemetery. Bobby?'

'What you're telling us is full of images,' Anna said. She looked towards the window, glass in hand. 'The woman dashing across the road towards her cat, arms outstretched, body lanced forward . . .'

'You saw this cat lying on her bed?' Ritchie was playing with images too. They were typical artists, Van thought, an ability to turn away from reality, make their own.

'Prone.' She too saw the image, the bunched-up paws gripping the quilt, the outstretched body. 'I told Alan he should get the vet in.'

'It sounds spooky to me. Poor chap. A grieving cat as well. Did you comfort him?'

'As best as I could. Of course I couldn't stay. I had Sam, and my classes.'

'Quite.'

Anna got up. 'My skin is itching. It's the grief in it. Was she very fond of this cat?'

'Oh yes, obsessively. I didn't like it at all. It's huge, and it stares at you. It's very . . . masculine. The stare is.'

209

'Do you believe in the transmutation of souls, Ritchie?' Hal asked.

'No, and you're not leading me along that path!' He laughed. 'You'll put it in my book.'

'Let's go down and have your clootie dumpling,' Anna said. 'I don't like this conversation.'

Ritchie carried it in for Bessie, who was flushed and anxious.

'I'm a wee bit oot o'practice wi' clooties, but I think it'll be aw right. It's no' for want o' help.' She threw a glance at Sam, her mouth turning down in a smile. 'But I've toasted it at the fire and turned it roon an' roon to get the skin crisped up, an' I've put three threepenny bits in it, so fur goodness sake, ony o' ye, don't swallow them.'

The huge, shiny, rich, brown-raisined, red-cherried golden globe on its platter was placed in the centre of the table. The steam from it was enough to make your head swim, Hal said, swaying in his chair to Sam's amusement. Anna cut a generous slice, sprinkled it with sugar and poured cream over it.

'There you are, Bessie. I think you've reached perfection this time.'

'Bessie's an artist,' Ritchie said, 'better than us, though she'll never admit that.'

'I'll away to the kitchen and sample it onyway,' she said, 'gie it ma considered opeenion.'

'Why doesn't auld Bessie sit with us?' Sam demanded.

'Whit an idea!' Bessie said before anyone could speak. 'No, thanks, young man. I know ma place and where I'd rather be. An' less o' the "auld Bessie" if you don't mind.' She went off with her plate. They smiled at each other.

'Wouldn't she have stayed if you'd asked her, Mother?' Van said.

Anna shook her head. 'No. I've tried at birthdays and Christmases until I realized she didn't *want* to, then I gave up. Besides she's queen in her own kitchen. She knows she wouldn't be queen here.'

'I hope she hasn't got all the threepenny bits,' Sam said.

'Not a chance.' Ritchie took a generous slice from Anna and passed it to him. 'Get outside that.'

'I'm going to wish and *wish* before I eat it!'

'When Bessie made one in the old days,' Anna said, 'us girls used to laugh at each other with our white moustaches from the cream. Happy days.'

'I can do that,' Sam said eagerly. He took a generous spoonful of dumpling and cream and slapped it into his mouth. 'I've got one! I'll go and show Bessie my white moustache!' He was off his chair and out of the room in a second.

'And so tradition is carried on,' Hal said.

Anna smiled at him. 'But we shouldn't have been allowed to leave the table. That's how times have changed.'

'Think what you've missed, Hal, with all those ordinary iced cakes on birthdays.' Van smiled at him, loving him. If they lived together they would establish their own traditions, and perhaps pass them on to their children . . .

Later, Bessie, Anna and Ritchie went off to St Columba's church to take communion, a three-monthly treat for Bessie. Anna and Ritchie were taking part, as Ritchie said, to please Bessie, not God. Hal bathed Sam while Van washed up. This was part of the treat for Bessie.

'Don't make a mess in ma kitchen,' she had said to Van, going off with her black toque and her fox fur, a present from Anna, knowing how Bessie had lusted after Nancy's. 'An' wring oot the dish-cloot and wipe aw roon, an' be sure and sine the dish-towels wi' a wee bit o' bleach in the water, and gie the taps a rub. Spick-an'-span. That's ma motto.' Anna had led her away by the arm, still issuing instructions. It was a quarterly event in her life, compared with meeting the Queen or setting off for the Antipodes.

When everything was finished and Sam had had two stories read to him by Hal and one from Van, they settled down in front of the fire in the drawing room.

'Bliss,' she said, 'bliss to find you here when I got back.' They were sitting on the sofa and he put an arm round her.

'To use a euphemism, do you want to sleep with me while they're out?'

'What's your decision?' she asked, turning to face him. He took off her glasses, laid them carefully on a table by their side and held her face in his hands.

'Regretfully, no. What's yours?'

'The same. It's a family visit, this. It would be like a betrayal of . . . using their house as a . . .'

'Not that Anna and Ritchie would mind or be shocked. Nothing like that. It's the . . . feeling.'

'I have it as well.'

'How nice that we share feelings too, a bonus.'

'Anna told you why I was in Kirkcudbright?'

'Yes.' He kissed her, and they settled back in the sofa, his arm still round her. 'Anna and I get on well. I quite understood. A friend, she said.'

'He's more than a friend. He wants to marry me.'

212

'How do you feel about that?'

'I don't love him and I love you.'

'Well, that's it, isn't it?'

'Yes, I suppose it is.'

'You don't sound very sure.'

'I feel so sorry for him.'

'He wouldn't like just that, this man – any man. It's an insult.'

'He would say that pity could turn into love.'

'Do you believe that?'

'I pitied Eb and let him make love to me. He didn't want the result, Sam, so I never found out.'

'I didn't come up because of your sad news, Van.' He changed the subject. 'I'm going to America next week. I have several books to arrange, including your father's. That's what my life is like, is going to be like. I enjoy it. Normally if you lived with me you could come on these trips – I mean, if you didn't have a career of your own, but you have, or are working towards it. I want you to think of this, what it would be like for you and for Sam. I know you want to have a settled life for him, and that you want to be independent of your parents, and so you should at your age. You have to decide who would give you the better solution, the man in Kirkcudbright, or me.'

'His name is Alan.'

'Alan or me. You have to think of our special and different kinds of need, his, and mine, and yours, and what kind of background you want for your son. My parents were different from yours. They were more detached. I have had to stand on my own from an early age. They sent me to England from Singapore to be educated. Then I was at Oxford. They have never been in the foreground of my life and I think that's how they want it to be. So, it's your decision.'

She couldn't say, 'But Alan is offering me marriage.' It was like saying, 'Alan's offer beats yours on points. Can you better his?' Instead, she turned to him, her face upraised. She felt his kisses, on her mouth, on her neck, and despite their scruples they slipped down on the rug in front of the fire. And she felt passion, heady passion. John Whitbread had said that was the most important thing. She had the feeling that Anna and Ritchie would say the same.

When her parents came back Van and Hal were sitting watching television. 'Don't tell me you've been looking at boring programmes all evening?' Anna said, touched perhaps into censoriousness by her brush with the Church.

'Would you have been very disappointed with us if we had?'

'Very.' She sat down and kicked off her shoes, breathed deeply. 'Well, that should do me for another three months.'

Twenty

Hal went off the following morning with nothing settled between them. He would be in New York until Christmas, and would go to see Mish. Van had to take Sam to school. Indeed he was at her heels in the hall, school cap on his black frizzy head, satchel on his back.

'Come on, Mummy! Leave him! You'll make me late for Miss Clewes!'

They parted. 'It's only three months,' Hal said.

'Three months!' There was the difference between an optimist and a pessimist. 'All *right*, Sam! Say good-bye to Hal. That's what *I* was doing.'

'I'm not going to cuddle him the way you were! Miss Clewes –'

'Goodbye, old chap.' Hal stuck out his hand and when Sam tentatively took it, he swung him into his arms. 'That's a hug for Miss Clewes. Look after your mummy for me, will you?'

He drove off, she got Sam by the hand and hurried him into Anna's car. Her parents were already at work in their studios. They had said their goodbyes, tactfully perhaps, at breakfast.

The headmistress was in the hall greeting the mothers. The last of the small private schools, Van thought. Soon Miss Clewes would be phased out,

215

soon Sam would be leaving for the rough and tumble of the Elementary, he wouldn't need shepherding, and his childhood would be over. She thought the woman looked pale and drawn, possibly ready for retirement.

'Are you looking forward to the half-term holidays, Miss Clewes?' she said.

'Indeed yes, Mrs Laidlaw.' She too retained the polite fiction that Van had been married, and Van had never corrected her, thinking that was far better for Miss Clewes' peace of mind than reality. 'Sometimes it looks as if it will be a long holiday. This school has been my life, but I'm getting to the stage where I can no longer afford to maintain it as it should be maintained.'

'Yes, prices go up and up.' Van remembered that as far as Clevedon Crescent was concerned, she took no part in maintenance, and felt a guilty stab. She thought fleetingly of Alan, standing in the wings, ready to assume responsibility for her.

'One thinks twice before calling in a workman now. And people aren't sending their boys and girls to private schools as much as they did. Your mother and sisters came here, and I believe their mother, which was before my time, of course.' Miss Clewes' winsome smile was a bit forced. 'But young parents can't afford the fees now, or won't. Perhaps they think they're entitled to get it off the Government.'

'Things aren't as they used to be,' Van agreed. It was a frequent remark of Bessie's, couched in more forceful terms: 'I don't know whit the world's comin' tae.'

'Indeed no. Well, I'd better get inside and start Assembly. I like to follow the public schools' régime in our own small way.'

216

'And I'd better get off to college. Good morning, Miss Clewes.'

As she was driving to Pitt Street she felt the familiar guilt that her parents should still be subsidizing her like this, paying her fees for the college, fees for Sam. She would rather he had gone to the local school at Byres Road.

She had wondered at the time if her mother had feared he would be taunted at a bigger school because of his colour. Ritchie had agreed because it wasn't an issue with him. In his case there had been no choice when he was Sam's age, and sometimes, Van thought, he showed a bemused bewilderment that he, a 'Glasgow keelie', should find himself living in one of Glasgow's most élite addresses, and even having a grandson who went to a 'private school'. There had been none of these where he had been brought up. Miss Clewes would have probably shuddered at his first school's dirt playground and outside toilets liberally besprinkled with graffiti, his first taste of art, he'd said.

She rounded the corner from Sauchiehall Street and saw the bulk of the Commercial College in front of her, squarely characterless, and because of its modernity out of step with the elegant old streets around it, Douglas Street, Holland Street, and the elevated green enclave of Blythswood Square. The college was functional without Rennie Mackintosh's sense of design. Ritchie called it her College of Knowledge.

It had had a chequered career, she had learned in the brochure, having been instituted by some public-spirited Glasgow business men in 1834 to fill the gap between the Mechanics Institute and the Glasgow University. Originally it had run classes at seven o'clock in the morning designed for those ambitious young men who had been thirsty for further education but still had to work all day. There had been a clockmaker in Glassford Street who advertised alarm clocks for those dedicated early risers.

The college was aptly named, she thought, parking the car. Glasgow was a city of commerce. Its aristocracy was composed of successful businessmen, who, having come up the hard way, wanted to provide better facilities than had been available to them. Ritchie said he always felt Glasgow had more affiliation with New York than London in its forceful attitudes to 'getting on in the world'.

Van's course hadn't started until 1962, and already there were moves afoot to scrap it for a university degree. She couldn't face the longer time this would take. She wanted to get her Diploma and be fit to work anywhere. Her future was still uncertain.

She went through the swing doors of the college partly buoyed up by the thought of those ambitious old Glasgow merchants with their thirst for knowledge and their recognition of it in others. She tried to banish ever-present thoughts of Hal.

There was plenty of field work now that she was in her second year, and in the big city infirmary where she was sent that morning she knew she had chosen the right métier. The whole ethos of her life had been concentrated on helping others. Now she was learning how to direct it.

She had no idea where this wish had come from – not from Anna, who was single-minded about her own work to the exclusion of everyone else. Ritchie was more impressionable, but his natural laziness, except where his work was concerned, prevented him from allying himself with any voluntary charity organization. One Dorcas in the family was enough, he said.

She thought perhaps it came from Ritchie's mother, Lizzie Laidlaw, whose death from cancer had been such a blow to him. For weeks afterwards her name could not be mentioned without the tears flowing from his eyes. He grieved deeply, but healingly, for the mother who had believed in him from the beginning.

Van thought of that spry little figure who had worked all her life doing menial tasks but had been so full of dignity, her compassion for everyone as well as her husband, Walter, who had accepted his redundancy from the pits, and settled down to put ships into bottles while she scrubbed those dark smelly closes which Van had found still existed in the domiciliary visits she paid as part of her course.

Anna had told her of going with Ritchie to their tenement flat in the East End of Glasgow, and how, when she had admired the pipeclay arabesques on the outside end of every step on the stone stairs, he had told her his mother made them, saying, 'That's where I got my talent.'

That morning Van sat at the bedsides of old men and women and wondered if there weren't any hidden geniuses amongst them whose ability had been smothered by the necessity of hard, grinding work which never quite made ends meet. One of the old women whom she was visiting reminded her of Lizzie Laidlaw in her birdlike appearance – a very old bird.

'Could you give me a little of your history, Mrs Tait?' Van asked.

Mrs Tait had no false teeth in, or simply no teeth. She had a woollen shawl wrapped firmly round the upper part of her body, which made her look like an Egyptian mummy. It reminded Van of how Bessie had once wrapped *her* up in a similar fashion when she had been visiting Grandma Rose. 'Your hug-ma-tight,' she had called it. She became aware of Mrs Tait's basilisk stare.

'What age are you, Mrs Tait, if you don't mind telling me?'

The woman hesitated, toothless jaws clamped, reducing her chin to nothingness, then snapped them open. 'Seventy-nine, miss, gaun on eighty, maybe. Aye, that's it.'

'Any children?'

Mrs Tait's wool bandaged torso heaved. 'Aye, plenty o' these! They never gie ye a minute's peace, men. Seven live weans, two deid, naw, three. Wee Aggie . . .'

'How many grandchildren?'

'Aw, I canny mind. Maybe twelve. The wee lassies urny bad, but, see, Easterhouse, it's a bad atmosphere there. We were better aff in the Gorbals.'

Van nodded sympathetically. Easterhouse reminded her of a painting of her father's he had discarded recently. When she had commiserated on the amount of wasted work, he had said, 'I've only myself to blame. I didn't spend enough time thinking it out first.'

Mrs Tait was describing with every sign of enjoyment the various disasters which had befallen her, her husband, her family, and now her grandchildren. Her hands waved as she spoke, her toothless mouth was a hollow cavern. It was unusual in someone of her class to be so theatrical in gesture. Her hands were graceful although the fingers were calloused, the nails ridged.

220

'Your own parents? Were they of British nationality?'

'Scottish. I don't know anything aboot British. This is Glesca.' She considered, massaging her small chin. 'Well, ma mither wis, but ma faither wis a Lascar seaman, noo I come to think o' it. They in their big boats at the docks. I've got his black eyes and the same fancy hands, ma mither used to say. When he came hame he used to teach me how to dance. The fandango, he called it. Mither used to get mad at him. "We don't want any o' your furrin tricks here," she would say. "I've had enough o' them to last me aw ma life." For years,' she said, looking up at Van with her inherited dark eyes in their wrinkled framework of yellowing skin, 'I thought ma mither was fat, till I got caught masel and then I knew she'd had a wean in there maist o' the time, yin efter the ither.'

'She couldn't have had much time to herself?'

'Time! You must be jokin'. The only one who had ony time wis ma faither, and that was haunded oot to him by the judge!' She cackled at her own wit, gums on display. 'She used to say she would never know how many brithers an' sisters we had at his other ports of call. I liked fine the thought. I always wanted to hop on a big boat that had a whole lot o' ports of call!' The phrase seemed to please her. 'See the world. But aw the hoppin' I'll be daein is into ma coffin.'

In the evening, at dinner, Van told Anna and Ritchie about Mrs Tait. Anna said, laughing at Ritchie, 'There's no saying where *you* get your dark eyes from!'

Ritchie was incensed. It always amused Van how they went for each other, hackles rising. 'Your tongue gets the better of you at times!' Van and Sam didn't

221

exist. 'If ever anyone stood by her man, that was my mother! God knows, I used to wonder why, and yet you couldn't help liking the old bugger – sorry, Anna, I know there's a child in the room, sorry, Sam. Him and his wee pliers and his glass bottles. That's art too.'

'He was sweet,' Van said.

'That's one of your Sassenach expressions, but, yes, it fits. You could forgive him anything. I never held it against him that my mother had to work while he sat at home. The sweetness was there.'

'Now things are different,' Van said. 'Equal responsibilities. That's why I want to be independent.' She saw her mother's acute gaze, then her hand going up to her mouth, suddenly.

'That reminds me, although I don't know why it should, but Alan phoned. He'll be here on Saturday. He'll call for you at seven o'clock. I didn't ask him to have a meal here. I know he'll want to talk to you.'

'This time I'll have to have the courage to tell him it's over.'

'Better sooner than later. It's a matter of commitment.'

Later, when Sam was in bed, Van asked her, 'What did you mean when you said it was a matter of commitment?'

'Oh, that!' Her black hair had swung forward over the book she was reading, and it swung back like heavy liquid as she looked up, her brilliant blue eyes wide. It was a moot point sometimes which twin was the beauty. 'I think what's bugging you is that *Hal* won't commit himself, but don't you see it's the same with you? Ritchie and I were committed to each other from the age of eighteen. We were desperate to get married as soon as he had a job, because, generally

222

speaking, and leaving aside my wayward sister, a husband had to maintain his wife, and, generally speaking, you didn't have sex before you were married. I think Ritchie was even more puritanical than I was, coming as he does from a lower class.'

'Oh, Mother! How terribly Clevedon Crescent!' Van laughed.

'I'm factual, that's all.' She waved her hand. 'You lot don't have to rush into marriage, because you don't wait to sleep together, but I think that makes it harder, not easier. Commitment, equal commitment, should exist.'

'You're right, Mother.' Of course . . .

But she hadn't the courage to tell Alan it was all off between them when he came to Glasgow on Saturday. He looked so woebegone, and so sad, that she agreed to go out with him for a meal. She listened to the saga of the cat, which had been half its original size when the vet came to take it away. 'Like a great empty bag of fur,' he said. 'I can't forget its eyes.'

She told herself she was a social worker listening to a patient who was ill from grief. You didn't turn a patient out of bed until he was better. She noticed, however, he was no longer dishevelled, he had become a lawyer again, and was going to work regularly. He had stopped taking the pills the doctor had given him. 'Everyone has been very kind,' he said. 'Of course, I hold a certain position in the town, Van.' He had regained an estimate of his true worth. And his chrysanthemums had never been better, he said.

Twenty-One

Hal liked where Mish lived. They had become good friends, and Hal had been assured that he would be welcome to drop in any evening. They were both too busy during the day to meet, and he had got into the habit of walking up Madison or Lexington Avenue from his hotel near the Rockefeller Center to Mish's apartment on East Sixty-Third street and dropping in for an hour or so.

He could live in New York, he thought. It wasn't the den of iniquity so often painted, at least in his experience. It was a question of sticking to the frontiers. Upper East Side was generally quiet at this time, the brownstone houses reserved, the little restaurants, mostly German, always busy.

There were plenty of good shops to browse around, individual little places, one particularly where he often chatted to the proprietor, a young man who sometimes sat on a chair on the sidewalk, as Hal had come to call it. He made little wire sculptures, 'poor Giacomettis', he called them. He even resembled him with his dark romantic good looks.

He seemed to know everyone who walked along the street, and there was often a coterie of young men browsing inside. 'Hi, Anthony!' he had heard one shout from the interior.

Hal had got to know him when he had bought a small sculpture of a girl who reminded him of Van because of the Afro hair, the thin, childlike legs and the thick waist, not waiflike, but incredibly appealing to him.

'Does she remind you of someone?' Anthony asked him when he was wrapping it up. 'I did it from life, you know.'

'Yes. There's a girl back home . . .'

'Lucky you!' His smile was charming; he was too beautiful for a man.

Hal asked Mish about him when he showed him the sculpture. 'He works from models, you know.'

Mish laughed. 'Is that what he told you? He buys them wholesale from one of his friends. Very kitsch, really, but good kitsch.'

'This one reminded me of Van. Maybe I was done.'

'You aren't done if you like it, and if there's some point of contact. I see people paying thousands of dollars just because it's a well-known name although it's an inferior painting.'

'Do you tell me that?'

'Hi! I'm a business man first and foremost. I'm not an idiot.'

'Neither is Anthony.'

'You're right there. Do you know, he collects old Rolls Royces? He's got three!'

'He showed me a sculpture of one of them, but I didn't quite believe him.'

'You'd better believe him – where the Rolls Royces are concerned. That guy's rolling.'

It was a mild evening for early November, and they sat out on the balcony drinking and listening to the New York noises, sirens, taxis, screeching, no voices from the street – it was a well-bred neighbourhood – watched with casual interest the movement of figures behind the screens of the apartments across the street. Not many people sat out on their balconies now that the weather was cooler.

'It's only when the temperature drops that you can breathe,' Mish said. 'And yet I'd be miserable living in the country. I'm truly urban. My job takes me to other cities, just like yours. How about you?'

'Pretty much the same. I know it can't go on, this life-style. It wouldn't suit my wife if I had one.' He felt Mish's gaze on him. 'How is Karin?' he said quickly.

'Living a life of deprivation along with the Biafrans. She isn't exactly scourging her soul, but it's a kind of penance for being well off. She has to see the other side of the coin, give something of herself before she settles down. I wouldn't dream of interfering with that. I wait patiently.'

'It's a strange thing, this, with women. Your sister has it.'

'Van's always had it. She would have made a tramps' hostel out of our house from the time she was five, or a cattery, if Mother would have allowed it. A real bleeding heart. They used to have awful rows.'

'She's still the same, but in a more disciplined way, with this training she's doing.'

'You can't object to that?'

'Good God, no! I'm one hundred per cent for it. No, what worries me is that she can't make up her mind about me, or rather, me in relation to another man she's involved with. She can't bear to hurt him. I understand her, and I don't want to push her in any way. She must come to me of her own free will.'

'You love her?'

'Like anything. For ever. And a day.' He looked over at the apartment opposite, saw two figures embracing at the window, taking their time about it. His throat filled.

'Mother used to watch that apartment,' Mish said. 'She came here when she was very miserable. Father had gone off with another woman, and I think she made little fantasies out of the couple across there. Don't know if it was the same one. She used to tell Karin and me about them when we came home at night. We were so sorry for her. I could have kicked my father up the backside!'

'I thought you were a loving family!' Mish laughed.

'Sure we are. We're involved. What's a family for but to become involved? Aren't you?'

'No. My parents are non-involveable. It's made me . . . suspicious.'

'Of what?'

'Happiness.'

'Married happiness?'

'I suppose so.'

'I think Van's suspicious of it too. She's never been sure of herself like me. I've had a big head since schooldays – quietly confident, it's called – but not Van. She felt disadvantaged in our family, not being interested in art. I knew where I was going, Father and Mother were work-oriented, our milieu at home was artistic. Van's interest was in people, in their suffering. God, did she identify with them! This black guy she lived with. Do you know, I think she had sex with him because she couldn't bear to feel he was disadvantaged, and then when she was pregnant the bastard threw her out. Wanting to be like other people didn't extend as far as being a father. He was a selfish git.'

'It's the imago thing,' Hal said, remembering.

'Come again?'

'We had a talk once along these lines, Van and me. She told me some young Spaniard she met at your father's place had explained to her that "imago" is the moment when a butterfly emerges from its chrysalis and becomes sexually aware. He had commented on her name, Vanessa – he was an entomologist or something. I think she's reached that stage now, feeling complete, if you get it.'

'She's a slow developer. Really rather like a butterfly. Not in her movements, bless her.' He laughed. 'Van as a little girl was clumsy, and then her glasses . . . she felt that put the kibosh on her.'

'I like her wearing them. A serious, beautiful girl in glasses is twice as beautiful. Besides, there are contact lenses now.'

'That'll be the day. She would think that was being dishonest, or half a dozen other things – misrepresentation, what have you. Van needs reassurance. She's never really got it from Anna and Ritchie. Anna has only a below-the-skin rapport with one person in the world and that's Jean, her twin sister. Everything else goes to Ritchie, I mean, all the intensity.'

'Observant.' Hal nodded.

'Van feels she intrudes on their idyll living with them. It's important for her to get her Diploma as an almoner, establish her independence, be responsible for Sam, and then think about you.' He looked at Hal. 'Have you ever asked her to marry you?'

'Not in so many words.'

'There are only four, "Will you marry me?" '

'It's not that easy. There's this man she's tied up with, and now he's leaning heavily on her because his mother was killed under his very nose, so to speak –'

Mish interrupted. 'If that's the only reason,' he gave Hal a sidewards glance, 'you could send him to hell in one easy movement.'

'How?'

'Ask her!'

They looked at each other. 'You mean, ask her, leave out the supplementary clauses, the parentheses, the reasons *why* I shouldn't ask her?'

'That's what I mean.'

'Like go to the phone and ring her?'

'No. Write. Write a love letter and solemnly, formally, ask her to marry you. You've put off so much time already that a few more days won't matter.'

Hal got up. 'Chilly here now, Mish.'

'Yes, chilly. Come in and I'll heat up some soup or something.'

'No thanks. I'll get back to my hotel. Got to write a letter . . .'

'Give her my love.' He slapped him on the back as they went in.

'I will. Give mine to Karin when you write to her.'

'Sure! We're a couple of bozos, you and me, hanging around like knotless threads, waiting. Maybe it's deliberate sadism on their part.' They laughed together.

Twenty-Two

'Into November now,' Van said at dinner time. 'Soon be Christmas.'

'We're all going to the pantomime at Christmas, aren't we, Sam?' Ritchie said. His curls were particularly grey this evening; one had a metallic gleam. He had taken to using a touch of gold paint in some of his abstracts. Anna didn't like it. 'It's an additive,' she had said, 'not pure colour.' 'It's for the Americans,' he had replied, looking sheepish, 'they like a bit of glitz.'

'We're going to the panto, we're going to the panto,' Sam sang, banging his knife and fork on the table. 'Are you taking a *big* lot of people, Grandpa?'

'Quite big. All the Pettigrews and us, and two extra tickets, one for your friend, one for Mummy's.'

'Could I bring Toby? He's definitely my best friend.' He giggled. 'He's so funny! And he doesn't do what Miss Clewes tells him. We run all over the school when we have our playtime. It's out of bounds!'

'That's naughty,' Van said. 'You shouldn't disobey Miss Clewes' orders. She would be very annoyed.'

He pouted. 'I wish I hadn't told you.' He appealed to Ritchie. 'Are you going to *still* let me bring him, Grandpa?'

'Well, if you promise your mother to be a good boy.'

'Of *course* he can bring Toby,' Anna said. 'Where does he live?'

'I don't know. His father is a cutting doctor in the hospital, that's all I know.'

'A *cutting* doctor?' Van echoed, laughing. 'You mean a surgeon? Which hospital is he in?'

'I don't know these things. We don't *discuss* fathers much because I haven't got one. I just know he's a cutting doctor and he slices legs off and he's my best friend, Toby is. Oh, he's funny! He –' He suddenly stopped, his eyes slid round the three others at the table, and not for the first time Van saw a look of Eb in his glance, a slyness, like an animal, and then it was gone and she told herself it was imagination. All children learned early to watch their step with grown-ups.

'And the other ticket is for me, is it?' She smiled at her father.

'You and partner. I leave it to you to decide who is the lucky man.'

'Hal will be home for Christmas.'

'And, of course, there's Alan,' Anna said, looking limpid. She was getting at her.

'He's all right now.' She was casual. 'He's got a new housekeeper, much friendlier than Mary, he says, and he's joined a bridge club. Oh yes, I think he's all right. The whole town will be supporting him in his loss.' She bent her head to her plate. The next time he came to see her she would tell him she was in love with someone else. He would be able to cope with that now. She could feel Anna's cool glance. Ritchie had never been able to read her the way her mother did.

After their meal she went into the kitchen to wash up. She had taken over that chore from Bessie now. Bessie was going to bed earlier and earlier, but still wouldn't hear of help in cooking the evening meal. 'Ur ye feart I'll pooshen ye aw?' she had said to Anna when she had offered to do it. Anna accepted this, but kept the menu as simple as possible. She knew how important routine was to her.

They were both upstairs when Van had finished, Anna seeing to Sam's school clothes, Ritchie reading to him. It was their time, the indulgent grandparents, and Van was relegated to the role of stern parent who went in and said severely, 'Lights out now, Sam. You've had a good time but you've got to be ready for school.' She tucked him in, kissed his brown cheek and smoothed his frizzy hair, like hers or Eb's.

His eyes were heavy with sleep. 'I *can* bring Toby to the pantomime, Mummy, can't I?' He reached up to put his arms round her neck.

'Grandpa said you could. What does he look like?'

'He's got fair hair, not like mine, it's smooth, and he wears a kilt, and his full name is Toby Graham because the kilt is a Graham tartan, he says, and he's got pink cheeks, bursting pink cheeks because he's always laughing.'

'Well, he sounds very nice. There's plenty to laugh at in *Puss in Boots*.'

'Oh, *Puss in Boots*!' He squirmed in ecstasy, snuggling down under his quilt. 'I'm going to dream of Puss in Boots, a great big cat in huge boots that stalks about the earth and frightens people. Oh, great!' He moved his shoulders with pleasure. His eyelids dropped.

'A great big cat, stalking about the earth . . .' She thought of Mrs McAlpine's Tom and how it had been

232

literally the death of her although she had given it all her love.

In her room she worked diligently on an essay about the social conditions in the thirties in Glasgow. That was when her father and mother had been at the Art School, but how little they ever spoke of the state of depression in the city at that time!

Her mother would have been unaware of it, her father was shielded from it by being spared the necessity of finding a job, thanks to his mother. Certainly he would see the results in the streets around his home, but his mind would be filled with two things only, Anna and art.

I wonder what I'll remember of *this* period, thirty years on, she thought, the promiscuous sixties. I did my bit . . . but hurt fades like everything else, and the result, Sam, made up for everything. But, thirty years on, I'll be mother's age. What will Sam's future be? Shall I be married to Hal, with a family? Where will we live? One thing was sure, she could not contemplate a future without him.

The college had opened in the thirties, and there was an old janitor who remembered how they had celebrated the occasion by a trip to the Firth of Clyde. 'Two boats,' he had told Van proudly, 'the *Duchess of Hamilton* and the *Duchess of Montrose*, packed to the brim, all food supplied. My, what a day that was. I'll never forget it.' Strange the magic the doon the water trip had for Glaswegians.

Once Ritchie had described to her the trip he and Anna had made when she was spending her holiday at Kilcreggan and he had a vacation job in a fruiterers in Hamilton. 'I sailed from the Broomielaw,' he said, 'the fare was one pound, and I'll never forget how my heart stopped when I saw her stepping along the

233

gangway when the *King Edward* called in at Kilcreggan, the neatness of her in her light dress and white cardigan, the trimness, and that smile and those eyes . . . She came into my arms like a homing pigeon.'

Mother had been guarded by her parents from the strikes, the unemployment everywhere, the Family Means Test, the general misery prevalent. She had never known any poverty at first hand, and with this in mind Van began to write passionately about the vast gulf which had always existed between the rich and the poor, because it was something she cared passionately about.

'The tragic years for Glasgow began in 1932,' she wrote, 'the year which saw the collapse of shipbuilding on the Clyde, the closure of the pits, when the dole queues became longer by the week . . .'

She was being too general, she soon realized, and she set herself to read a copy of the report on the situation then by the Glasgow Chamber of Commerce. One hundred thousand men unemployed and no constructive policy on how they could be reinstated. Heavy industry had had its day. Only the cynics allowed that Germany's unconcealed rearmament was going to reverse that trend before long.

Thousands of able men were defeated, morally and physically, she thought. Walter Laidlaw had been one of these. Where had Glasgow's enterprise gone to? Was it that so many of the young men who would have thought actively and creatively about the Depression and how to combat it had been killed in the First World War? It was ironical, to say the least, that the thought grew at that time that only another war could change the country's fortunes.

She sat reflecting on the cycles of any great city, the ups and down for its people, and how few of them were able to change their circumstances. All the old men and women she saw in the Glasgow hospitals had lived through the Depression. They had known poverty and hardship to what seemed to be an unacceptable degree. And in Clevedon Crescent Granny Rose had continued with her bridge parties and her sorties to Daly's, not knowing or caring what went on in the city unless it affected her directly.

Anna had once said that her father had changed during these years. He had always kept his worries to himself, and he had continued to do so. She said that sometimes she surprised a wistfulness in his expression as if he was thinking longingly of the mountains of Ross where life had been simple and clean and where there were no tenements stinking with overflowing drains and overrun with rats, and where the Corporation had neither the money to repair them or dismantle them in spite of the protests of architects like himself. Perhaps Rose preferred a lighter subject at the dinner table with its perfect appointments and its wee silver bell to summon Bessie to clear the plates.

Bessie, Anna had said, had always shown a sturdy independence of spirit as if she saw through her mistress's foibles. 'I got more information about the other side of things from Bessie in the kitchen than I ever got from Mother.'

Later, Van lay in bed planning tomorrow. She would take Sam to school then get the bus to college. She had to attend a conference in St Andrews Hall to hear a well-known psychologist speaking on 'The Social Concept of Morality', and then make her way back to Pitt Street for afternoon lessons. Afterwards she would hurry back to pick up Sam at school.

And, having settled the practicalities, she allowed

herself to think of Hal. She wrote a letter to him in her mind.

My love, *she would say*, I miss you, but in a way it's a good thing. Sometimes, time is on one's side. Things settle. My anxiety about Alan McAlpine is beginning to go. I'm waiting for his next visit to tell him that I can never marry him. I feel this even more strongly when you're not with me. *Then* you bowl me over. I would dance the Highland Fling for you if you asked me, stand on my head, turn cartwheels. But when you're so far away I can see you differently, although never objectively, because I realize my life is incomplete without you and always would be. I don't go any further. Everything falls into place when I realize that fact . . .

They were late the following morning, and Van was short-tempered with Sam for not hurrying. 'I've got a school to go to as well as you, you know. I can't afford to be late. I've got to sit an examination and then get a job so that I can keep us.'

'Grandpa does that,' he said, pouting.

'We're not beggars. Come on, hurry up!' When they got to his school she waved briefly to him and went off.

The morning was spent at the conference at St Andrew's Hall, and she had to rush back to be in her classroom for the afternoon lessons. She was bent over her books when another teacher came in, excusing himself. He spoke to their tutor, and Van got the impression they were looking at her as they stood. There was a sudden coldness in her heart.

'Miss Laidlaw?' She had been right. 'Mr Thomas would like to have a word with you in private.' She got up trembling, still cold. Sam . . . her parents . . . Hal . . . she was outside the door, Mr Thomas was speaking to her, kindly.

'There has been an accident at your son's school, Miss Laidlaw. He's been hurt. I don't think it's too serious –'

'Accident?' Her hand went to her mouth. 'What's happened?'

'I think he's had a fall. I'm sure –'

'Is he . . . is he still in the school?'

'No. They've taken him to the Western Infirmary. That's the message. I shouldn't worry.' His face expressed his kindly concern.

'I'll go right away. Will you tell Mr West? I have to go . . .'

'Of course. I'll get you a taxi first. Come along.' He took her elbow. 'I have children myself. I know how you must feel.'

'Didn't they say how it happened?'

'No. There were no details. Just that he was in the –'

'Mr Thomas, do you think you could ring home for me – they'll have the address in the office – and tell my father or mother? Let it ring for a long time. They work upstairs and our housekeeper is a bit deaf.'

'Maybe they know already?'

'Would you ring just in case? I'm sorry to give you this trouble.'

'It isn't any trouble. I know how anxious you must feel. It might just be a knee needing a stitch or two in it. One of my boys had ten stitches after a football game. I felt like banning him from the game but he cried. He would look stupid in front of his friends, he said . . .' He chattered on as they got to the front of the college.

And I was short-tempered with Sam, she thought. Oh, I wish . . .

There were no taxis in sight, but rather than go back and telephone from the office they walked quickly to the King's Theatre where there was a taxi rank. There was a solitary taxi there, the driver sitting inside reading a paper, and Mr Thomas helped her in.

'You have enough money?'

'Yes. My purse's in my pocket. Thanks . . . thanks very much . . .' She suddenly couldn't remember his name. She heard him give the driver the address, and gave him a small wave as they drove off.

She was composed now. The first shock had gone. Perhaps it wasn't so bad as she had at first thought, but that didn't help her feeling of guilt. She remembered the little face, the truculence, her hand on his back, hurrying him along. Miss Clewes would be easily alarmed. She might have rushed him to hospital when there was no need. She was getting too old to deal with any emergencies. When she got to the Infirmary Ritchie was inside the door waiting for her.

'Oh, Daddy!' She went towards him and felt his arms round her. He was a more comforting parent always than her mother. 'Do you know what's happened?'

'Not really. We've to go to the waiting room until they call us.'

'Where's Mother?' They were walking along the corridor, following the signs for the ward to which they had been directed.

'She wasn't in. I think she's hit a block in her work so she decided to go shopping, to clear her head. I jumped into the car when they phoned me.'

They sat in the waiting room amongst people with

downbent heads, as if they were contemplating the state of the world, or hiding their suffering, or having a nap. They didn't want to meet other glances, become involved. Van had thought people talked incessantly, but that wouldn't be in the waiting room of an emergency ward. Here the unknown hung heavily in the air. She and Ritchie followed suit, sat silently and kept their fear to themselves.

One by one someone was called and left the room. Those who were left moved their shoulders, rustled, resettled. After what seemed an unconscionable time, when the room had emptied except for themselves, a nurse appeared at the door.

'Mr and Mrs Laidlaw.' A corner of Ritchie's mouth went up. He turned to Van.

'I'll come with you since I'm included.'

They walked behind the nurse who wasn't talkative. Either she was naturally so, or she had something to hide. Van's fears returned doublefold. She began to tremble. Just when she had been so happy with Hal. It was always the same with life, this constant seesaw. Was she going to be like Aunt Jean, a punchball? How nice to be like Mother, who even at this moment was happily shopping.

Ritchie sensed her mood and took her elbow. 'Don't worry. It will be all right.' She smiled wanly at him. Always the optimist . . .

'Here we are,' the nurse said, turning to them. She was older than Anna, with a tired face. And her ankles had been swollen.

'I should tell you your son is still unconscious, so you are only being allowed in for a minute or two. But your husband can go with you.'

'He's my father.' She saw the look of surprise on the woman's face.

239

They both went into the small room. Sam lay on his back. His eyes were closed. His face was yellow-brown, the smooth colour marred by what looked like faint purple bruises on his cheekbones and under his eyes. There was a cradle over his legs and his arm was in a sling.

They stood looking at him, Van searching for a flicker, a movement of his eyelids. There was none.

'Can I . . . can I . . . ?' She turned to the nurse. 'Can I touch . . . ?'

'Yes, sit down and hold his hand. It will be a comfort.' She didn't say to whom.

'What's happened to him?' Ritchie's voice was hoarse.

'You've to see the doctor. He'll explain. He's had a fall . . .'

Van sat, numbed, clasping the brown hand. 'Had a fall?' An accident? But she had taken him to the school herself . . . Afterwards? When they were outside playing? A fight with someone? She wanted to say, 'Open your eyes, Sam. Tell Mummy . . .'

She heard Ritchie say, as if he couldn't bear the silence, 'Will he soon come out of the . . . ?'

'Coma.' The nurse sounded grateful at having been asked. 'Loss of consciousness due to the fall. We hope so. You'll see the duty doctor on your way out. He'll explain everything.' Van felt the nurse's hand on her shoulder. It was kindly. 'He's in good hands, Mrs Laidlaw. You can come in any time you like, and if there's a change we'll get in touch with you right away. He'll want you there. Do you live near?'

'Yes, quite near. I could be here in ten minutes.'

Ritchie took her out of the room. She was weeping unashamedly, like a child herself. 'It's terrible, isn't it? He was all right when I left him. I wish . . . What was Miss Clewes thinking of? Did she take them somewhere? I can't understand it.'

'We'll go and see her afterwards, if you like, get the full story.'

'Yes, we'll do that, Daddy.' She wiped her eyes, controlled her weeping. Strange that she should revert to 'Daddy'. She was in training as an almoner. She mustn't let the doctor see her like this. 'He's my life,' she said, as they walked along the corridors. 'I couldn't live without him.'

'Yes, you could,' he said surprisingly, 'but nobody's asking you to. Sam will be all right. Come on and we'll have a cup of tea while we're waiting. It'll be half an hour at least, the nurse said.'

They went to the tea bar, a dingy room in the basement and were served with tea in plastic mugs by a long-faced, tired-looking woman. Were they *all* tired?

'Thanks,' Ritchie said, paying her. 'You do a good job here.' He smiled, and the woman's face relaxed. No one could ever resist her father when he smiled. It was a mutually exclusive, sharing smile. Van tried to emulate him.

'He's right,' she said. 'When are you off duty?'

'Just another hour before Jessie, my stand-in, comes. It's not so bad. I'm only here in the afternoons, but ma wee boy died here five years ago, and I've done it ever since. Wanted to repay them for all they did.'

'Oh, I'm sorry . . .' She looked at Ritchie. 'Where will we sit?' He guided her to a table topped with red plastic in the corner of the room.

'She says that just to cheer everybody up,' he said.

'Oh, for God's sake, Father!' She became adult again, laughed, and then sobered, stirring her tea.

'We have only one tragedy queen in the family,

241

and that's your Aunt Jean. Remember that. Anna said she used to envy her. Can you imagine?'

'Funny, I was just thinking of Aunt Jean earlier.'

'Everything seemed to hit her. Then Roderick had to die as well. And your mother, in between feeling Jean's pain as if it were her own, said she envied her! Can you beat that?' He looked proud. 'And then she's missed *this* by gallivanting into town.'

'She wasn't to know.'

'She went to buy shoes, I bet. She always buys shoes when her work won't go right. She has more shoes than I ever had hot dinners when I was a lad. Anyhow, that's your Aunt Jean. But you and your mother aren't like that, believe me, Van. Your lives are in quieter waters . . .' He was running out of steam in his attempt to comfort her.

'Eb died.'

'But you weren't with him when it happened, like Kleiber drowning.'

'No,' it was becoming an argument, 'but I can't lose Sam too!' She felt her mouth tremble.

'Don't,' he said, as if he couldn't sit and watch her. 'Bear up.' He put his hand over hers.

'Mr and Mrs Laidlaw.' They still hadn't got it right. It was another nurse at the door. 'The doctor will see you now.' They followed her out of the room.

Twenty-Three

They sat silently in the car as Ritchie drove up Byres Road towards the school.

Van was afraid to speak. The doctor had been factual, although kindly. 'The prognosis in a case like your son's is always difficult, Mrs Laidlaw.'

'It's Miss Laidlaw,' she said, 'and this is my father, not my husband.'

'Oh!' At least it had the effect of making him regard her as a person, not just a patient's mother. He looked at his notes. 'Fall. The school will give you the details. The injury to his arm and shoulder will heal. There is severe bruising to the arm and the shoulder is dislocated, the ankle will take a little longer, they always do. But the lack of consciousness, that's a different matter. He's suffering from severe concussion and until he has an EEG done, that's an electroencephalogram, a graph of the brain, we won't know if there is permanent damage. There may be a small bleed . . .'

Van put her hand to her mouth. 'Oh, that's terrible!'

'Not necessarily. He seems to be a healthy little boy. What nationality is his father, by the way?'

'West African, but he had British nationality. He's dead.'

'I see. What's called for, Miss Laidlaw,' he gave her

243

a quizzical glance, 'is patience and hope. Everything will be done here. We've had many similar cases where the patient was quite normal when he came out of a coma, so don't distress yourself unduly.'

There was the word, 'normal'. What would she do if Sam at last regained consciousness, but was an imbecile, all his brightness gone, his mischievousness, far worse than a mongol? Could she enter then for the stakes of a tragedy queen?

'Don't be too hard on Miss Clewes,' Ritchie said as he stopped at the gates of the school. 'She must be suffering too.'

'Yes, I know that.' But it didn't lessen the pain in her heart or the gnawing anxiety.

Miss Clewes opened the door to them. She looked distraught, her hair needed brushing, her manner was nervous, her white face had developed a tick. She looked like an old woman.

'Come in, Mrs Laidlaw, and Mr Laidlaw.' They were irrevocably coupled today. 'I saw the car arriving from my window. I've been sitting there unable to apply my mind . . .' She led them into her drawing room, huge, dull, faded fabrics and walls, with tall narrow windows on to the little square. It smelled of chalk. Perhaps it had been the original classroom thirty years ago, before the school expanded. 'Please sit down. Would you like a cup of tea?' She was twisting her hands nervously together.

'No, thanks,' Van said. 'We've just come from the hospital. We must get back home. My mother will be terribly anxious.' She couldn't restrain herself: 'Miss Clewes, how could it have happened? What kind of fall? I can't understand how he's so badly injured.'

'Oh . . .' The woman moaned and sat down. 'Is it very bad? The whole thing's incredible to me. I'm still in a state of shock.' Van saw the tremor in the hand which she put up to her hair, as if suddenly aware of its untidiness.

'Perhaps if you could tell us from the beginning, Miss Clewes,' Ritchie said. 'We're not here to blame you, don't think that, we just want to know from you what happened.'

'Yes, I'll do that. That's what I want to do.' She sat up straight. 'That's what I want . . . You see, I take the children in Sam's class for story-time once a week, and try to make it interesting. I was telling them the story of a little Italian puppet-master . . . Italian marionettes have always been popular all over Europe. They often perform Harlequin and Columbine, which are traditional sixteenth-century . . .' She shook her head as if to collect her thoughts. 'I suddenly remembered I had some old puppet gloves in a box in the loft, and was annoyed at myself for not looking them out the previous evening – I'm sorry, I'm taking too long over this.'

'So you went and got them,' Ritchie said, 'but . . . ?' He looked puzzled.

'No, I didn't, Mr Laidlaw, that was my great mistake. I thought to myself that the class would probably misbehave during my absence, so, well, you know what children are like, I said . . . I'll never forgive myself for that . . . "Who would like to go up to the loft for me?" Well, needless to say, every hand shot up,' she smiled wanly at Van, 'but I caught sight of Sam's bright face – he was a very attractive little boy . . .' He still is! Van wanted to shout. He still is! '. . . and said, "All right, you go, Sam, but be careful."'

'You *remember* warning him?' Van said.

'Oh, yes, once or twice. It's a very easy access to the loft, no Slingsby ladder or anything like that – I

245

shouldn't have dreamed of it otherwise – but you go upstairs to the attic floor and there's a smallish door in one of the rooms which leads directly into the loft on the same level. I warned him that the loft was only partially floored, and he would find the box with the gloves in it just inside the door – where it *is* floored – and on no account,' her voice shrilled in agitation, 'on no account to venture on to the other part where the joists are exposed.'

'Had he ever been up there before?' Van asked. She remembered the conversation with him only the previous evening, at the dinner table.

'It's out of bounds, of course, but I have to tell you, Mrs Laidlaw, although it doesn't mitigate this dreadful accident, that I wouldn't be surprised if he hasn't been up there with Toby Graham. He's a naughty boy, Toby, a natural ringleader, and lately my housekeeper has complained about them running about the house when they should be outside at play-time. I warned them about it. Sam is easily led, but is generally obedient. I think he paid attention to my warning, I don't know. Certainly Mrs Ellis didn't hear him again, but they may have been very quiet. Toby's – I don't like to say this about any child, but he's sly . . .' She put her hand to her eyes. 'I should have punished him, but he's one of those boys who twists things, and his mother is a little aggressive. Mr Graham is a surgeon. They're very rich . . .' She fumbled for her handkerchief.

Van felt a rush of sympathy for the woman, but steeled herself. She had to hear the rest of the story.

'Take your time, Miss Clewes,' Ritchie said. 'We want to hear everything. We know what boys are like.'

She raised her face. 'I'm so worried. And Sam hurt

. . . badly, you said. I hope . . . I hope you aren't going to sue me, Mrs Laidlaw. It would finish the school. I know your first concern is for Sam, and it is mine, but I do feel guilty. My mistake was in sending him there in the first place, but I knew the class would misbehave if I left them while I went myself. I should have been thoroughly prepared beforehand, but the previous night I had been immersed in my accounts.'

'He stepped on to the unfloored part of the loft. That was it?' Van tried to keep her voice level. The stupidity of the woman! A wave of anguished irritation swept over her, immediately followed by sympathy as she saw the white face, listened to the trembling voice. To blame Miss Clewes didn't alter the fact that Sam was lying motionless on that bed.

'Yes. What I think, knowing children, is that Toby and Sam had been up there several times without being caught. It's the kind of game that boy would think up. "I dare you to walk on the joists, Sam." I can just hear him say that.'

'And, of course, the floor wasn't sound between them,' Ritchie said.

She shook her head. 'This is where I blame myself bitterly. It should have been inspected. Maintenance. I think I was speaking about it to you not so long ago, Mrs Laidlaw, but the expenses keep on mounting and when I got each day over the effort involved in writing letters to tradesmen . . .' She drew herself up into a semblance of dignity. 'But you want to hear the rest.' She took a deep breath and looked directly at the two of them opposite her.

'We were waiting for the gloves, and I was giving the children a little dissertation on the origin of puppets, trying to keep their attention, when there was a loud crack. It came from directly above us. We all looked up at the ceiling, horrified. Some of the little girls screamed. I was terrified myself, but tried to quieten them. Then there was a shower of plaster and dust and I knew what was going to happen. It was like waiting for thunder, the same awful quiet because *everyone* was quiet. Then, Sam's leg came through the ceiling! It was so awful, so frightening. The screaming started again, pandemonium, everyone jumping up, shouting, I tried to shout above it, "Quiet!"'

'Didn't you call to him?' Van asked. A fall, they had said, not *this*.

'Yes, indeed I did, Mrs Laidlaw. I calmed myself, and my voice. I shouted, "Stay there, Sam! Hold on and I'll come up right away." He wailed something, so pathetically, and I called again, "Don't move. You'll be all right!" I was halfway to the door when I heard that dreadful sound again, and when I looked up I saw the crack was growing bigger, wider, quite slowly, and . . . his other leg came through. "I can't," he was shouting, wailing. "I can't, there's nothing . . ." Then, oh dear, oh dear, that terrible tearing noise, the clouds of plaster and the lower part of his body appeared. He was moving frantically, wriggling, trying to get a hold. He seemed to hoist himself up again, and then . . .' she looked at Van and Ritchie, her eyes wide '. . . he seemed to . . . to somersault in some way because his *head* was hanging downwards, his face terrified, his black hair white with dust. He hung for a moment, wriggling like a fish before either his hold slackened or there was nothing to hold on to and he fell.'

Van covered her face with her hands. The picture of Sam, the thought of what he must have felt, his terror, was unbearable. She wanted to get up, to strike this woman.

'He missed my desk by inches. I suppose that was a small miracle.'

Van felt Ritchie's arm on her shoulders. She raised her head, looked towards Miss Clewes. The woman was going on.

'The children were shrieking, out of their places, crowding around Sam. Other teachers arrived and I told one to march them out, and to telephone for an ambulance right away. I kneeled beside your boy.' Her eyes met Van's pleading. 'He lay amongst the dust and plaster on the floor, not moving. I thought how awkward his limbs looked but daren't straighten them. I thought he had died, Mrs Laidlaw. Can you imagine my feelings? I know it's nothing compared with yours, but I felt my heart would break. I was kneeling beside him, holding his hand when the ambulance arrived. I must have been there for at least fifteen minutes. My knees were so stiff that I had to be helped up . . .'

She wants sympathy, Van thought. Just a little show of sympathy. She kept her eyes on the woman.

'The ambulance men were comforting. They told me he was breathing, and one said, "You can count yourself lucky, miss, his head didn't strike your desk." The other one told me to leave it to them and go and phone you immediately wherever you were, and then Mr Laidlaw. I've been waiting here ever since.' She put her hands to her face and the sobs were that of an old woman, guttural, phlegm-filled.

Van got up. She put her arms round Miss Clewes' shaking shoulders. 'I know how you feel. He's in a coma. I can't say any more. I'm trying hard to take it in . . .' She turned to Ritchie. 'We'll go now, Father.'

He got up, pausing for a second to give the woman's shoulder a pat. 'Right.' He followed Van to the door.

In the hall she stopped, said, 'Wait a minute,' and went towards the kitchen, at the back of the house. She was back in an instant. 'I was telling the woman in there to take her a cup of tea.'

'Good.' He opened the door. They went down the steps to the car.

'She says Miss Clewes will never get over it. She'll shut up the school.' The air felt fresh on her face and cleared her throat, as if it was choked with plaster dust.

'We'll get home and tell Anna. She'll want to go back with you to the Western.'

'Yes. I'm going in any case. I'll ask if I can spend the night there.'

'If you do, I'm sure your mother will stay with you.'

Speaking was too much of an effort. She sat beside Ritchie while he drove as swiftly as he could to Clevedon Crescent. She couldn't get rid of the images of Sam falling, of his face, terrified, of the plaster-whitened black hair. She wouldn't be able to sleep for them.

Anna was waiting in the dining room when they got home. They had seen her at the window. 'For God's sake!' She came towards them. 'Where have you been? Sit down, Van, you look all in. I got your message, Ritchie. Van,' she turned to her, 'what's been happening? What kind of accident?'

Ritchie took her hands and led her to a seat beside Van.

'Calm yourself. We've been to see Miss Clewes. Sam fell through the ceiling –'

'Are you out of your mind? Fell through the ceiling? It doesn't make sense!'

'It's true, Mother,' Van said. 'He's in the Western. Father will tell you all about it. I'm going upstairs.

I'll be down again in five minutes. I just want to go to the bathroom . . .' She couldn't speak.

'You do that, Van.' Anna was suddenly calm. 'You'll feel better.'

Van saw in the mirror above the washbasin a face which hadn't changed since this morning when she had set off full of good intentions to do well in her course . . . but who the hell cared about her course or her great independence when her child was lying motionless on that bed?

She watched her face dissolve because of the sudden rush of tears blurring her vision. She bent down and splashed cold water fiercely, wetting her hair in the process, grabbed a towel, put it over her head and wept as Miss Clewes had done, only more violently. She was in utter blackness in her mind and in reality. She was almost beyond feeling, a new country to her, the country of despair. After a long time she took the towel off her head and wiped her face with it. Her tears had dried as if she had turned a tap. She had to keep presentable for going to the Infirmary. A command seemed to have been issued from somewhere. She was a trainee hospital almoner.

When she went back to the dining room her mother was just putting down a tray with a plate of sandwiches on the table, and a pot of coffee. 'Come on, Van,' she said, still calm, 'have something and then we'll go.'

'I don't want anything.'

'You're no good to anyone half starving. We might be there for a long time.'

'Are you coming?' Her heart lifted.

'Of course I am. You drive me there.' She began pouring the coffee. You can't fool me, Mother, with your businesslike pose . . . Van took a sandwich.

They were good. If the roof fell in Anna would still make good sandwiches, buttered right to the edges, proper flavouring. 'If the roof fell in . . .' The bread stuck in her throat.

'I can hardly believe it,' Anna said, 'falling through the ceiling.' She had a half-smile of disbelief, almost of admiration.

'I think it was faulty.'

'That doesn't excuse Sam walking between the joists.'

'He would probably agree with you if he weren't lying unconscious.'

Anna put down her cup and came towards her, put her arms round her. 'Oh, I'm sorry, pet. I don't know what I'm saying. I must be in shock.'

'I'm still not out of it. Let's go, Mother.'

'You wouldn't like me to drive you?' asked Ritchie.

'No.' Anna was definite. 'You have a sit-down. If we aren't back before midnight drive over and come up to the waiting room. Maybe one or the other of us will go back with you if Sam's out of the . . . coma.' She said the word fearfully.

'I was going to ask you if you'd ring Hal,' Van said, 'but on second thoughts, I'll leave it till we see . . . I don't want to alarm him unnecessarily.'

'Nor Mish?'

'That's up to you.'

'Right,' Ritchie said. 'Give me a ring if there are any developments. I'll not go far from the phone.'

As they went down the steps Anna handed Van the keys. The little act made her feel responsible. She had always liked driving. It was one of the things she did well. Perhaps Anna had recognized it.

Twenty-Four

That day began the daily visits to the Infirmary,
meaning all day more or less as far as Van was concerned, and a part of each day by Anna and Ritchie,
sometimes singly, sometimes together.

They sat with Van – they were allowed in one at a
time, properly gowned, and watched Sam lying like
death, deeply unconscious, breathing shallowly, his
skin when they gently touched his hand or cheek
cold and clammy. The doctor was unwilling at this
stage to make any prognosis.

'His blood pressure is low, he's in a state of flaccid
paralysis. He may have suffered a major contusion
because of the fall. Time will tell. In the ordinary
march of events he should have a fairly rapid recovery, say two or three days, then we can review the
situation. We have done a lumbar puncture. This will
be repeated if necessary.'

Their anxiety was great. They sat silently in the
waiting room while Sam was being attended to, saying the occasional word, afraid to say too much. Anna
brought titbits from Bessie, her fruit loaf which generally Van couldn't resist; she herself made up sandwiches with strong individual flavours which were
her special forte. Everything tasted like sawdust in
Van's mouth, or plaster dust.

There were flowers from Nancy, from Wendy and Gordon, from Jean and John in Kirkcudbright, from the school. In the middle of it all, Sam lay motionless.

Van sat and studied his face, the yellow-brown colour accentuated by the whiteness of the head bandage, the nose slightly flattened across the bridge reminding her of Eb, the dark eyebrows, the full mouth, blue-tinged, a travesty of the appearance of death.

The doctor didn't prevent her from coming. He felt her presence was beneficial, the smell of her, the perfume of the flowers, the soft stroking of her hands on his, any one of these might be a trigger. Even the words which he showed no sign of hearing.

'Sam, it's Mummy. Open your eyes for me, darling, there's a good boy. Just raise your finger, anything.' He lay like a Minoan statue of a boy she had once seen, the lines of his face noble in their immobility, like a stricken young god.

Each day her heart seemed to break afresh, and then the daily round of getting up, driving to the hospital, spending the day there, reasserted her identity, her determination to do everything in her power to aid his recovery. She daren't go down any other road in her thinking.

One morning halfway through the week, she made herself call to see the bursar of the college, although she grudged the time.

'I know how worried you must feel, Miss Laidlaw,' he said, 'but in your own interests I think you should try to resume your classes for at least part of the day. We're in a state of flux here, and we're urging everyone to get through their courses as fast as they can before changes are made. It may be necessary to take a degree course at the university in the future as we're liable to split up or be closed.' She listened impatiently, her mind with Sam.

He went on: 'From your own personal point of view you have to keep well for your son's sake. You don't want to be looking like a wraith when he regains consciousness.' She would have to avoid pity, but he was right. It was a wraith who had looked out of her mirror this morning. 'You'd be better able to be with him by taking a short break here.'

'I can't,' she said. 'If I weren't there if . . . when . . . he wakes up, I'd never forgive myself.' She was getting to her feet as she spoke, driven by this urgency.

'I understand.' He nodded. 'Well, supposing I arrange for you to do some interviewing at the Western while you're there? You would be on hand for your son. Would that suit you?'

She agreed, partly to please him, and then drove through the busy traffic of Sauchiehall Street, through Charing Cross and along past the sedate terraces on either side, with the tower of the university grey behind the red sandstone of the art galleries, risking being stopped by the police for her speed. She wanted Hal beside her, badly. He had suggested it when he had telephoned, but she had said she wouldn't dream of it. She was all right. He would be pleased if she went back to the college part time. He had said something about her 'diffusing her emotion'.

They'd been right. She found the visiting of patients therapeutic, and reassuring also to her wish to be within call. She could be summoned in a minute or two. She was in the same building. She found, as the bursar had said, that to concentrate on other people's problems helped her to deal with her own.

She saw old men and women who had lost their

children in infancy or adolescence and treated it only as a distant memory. She asked one woman, 'How did you cope at the time with your son dying? Did you ever feel you couldn't go on?'

The woman looked at her. There was puzzlement in her eyes. 'It's not so bad when it happens as imagining it. A think A had a guid greet when A got back from the Infirmary, but there were the ither yins to be seen to, clamouring fur their teas, an' ma man sitting grumblin' at the fire because his dinner wisnae ready. And wi' the long journey in the caur and gettin' the weans to bed A wis fair worn oot. When they telt me wee Johnnie had died, it was kind o' relief. A think ma first thought wis, well, that will put an end to the waiting fur a caur an' strugglin' hame in the cold and wet.'

'Did your husband never go with you?' Van asked her.

'Naw, he canna abide they infirmaries. But my neighbours rallied roon. Ye don't get the same in them high rises, stuck like a canary in a cage up there, and that lonely . . .'

'Where are you children now?' The woman had no financial support except from State benefit. Her husband had died.

'God knows,' she said, 'scattered. The only yin that comes to see me sometimes is ma daughter. They always cling, but she's trauchled wi' weans and cleaning offices at nights and a lazy man like mine wis. She never saw ony better so she made the same mistake as me. Wid ye like to hae a look at ma ankles? They're swollen up like puddocks.'

It didn't lessen Van's grief, but it put Sam out of her mind for a short time.

The results of the EEG came. There was a small

bleed and the prognosis wasn't very good. Van was sent for. Anna and Ritchie insisted on going with her although she would rather have gone alone.

She was numb. She told them to go back home, that she was going to sit with Sam. 'No point in three mourners,' she said, and then was horrified at the implication in the words. If Hal had been with me it might have been easier, she thought, but knew that nothing would have made it any easier. When she had rung him the evening of the accident he had asked her if she wanted him to come over, but she had said, no. She had been more optimistic then.

Ritchie or Anna had taken subsequent calls from him. 'He's thinking about you and Sam all the time,' Anna said. If Sam dies, she thought now, will I want Hal? The three-part idyll, Sam, Hal, herself, would be shattered. Would she be able to recover from the blow?

A nurse came in and put her hand on Van's shoulder. 'I don't think you're doing him or yourself any good sitting there,' she said. She was young, brisk, very pretty, a no-nonsense, destined-to-be-matron type. She could run rings round me, Van thought.

'He might . . .' She thought she whimpered.

'Take my advice,' the nurse said. She had dark, beautiful eyes. 'Go home for a night. Have a good drink and come back tomorrow. You can't see the wood for the trees in your state.'

'Well . . .'

'Go on. It's good advice.' She smiled. She had perfect teeth. She would have done for a recruitment poster.

Van went home. She surprised herself by getting mildly drunk over dinner, being taken up to bed by Anna and tucked in.

'You look worn out,' she said, as brisk as the pretty nurse had been. 'Have a good sleep.' She felt Anna's lips on her cheek and was a little girl again. She sighed.

The next day, which was the fourth day, when she was sitting beside Sam his hand moved under hers, his eyelids flickered. She bent forward, her heart racing in her throat. 'Sam, it's Mummy. Sam . . .' He opened his eyes as if he was at home, slightly irritable as he usually was when she told him it was time for school.

'Mummy . . .' And then, taking in the unfamiliarity of his surroundings, 'This isn't . . .' His head moved. 'Where . . .'

'You're in hospital, darling.' She stroked his cheek as she spoke. 'You've had an accident.' She saw the frown, 'But you're getting better.'

'I want to go home.' He began to cry weakly. 'I don't like . . .' She realized there was a nurse at her side, that there had been movement around the bed.

'The doctor's here, Miss Laidlaw. We've told him.' She heard the voices, and keeping her eyes on Sam, she got up.

'Stay near so that he can see you.' The doctor nodded approvingly as he bent over Sam. He had his stethoscope round his neck. The nurse exchanged reassuring smiles with Van.

'I think he's going to be all right.' The doctor had straightened. 'He'll have to be thoroughly examined, of course, and kept under observation.'

Van saw Sam's eyes had closed. 'He's not speaking now.'

'That's all right. He'll sleep and waken alternately, but he has to be kept very quiet. You get off home and come back tomorrow.'

'But – he'll *miss* me.'

'No, he's not at that stage yet. Leave him to rest. Children have tremendous powers of resilience. You'll see a great change when you come back.'

'You're sure . . . he won't miss me?'

'Quite sure.'

She was jubilant when she got home. Anna and Ritchie downed tools to hear the news. 'I can hardly believe it! I began to think . . . and after they'd said there was a small bleed . . . I was terrified . . .'

She went straight to the telephone and dialled Hal's number, praying she would get him in. It was her lucky day. He answered immediately and the sound of his voice filled her with almost forgotten happiness.

'Van! I was actually sitting at the phone. I was going to ring you. Go on, you speak.'

'He's out of the coma! I've spoken to him tonight. The doctor said I had to come home and go back tomorrow. He thinks the danger's passed.'

'Great news! So, what do you know! I was going to tell you I wanted to be with you. I had looked up planes.'

'No, there's no need now. Honestly. But, Hal, the relief . . . I can't tell you.'

'I know, I know. I've lived with you over this. Every moment. Are you sure you don't want me?'

'Oh, I *want* you, but there's no *need*. Mother says, will you let Mish know?'

'Sure thing. And, Van?'

'Yes?'

'I've written a letter to you. It's in the post.'

'That's sweet of you.'

'It was to . . . well, no, you'll get it soon.'

'I'll have to go, Hal. I tremble to think how much I've cost them. They've been so good.'

They spent the rest of the evening telephoning round friends and relatives, and especially to Kirkcudbright where John was able to clarify and reassure. 'He'll be on the mend now. The main thing, he's conscious.'

Jean asked if she should come to Glasgow, but Ritchie was the one who said no. 'I'm no doctor, Jean,' she and Anna heard him say, 'but he's still confused. Other faces might confuse him further. I'm sure he needs calm all the time.'

'I'll go on phoning, then, and when I can't bear it any longer I'll come, but just to see Anna.' Ritchie smiled when he repeated her remark. Anna said, when told, that she would have said the same thing.

The second day after Sam had regained consciousness he was still confused. He lay in the foetal position, wouldn't look at Van and grew irritable when she said she couldn't take him home. The nurse said they were all difficult to manage at this stage, but not to worry. Dr James was seeing him every day.

The doctor who sent for her the following morning was not Dr James. He was an older man whose grey hair seemed to have tinged his face with the same greyness. He was precise, treating Sam as a 'case'. Perhaps it was the only way he could manage a difficult situation. Van tried not to feel apprehensive.

'I have to tell you, Miss Laidlaw, that your son is for the most part still stuporous. We should have expected him to shake that off by this time.'

'But he spoke to me,' she said, fearfully.

'Yes, I know, but there are other signs. His pupils are unequal, there's a rigidity in the neck muscles, and the nursing staff tell me he's incontinent. I'm afraid if his condition further deteriorates, a craniotomy will have to be performed.'

'I see.' A bird of terror was in her throat, in her chest, now it was beating against the wall of her ribs. 'I see . . .' she said again. 'Is . . . is that . . . very . . . serious?'

He drew in his breath, caught his lip with his lower teeth, his head on one side, like a man on a weighing machine. 'I have to warn you that sometimes it can be fatal.' He didn't stop speaking. 'That's why it is a very important decision, a step not to be taken lightly.'

'I thought he was getting better.' She knew she wailed rather than spoke.

'Yes, we had great hopes when he recovered consciousness within the statutory time – or what we like to call the statutory time. Now, I want you to be brave. And wise. We're going to do further tests and a final lumbar puncture which will decide us whether or not to operate. I want you to stay away during this period. Have you any relatives?'

'Yes.' She was numbed by shock. 'I live . . . I mean, Sam and I live with my parents.'

'Good. The boy's father? He should be told.'

'He died.'

'Ah . . . Go home to your parents' house then, and come back in twenty-four hours. This will be hard for you, I know, but we shall be able to tell you then if it is necessary to operate. Your son is suffering from the effects of a major contusion sustained when he fell from such a height.' He shook his head, looking human for once. 'A strange accident. But we are always hopeful, and so must you be. Your permission will be sought, of course, before an operation is performed.'

261

He got up, walked to the door and opened it for her. 'Try not to worry,' he said.

She had no alternative but to go out. She walked in a daze along the gloomy corridors, out and across the road to where she had parked the car, and got in. When she got back home Jean was there.

'Jean!' she said, going into her arms held out to greet her. 'Father said you *weren't* to come!' She was almost frivolous.

'Did you ever know me doing anything that man Ritchie told me? I thought you needed me.'

'Needed her to boss us about,' Anna said, smirking with pleasure.

'They're a pair!' Ritchie looked at Van. He had guessed there was something wrong. 'What's the news?'

She sat down. She wasn't going to weep. Jean's presence helped in some way. She could look after Anna and Ritchie, for one thing. Van had enough to do to look after herself, act like a human being, not a stricken animal.

'Not good,' she said, having to twist her hands but otherwise composed. 'He says it's definitely a major contusion, and they . . . they might have to do a . . . craniotomy. I have to keep away for twenty-four hours.' She bit her lip, looking down. Ritchie had been busy at the table where he kept his selection of bottles. He turned, a tot of whisky in his hand and came towards her.

'Drink that. It will help.' His eyes were full, saying everything he felt.

'Oh, you!' she said, feeling half-crazed. 'You're going to make me drunk again on top of everything!' But still she didn't weep, still she went through the pretence later of eating, and was amazed at how her aunt took

262

the edge off her terror. Her personality was strong, she dominated the table, telling them about Kirkcudbright and retailing its gossip, about the fishing boat that went on fire, knowing they couldn't really care, but trawling the town for snippets of interest, so that, against her wishes, Van *did* become interested.

'What about Alan?' she asked.

'He sends you his love and sympathy. He has been afraid to telephone or write knowing how you have no time for that. I was amazed at how understanding he was. He's asked me to phone him when I get back. He's a sensible chap. It may be my imagination but he's been more relaxed since his mother died.'

'I wonder what happened to the cat?' She saw it again, the size of it, its frightening stillness, its eyes . . .

'Oh, Johnson, the vet, would see to that. He'd probably give it to a farm, for ratting.' It would grow bigger and bigger, on rats.

They talked, and Anna and Ritchie plied them with good food and wine. Van announced that she wouldn't telephone Hal, or Mish, but wait until the twenty-four hours were up. There was no point in spreading her anxiety. Anna agreed. Van knew her altruism was partly fuelled by Ritchie's claret, but they all nodded in agreement. She felt she looked strange to them, half deranged by her extravagant waving of hands. She got up abruptly and said she had better go to bed while she could still walk.

She heard Bessie calling her as she passed the kitchen. She went through it to Bessie's little room. She was seated upright in bed with a shawl round her shoulders. Her nutcracker face without her teeth was accusing. 'You might hae cam in an' telt me. When's the wee lad gettin' hame?'

'I don't know, Bessie. There might be an operation.' She had sat down on the bed and she knew the tears were streaming down her face as she raised it. 'He might die . . .' Bessie drew her against the brown and grey shawl. She felt the rough hands stroking her hair as she wept.

'I never heard such nonsense in ma life! Dee? That yin! He'll be jumpin' aboot the hoose like a wee monkey afore ye know it.'

Van cried the wine she had drunk out of her in her tears. She imagined she smelled it as she blew her nose eventually and sat up.

'You've cheered me up, Bessie,' she said. 'Would you like a cup of tea?'

'No, I made it for masel'. You were aw laughin' in there owr your dinner and I knew you'd forgotten all about me.' There was no rancour on her face.

'What a hope! Lie down and I'll tuck you in.'

She fell asleep the moment her head touched the pillow, but her last thought had been of Sam.

Twenty-Five

The next thing Van knew was Anna's hand on her shoulder. 'It's nine o'clock, Van. I let you go on sleeping. It'll do you good.' Everyone was intent on doing her good. She was ashamed. 'Now get dressed after you have your breakfast. It's all on the tray, orange juice, toast, coffee. I know you won't take anything else.'

'Thanks, Mother. It looks good.'

'We're having a day off since Jean's here. A trail round Glasgow. We used to do that as girls. We're taking you, and Ritchie's coming to pay the bills.'

She shook her head. 'I'll just stay at home in case –'

'The surgeon told you to stay away for twenty-four hours. There's nothing worse than people who won't do as they're told. Jean wants to go to the art galleries, then we'll have lunch somewhere, then Ritchie's taking us to see an old man in Anniesland who has a few pictures by the Glasgow Boys. After that we'll go back home, drop Ritchie and Jean, and you and I will go on to the Western.' She saw Van's hesitation. 'Come with us, Van. You'll only make yourself miserable hanging around the place.' If she had been less Anna-ish, Van would have still refused, but it was her mother's very matter-of-factness which persuaded her. She didn't want to hang around and weep on Bessie's shoulder all day.

'Okay,' she said. 'Someone will have to keep Father company when you sisters get together.'

'And put on your best outfit. You know Jean. She likes to dress up for Glasgow. We've to keep up with her.'

Van smiled. 'You want me to say you're just as smart as she is. All right, I'll say it.'

She selected her clothes with care, so that she wouldn't spoil the party. She also made up her face, especially her eyes, and saw how, behind her glasses, it lent importance to them. Yes, she decided, maybe she was a little like her exotic Aunt Jean with her black frizzy hair and those eyes. She put on a bandeau – Jean had given up wearing them now – and saw that it suited her.

She didn't have a big wardrobe, but she had a decent pair of high-heeled shoes and fine stockings. The result in the mirror pleased her momentarily, helped to push back the lurking terror, and she managed a smile when she went into the drawing room. She was rewarded by Jean's admiration.

'Well, well, will you look at what the wind's blown in! We'll have to look to our laurels today.'

They were both beautiful in their different ways, Van thought – her mother dressed in her simple well-cut clothes, her hair shining, her face immaculately painted, Jean all bits and pieces, floating scarves, jangling earrings and bracelets, looking like Carmen ready to burst into an aria. She only needed a fringed shawl.

They went first of all to the art galleries and quartered it from top to bottom, Anna and Jean reminiscing about being taken there by their father as a

Saturday afternoon treat. They had liked the dinosaurs best (or perhaps they had been steered away from the male nude sculptures), and had vied with each other as to who had the most horrific dreams afterwards about skeletons with rattling bones.

In the great hall Van stood in front of Sir Roger, the preserved elephant who had ended his days here. Each time they came, Sam demanded the story of Sir Roger's happy days in Bostock's circus and his sojourn in the zoo until he became ill and was stuffed. 'With straw?' he had asked.

They searched out any painting on show done by the Glasgow Boys or Glasgow Girls, while Ritchie remained with the skeletons, busily sketching. The framework – he didn't say 'skeletons' – appealed strongly to him. He said he could see all kinds of possibilities in them. He had to be dragged away when they came down again to the ground floor.

'We'll have lunch now,' he said, 'and then we'll go to see the old man's collection.'

'Have we time?' Van asked, her anxiety flooding back. 'I want to be at the Western in the afternoon.'

'Five o'clock's time enough,' Anna said. 'You don't want to sit biting your nails in the waiting room all afternoon.'

'I could have gone to the college at that rate.'

'Leave it, my love,' Ritchie said. 'Your mind wouldn't be on your work today.' He had only recently started calling her 'my love', she noticed. 'You'll get back into the routine in no time.'

Jean had wanted a Miss Cranston tearoom for the ambience, she said, but Ritchie knew a good howff in Blythswood Square where he sometimes met fellow painters. The bottle of wine they shared kept the terror from snapping at Van's ankles, although it was there, hovering. But she reminded herself that Jean was the tragedy queen.

And it was Jean who kept the terror at bay by telling them of Kate Cranston, that redoubtable banner-carrier of the Glasgow style, who had taken George Walton from bank clerking and set him up as an interior designer.

'The forerunner of Charles Rennie Mackintosh,' Anna reminded her.

'Yes, smartie. But you can see the link, the perfectionism in both of them, and, of course, in Kate Cranston herself. Wallpaper had to be specially designed, as had the furniture, the lighting, the flooring, even the cutlery. The Walton girls did the glass and china, and the painting brother, E. A., supplied a few pictures.'

'I think the old man I'm taking you to see today has one or two Waltons,' Ritchie said.

'Who was it who said genius was an infinite capacity for taking pains?' Jean was into her stride. 'Kate Cranston ran her tearooms like a commander, two clean aprons each day for her waitresses, their bows tied by herself or the manageress, the girls vetted in their homes before they were engaged, hands inspected daily for clean fingernails. Do you think that's what it's all about, Ritchie? Taking pains?'

'Sure, sure. But there's the other component, having an eye. That's a gift.'

I have no 'eye', Van thought, but I can see what you lot are doing. You're trying to take my mind off Sam.

'And she didn't let marriage get in her way,' Anna said. 'She took her husband with her every day to have lunch in one or the other of her tearooms so that she could keep that famous eye on how they were being run.'

'Poor henpecked soul,' Ritchie said.

Hal wouldn't be henpecked, Van thought, but we could have an ideal life together – his work, my career, my beautiful career – once this terror-bird had stopped hovering.

'You're outnumbered here, Ritchie,' Jean said, 'so you'll just have to sit back and listen to us for once. What Kate Cranston did was important in that she recognized women's needs, not only that they should have a decent place to meet, but the place they should occupy in society.'

'Do you remember being taken by Mother, Jean?' Anna said. 'Even as children we felt the atmosphere she created, the sense of occasion, fresh flowers, gleaming white tablecloths, wall coverings which pleased your eye . . .'

If Sam got better, Van thought, *she* would be a woman in her own right, complementing Hal, not dependent upon him. She was glad she hadn't telephoned him again, wept over the wires like a child. She was a capable woman as well as a mother, the future stretched ahead, beckoning. If only Sam . . .

They drove to Anniesland where Ritchie's old friend lived, a modern council estate house but furnished inside exactly as his wife had left it with antimacassars on the armchairs and beaded footstools. This time Van looked carefully at the paintings on the walls, done by artists like Peploe and Walton, tried to see where this genius lay which they talked about, and thought she was beginning at last to get the hang of it.

You had to look and look, take your time, stand back and look again. She tried to walk into the landscape and found a little one of a river in Dumfries rested her, she climbed the smooth hill with the painter and got the same sense of space.

Ritchie gave his old friend a small sketch of his own, framed, and he accepted it with trembling hands. No, he wasn't going to sell the pictures, they would go to the city when *he* went.

They said their goodbyes, the afternoon was over, now they were speeding towards Clevedon Crescent, now they had dropped off Ritchie and Jean there, Anna was driving, Van was sitting beside her, white-faced and silent.

'Relax,' Anna said. 'You've got through the day.'

They sat in the waiting room and saw people come and go, elated or cast down. After an hour Anna went to the tea bar and came back with two plastic mugs of some kind of brew. It didn't taste like tea, but it was useful for easing the dryness in Van's throat, so that she could speak. 'Thanks, Mother. I could do with this.'

At six o'clock they were told to go up to the ward. The Sister would be looking out for them. They climbed the stone staircase saying useless things like, 'Not before time,' and 'Well, at least they've had the decency to send for us at last,' and Anna being positive and making a little speech at the top. 'It'll be good news. He's tough, that lad. Ritchie says that, and he should know.' Although how *he* should know Van failed to understand. Mish had never been tough, he had been smooth and self-contained since the day he was born.

The Sister was a youngish, Sisterish woman with a cool, kindly manner. 'Mr Crossley won't keep you long,' she said. 'He's been operating all day.' Did she mean on Sam?

'How is my grandson?' Anna said. Van was afraid to ask.

'I know he would like to tell you himself.' She gave a cool, kindly nod as if that was outside her province. Of course, that cool kindly manner could hide bad things as well as good. Would it remain the same if she was intimating death? She went out of the side room and they sat once more, afraid to meet each other's eyes.

'It's a torture chamber, this,' Anna said suddenly. 'If Ritchie were here he would complain, loudly and bitterly, that he wasn't going to be treated as an imbecile, but, do women? We're so mealy-mouthed!' She was talking to herself. 'We need a Kate Cranston here!'

They listened to the noises of the ward, the clattering from the sluice room. Sam had been incontinent, the nurse had said. He had never been like that, even as a little boy. Van knew some mothers had a problem. Roderick had wet the bed even when he was grown up . . . poor Roderick.

She thought of that twisting road outside Dumfries, and the fields on either side, and then that large green mound, crag-crowned and ringed with bushes which had alerted Jean, made her stop the car. If Sam died she would throw herself from something like that, perhaps a higher cliff, Portpatrick would do.

Life would not be worth living. It would be the pointlessness of the whole thing which would defeat her, his grandparents in their desire to provide him with a private school actually paying for his death! Sam, her son! What was happening? She looked wildly round the room, losing control for a second or two, and was on her feet when Mr Crossley appeared at the door. He didn't look anything, only distrait, as if he had half a dozen other matters on his mind.

'Sit down, please, Miss Laidlaw,' he said. She hadn't realized she was standing up. He sat down opposite her, moving his back as if it were a relief. 'I expect you're pretty anxious . . .'

'Yes.' She cleared her throat. 'Yes,' she said again.

'Well, I'm pleased to tell you that the last lumbar puncture we did shows definite improvement.'

'Definite improvement?' She had to get it right. He nodded. 'Oh, that's good. Isn't it, Mother?' She looked at Anna. 'We were beginning to –'

He interrupted her. 'In fact, the result was better than we had hoped for. In view of this I've decided not to operate. He'll be on treatment, of course, particularly glucose with saline . . .'

'Yes, of course.' She would have agreed to bull's blood if he had said so.

'He will have to rest quietly in bed until the headache and giddiness have passed, and then, of course, there are the physical injuries, his ankle and shoulder. I'm afraid he's going to be a wounded soldier for some time,' he smiled at his little joke. 'But he's a healthy boy and I don't expect any relapse now. I have to tell you though,' he nodded once, 'it was touch and go.' He looked as if a little applause might be in order.

'And no operation, Mr Crossley?'

'No. It shouldn't be necessary now. Rest and quiet, although that may be difficult with someone of his temperament.'

'Oh, thank you! The relief! Isn't it, Mother?' She looked at Anna.

'Yes, it is. We have to thank you, Mr Crossley. You can guess how worried we all were.'

'Naturally.' He rose, unrolling his back.

'Can I see him?' Van asked.

'Just for a few minutes. Don't excite him in any way.'

'And my mother?'

'No, just you.' Van got up, floated up, it seemed, feather-light. She heard him say to Anna, as she went out of the door: 'It's a pleasure to meet you, Mrs Laidlaw. I know your husband's work . . .'

Van telephoned Miss Clewes when she got home. She could feel pity now. 'He's going to be all right, Miss Clewes. I've seen the surgeon.'

'Oh, thank God.' *She* remembered to thank God, Van hadn't. 'Thank God,' she said again on Van's behalf. 'The relief is tremendous. I'm so happy for you.'

'Yes, it's been awful, not knowing. Of course, he won't be back this term.' She didn't add, 'If at all.' 'His ankle will be in plaster, and his arm will be in a sling. It's his right one too.'

'A real little wounded soldier, bless him!' Miss Clewes thought along the same lines as Mr Crossley.

'Yes, he'll have to be kept quiet for some weeks. Over Christmas, I imagine.' She saw Miss Clewes quietly disappearing, an episode in their lives.

Jean and Ritchie expressed their joy quietly, almost as if she were brain-damaged, which in a way she had been.

'Of course I always knew there would be a happy ending,' Jean said. Her title was safe. 'I'll get the lunchtime train tomorrow, Anna, if I could phone John. He might be able to meet me at Dumfries. That

273

man Beeching has something to answer for, closing our station.'

'You do that. And I'll telephone Mish and he could get in touch with Hal. Unless you know where he'll be, Van? It'll only be lunchtime there.'

'No, I don't know his business address. But if you could ask Mish, and then he'll phone me tonight, I know.' The pleasure, she thought, the *pleasure* of telling him the good news . . .

'Did you see the letter for you on the hall table?' Ritchie said.

'No? For me? I was so excited I didn't notice it.'

'Well, you go and lie on your bed and read it,' Anna said, 'while I get into the kitchen and help Bessie. Would you phone Nancy, Jean, and give her the good news? She's been very kind . . .'

Van was out of the door and running to the hall table. There the letter was, half tucked under the leather blotter. A USA stamp. She tripped going upstairs in her hurry to get to her room. She was opening it as she ran.

Dearest Vanessa, Van, Girl of the Limberlost, Butterfly Girl, Girl of my Heart,

This is my first love letter. Isn't it ridiculous at my age? But I've been so afraid of committing myself, seeing the way my parents lived. They didn't row. They went through an elaborate pantomime of not rowing, of being madly social, of going everywhere and being seen at the right places, of coming home and saying to me, 'Aren't you in bed yet?' Or, 'No, darling, I haven't time to read you a story now. What's Mary doing?' Or Rachel, or Cathy? 'God knows we pay her enough . . .'

There I go, off on the side issues, the parentheses. I think people who have unhappy memories of their childhood cherish them almost more than those who have happy ones. The happy ones take it as normal. People like me use them as an excuse.

Your brother and I get on like a house on fire. What a level-headed chap he is – just like Anna – and how easily he accepts his wife working her guts out with the Biafran kids, 'paying her dues'. There's a quality about the Laidlaws which makes me feel ashamed. Could I tag along with them, do you think, say, for the rest of my life? Ritchie, who is quite something – I am in danger of hero worship there – Anna, who is beautiful and sees right through me, but then I see through her and know she adores her husband (Have you ever watched her eyes when he comes into the room?), Mish, who could be a great buddy, but, most of all, you.

Mish tells me that you suffered from low self-esteem because they were all arty and you weren't. So you and I have a lot in common right away, in the low self-esteem stakes. I've concealed mine by cultivating a jokey front, you took a far nobler path by devoting yourself to the needs and problems of others.

Don't you think that now we could devote ourselves to each other? You're much more mature than I am, but that is only a repetition of your own parents where Anna is the fulcrum and Ritchie is the eternal Peter Pan.

Do you need any more persuasion? I love you, and I love Sam. I would like to be your husband, and Sam's father. I'm a firm supporter of women fulfilling themselves in whatever way they wish, be it in the home, in a career, or both. In the end it isn't your views I want you for, it's you, you, and only you . . .

And there's the imago thing. Remember we talked about it once? Yes, you'll never be more 'right' than now, so Mish, your wise brother says I've to cut the cackle, that there are only four words . . .

Will you marry me?

Hal.

P.S. Everyone says there's always something you forget. Well, of course there is, there's the other man in your life, Alan McAlpine. It's your decision. You have to choose. But, remember you love me, we love each other, we have been lovers. There's no more room in your life is there, for other men? There's just you, me, and Sam.

She lay still on her back, and occasionally she smiled, occasionally she laughed out loud, once she drummed her heels on the bed in sheer delight.

'Will you marry me?' Four words. 'Four Little Words . . .' Hadn't there been a song with that title? She hummed an experimental bar. 'Will you marry me?' She got up suddenly and whirled about the room, then went dashing downstairs and into the kitchen. Anna was standing at the table with a slim glass bottle of oil in her hand. She was mixing a dressing for the salad. Bessie was stirring something at the stove.

'Is anyone going to be using the phone, Mother?' she asked.

Anna, bottle poised, looked up. 'No. Why?'

'Just thought I'd ask. Are *you*, Bessie? Are you going to be ringing your boyfriend?'

Bessie looked at her as if she were crazy, as indeed she was. 'I've mair sense. But even if I hadny, chance would be a fine thing. It's like the Glesca Telephone Exchange in that loaby, blabber, blabber, blabber aw day.'

'I wanted to telephone Hal, Mother. He's asked me to marry him. Oooh!' Her voice ululated, rising in a crescendo. 'Four Little Words . . .' she sang, waltzing round the kitchen, giving Bessie's cheek a pat as she passed her.

'Fair oot o' her heid,' Bessie commented, 'because somebody wants to make an honest wumman oot o' her.'

'The song's "Three Little Words",' Anna said.

'Whatever. He's asked me to marry him. It was in the letter.'

'Well, he's showing a lot of sense, isn't he, Bessie?' She put down the salad servers she was holding. 'Come and give me a hug.'

'He could dae worse,' Bessie said, smirking at the two of them embracing. 'Away an' phone him afore he changes his mind.'

'You deserve a hug for that one too, Bessie.' She put an arm round her waist, rigidly encased in her stays. They were Bessie's bulwark against unexpected tendernesses.

He must have been sitting at the telephone. 'Van,' he said immediately, sounding unlike himself, anxious. 'Did you get it?'

'Oh, I got it!' she said, wanting to make that peculiar sound again, that ululation, half-scream, half-wail, of delight.

Jean said she was glad she knew before she left. It would be something to think about on the train.

Twenty-Six

Sam was still in the Infirmary but, mindful now of her commitment to her studies, Van went back to the Commercial College. It was a critical time. There would be the examinations at the end of the year, and she would then be into the straight run for next July when she would sit for her Diploma.

The college was now in the process of being split up, and she would be one of the last students. She wanted to do well for its sake, for her own and for her parents'. Anna was the one who had followed her progress with keen interest. It must be especially gratifying to her that her self-willed daughter was at last 'seeing sense'.

'You won't have a conventional life with Hal,' she said. 'He'll be very loving, like Ritchie, but it won't prevent him going away, I mean, having to go away. They're both blithe spirits. It's part of their job, but, as well, they need the excitement that goes with it. You have to guard against becoming a moaning Minnie, complaining about being left on your own. That's why you must have your own career. Don't make him the centre of your life – the heart of it, but not the centre.'

'I can't hear Aunt Nancy giving the same advice,' she smiled.

'She's not a creative thinker, Nancy. But then she hasn't a daughter.'

'Hal understands.'

'Yes, you're lucky there. He will. Alan McAlpine wouldn't. He has a small-town mentality.'

'I wish you could take my place tomorrow,' Van said. 'I'm meeting him for dinner. I have to tell him it's really over.'

'You knew that right from the beginning. You weren't honest with yourself, or him, even before Hal.'

'I was sorry for him.'

'When you stop saying that, I'll know you've really grown up. Misplaced pity does no one any good.'

'Yes, Mother.' She pulled a face and they both laughed.

Sam was still weak and giddy when he tried to sit up, and he was being kept in hospital for another week, but Dr James assured Van that his convalescence was proceeding normally. The fact that the surgeon, Mr Crossley, had sunk from view like a submarine was a sign of this. There was no danger now. Sam was no longer a source of concern to him.

'Sam,' she said to him one afternoon, 'do you remember Hal?'

'Hal from London? Yes. He's funny.'

'You liked him?'

'He's all right.' His brow furrowed, and she was sorry she had brought Hal up. He had to be kept calm. Any new idea . . . 'I remember the great times we had in Grandpa's place far away, you know, Mummy, with the swimming pool and the ladybirds that got in it. You know the place.'

'Arenys de Mar. It's in Spain.'

'Yes, Spain. And he took us out. He was very . . .
generous.' He pronounced it 'geneross'. 'Yes, I like
him. Better than the other one who comes.'

'Alan McAlpine.'

'I don't know his name.' He was irritable. 'He
wasn't like Hal. He was like the man who comes to
our school to examine us and he tells us to sit up
straight and Miss Clewes gets all fidgety. The Inspector. Don't talk about men, Mummy. I'm tired.'

'No, we won't talk about men, darling. You turn
over and have a nice little sleep and I'll be in
tomorrow again.' She noticed he didn't ask when
he was getting home. It was a warning to her not
to tell him yet that Hal would be coming into their
lives permanently, however 'geneross' he thought
him.

She met Alan that evening for dinner. He would
be staying at a solicitor friend's house that night, and
he would call for her at seven o'clock. He particularly
wanted to see her, he had said on the telephone.

She dressed with a fair degree of trepidation. It
would have been kinder at least to refuse dinner since
she would be eating it under false pretences. She told
herself she would heed Anna's advice and not insult
him with pity.

He looked well. Anna and Ritchie were out and he
said he wouldn't come in. The taxi was waiting. They
would go right away to the Malmaison. Life, she told
herself, as he solicitously helped her in, is very different from working with battered wives and rushing
back to cook for Eb. Eb was her youth. She was a
different person now, no less caring, she hoped, but
thinking straight. The main thing was to have no
regrets.

'So you're managing quite well on your own,

Alan?' she said when they had chosen from the menu and the waiter had stopped hovering.

'Very well, as I told you. I think that's the great advantage of living in a smaller community. Glasgow is too impersonal. In Kirkcudbright I'm well known, and if I may say so, respected.' He said with a rare flash of humour, 'At least I haven't robbed a bank yet!'

'Will you keep on your house or look for something smaller?' she asked. For some reason the question seemed to discomfit him.

'Well, that has to be decided . . . but don't let's talk about me all the time. You look well too, Vanessa, in spite of the worrying time you've had with your son.'

'Well, that's all over, thank goodness.' Should she have left off the makeup? She was becoming another 'painted lady'. It was fatally easy, once you started, but no amount of makeup, she thought, could have given the sparkle to her eyes she had noticed in the mirror when she was getting ready. She was in love. It showed. Hal wanted to marry her. The happy scream seemed to lie in wait, ready to be let out, but not in the Malmaison.

'In fact, if I may say so, you look quite radiant,' Alan said, buttering a roll meticulously, up to the edges. She had to tell him, to explain her radiance, but it seemed cruel and would quite put him off his dinner.

'Perhaps it's the relief about Sam. We had a very anxious time – I expect Aunt Jean told you – and to know that he's going to be all right – it's such a load off my mind.'

'Of course you're going to sue the school?'

'Oh, no! Ritchie and Anna are quite against it, and they've been paying the fees. Ritchie especially thinks

281

it would be cruel. Poor Miss Clewes. She was as anxious as I was. It's difficult for those little private schools to keep things going.'

'She needs a good accountant. Probably she's running it badly. There's no reason why a school in a good area like that shouldn't pay. There are always people who don't want their children to mix with the riffraff.' No, he would never have suited.

'I didn't want Sam to go there at all,' she found herself saying. 'My mother went, so I think it had sentimental appeal for her. I don't think children should be encouraged to be elitist.'

He looked at her with benevolent good humour.

'Well, that's a new name for it! I must say that any children I had would certainly attend a similar establishment. Indeed, I'm all in favour of boys going away at eight. You can't meet the right people too soon.' The waiter arrived followed by a minion pushing a trolley laden with silver entrée dishes. Van held her tongue.

Conversation was difficult, which was new for Alan. Generally he talked about his work, the people he knew, asked politely about Ritchie's latest painting, rarely about Anna's work. She thought he might be grieving for his mother. She was talking lamely about her course when the coffee came. She had eaten the food but hadn't tasted it because of her nervousness. She should have told him about Hal at the beginning of the meal, got it off her chest.

'Had I not decided *now* to take this Diploma,' she said to him, 'I might have had to go to the university instead. They are talking of changing to degree courses for almoners, and that would have taken three years instead of two. You went to Glasgow University, didn't you?'

'Yes . . .' He brushed that away. 'Vanessa, I should have told you about this sooner . . .' He stopped, looking worried.

Mystified, she tried to help him out. 'It's not always easy to raise a subject. I have the same difficulty.' He wasn't listening. He was looking at her, looking away again. He lifted his spoon and began to stir his coffee vigorously, which was unnecessary as it was black and he didn't take sugar.

'It's . . . do you remember Cissie Crichton?'

'Cissie Crichton?' She racked her brains. 'Oh, I think your mother mentioned her name. They were friends of hers, weren't they?'

'Yes, the mother and daughter. Mr Crichton died a few years ago, Royal Bank manager. Greatly respected. Cissie is a teller in the same bank. Very efficient.'

'I'm sure she is.'

'They have both, Mrs Crichton and Cissie, been extremely kind to me since my mother's death, arranging help for the house, coming in with titbits, soup and the like, frequent meals at their house, greatly appreciated when one is alone. Why I didn't learn to cook when my mother was there I don't know, but she was always so efficient.'

'Perhaps she wouldn't have liked you in the kitchen. Bessie was like that until she became frail.' He looked at her gratefully.

'That's right. It was her territory. "Not a place for a man," she would say.' He looked at her appealingly. 'I was lonely, Vanessa. I think you could appreciate that. I took Cissie out once or twice, purely for company – at least that's how it started. But, well, she seemed so eminently suitable for my requirements, and she liked our house, often said she could make a lot out of it, but she would leave the garden to me . . . well, I'll be frank with you, one evening she called, with a flask of delicious watercress soup, I remember, and she was so sympathetic and . . . and . . . one thing led to the other, and I asked her if she would like to take on the house . . . and me.'

'You mean you asked her to marry you?' She couldn't hide her astonishment.

'Yes, that's it. Exactly. The words were out of my mouth before I realized I'd said them.'

There was a dawning delight in Van which she kept in check. 'Did she accept?'

'She was bowled over, she said, quite bowled over. And then she confessed she had loved me from our schooldays. It was very touching.' He looked touched at the thought.

'I'm bowled over too, Alan. It's the last thing I should have thought of. And yet I don't know why I didn't. You're an attractive man, in a good position,' she looked at him drawing himself up, 'well-respected. Anyone would be.'

'You're very generous, Vanessa. Somehow I thought you would see it that way. I felt so guilty afterwards. I know I've been courting you, at least making my intentions clear, but right down at the bottom, I never thought you'd fit in with my style of life in Kirkcudbright. Perhaps that was your attraction, you were so different, so strange, an enigma. But, then, when I was sitting beside Cissie on the sofa,' she felt the side of her mouth quirk, 'I knew that this was what I really wanted, to go on exactly as I was doing, with a nice wife who would be there when I came home in the evening, ready to fit in, in every way. Have I hurt you badly?' He took her hands across the table, and she felt nothing but gratitude that she didn't have to hurt *him*.

'I'm glad for you, and Cissie. I see she's right for you. So much better than I should have been. A complete disaster.' She took off her glasses, as his face, so close to her own, was making her squint.

'You're being very noble, Vanessa.' He actually kissed one of her hands. Of course, the relief to him must be great. She had to be honest.

'You haven't hurt me badly, Alan. I have to be frank. I thought I was going to have to hurt *you*. I'm so glad about Cissie. You see, I've met someone else as well. He's in America at the moment and he lives in London usually, but we spent a few days together in Spain,' she saw him frown slightly at this extravagance, 'and we knew we wanted always to be together pretty soon. I was dreading telling you.'

He had released her hands rather quickly and was sitting back, looking slightly disapproving. 'Well, it's turned out all right, as it happens. You're sure this is a wise decision you're making? I've always felt a little . . . responsible, as far as you're concerned. It's something in your temperament.'

'Oh yes, Hal's right for me. Absolutely. And Sam likes him and Hal likes Sam. He talks about "the three of us". I couldn't have thought of anyone who didn't include Sam . . .'

'Naturally, but he'll need a stern hand, a good boarding school.'

She decided not to argue that point since he would have nothing to do with Sam's upbringing.

'Well, everything seems to have turned out all right for both of us. I'm sure you'll be very happy with Cissie. When will you get married?'

'There's no need to wait. I thought Christmas, but

Cissie fancies a spring wedding. Daffodil yellow for the bridesmaids. And she'll have to give notice at the bank, of course.'

'She won't be staying on?' She couldn't resist it.

'Oh dear, no! She'll have plenty to do running our home, and we've lots of plans. Cissie thinks we could make a dressing room off the main bedroom – there's a box room next door – and she would like crazy paving in the garden where you step out from the French windows, and . . . well, who knows?' There was a prospective father gleam in his eyes.

'We haven't made any plans. Probably start off in Hal's flat in Bayswater.'

'Yes, of course.' He looked sympathetic as he sipped his coffee, secure in his double-fronted villa in Kirkcudbright with its crazy paving round the French windows, and possibly, later, a sandpit. 'May I ask what he *does*?'

'He works for a publisher, chiefly of art books.'

'Ah, I see,' he said, looking wise, '*that*'s the connection.'

Alan, she thought, has to have a logical explanation for everything. They would never have been compatible.

Twenty-Seven

The first engagement Van and Sam had after he had been home a few days was to see Wendy's new baby. The visit was considered tranquil enough for a convalescent. Dr James had warned Van. 'Nothing too exciting for a month. There has been a severe shock to his whole system. Gently does it.' Van had gone to see Miss Clewes on her own to report progress.

'He won't be coming back, Miss Clewes. His days with you were nearly over in any case, and after that it's time for him to move into the bigger school near us.'

'I quite see,' she said. 'You wouldn't want him to come back here.' She wasn't spiteful, only sorrowful.

'To be truthful, no.' Van had noticed since she became involved in her course that she had found it easier to be honest with people, even at the risk of hurting them. In the end it was kinder. 'It might be traumatic for him after the accident, but please don't take it personally. He enjoyed his stay with you. It prepared him for a larger school and now it's time for him to move on. Tell yourself you have fitted him for that move.'

'Those rough boys . . .' Miss Clewes shuddered. Yes, it was time for Sam to move on.

'A baby!' he said when Van told him they were

going to visit the new Pettigrew arrival. 'I don't like babies! I like Gordon. He's a *real* boy.'

'Babies grow up to be real boys,' she assured him. 'You were one once.'

'Ugh!' He shuddered, like Miss Clewes.

But he was enchanted by the new little Graham, how he grasped his forefinger in a grip of iron and wouldn't let go. 'He's a strong baby, Aunt Wendy,' he said. Wendy, motherly in pink and smelling of milk, agreed.

'The way he pulls,' she said to Van giving her a meaningful glance. 'I'm so sore, down *there*.'

Over tea, when Sam was waiting eagerly at the gate for Gordon coming from school, Van told Wendy she would be getting married to Hal.

'Not Mr McAlpine?' Wendy asked. 'He seemed so suitable.'

'He wasn't suitable at all,' Van said, comfortable with her new-found honesty, 'he only *seemed* suitable. And I wouldn't have suited him. He needed a Worker for Kirkcudbright,' she thought of all the attributes in capital letters, a Baker of Prize Sponges for Jumble Sales, an Organizer of Fêtes, a Church-goer, a Bed Warmer. 'No, I shouldn't have done.'

Wendy said surprisingly, 'Maybe you're right. That's what I'm expected to be for Gordon. I'm an unpaid partner of the firm, giving dinners to woo the contractors. It's new "freeways" now. They borrowed that idea from America. Gordon actually thinks it's a crime to chop up the city, says behind their backs that they're making a bombsite out of the place, but he sucks up to them to get the work.'

'Well, you can always have babies.'

'No, that's hell too, absolute hell, but once they're here, it's good. I'm in charge there, you see. It's *me*

288

they look to for their happiness. It's one world Gordon can't enter, thank goodness!'

'I never thought of you like this,' Van admitted.

'Didn't you? I feel trapped sometimes. Gordon and I had to get married, you know, and sometimes I think that was *my* fault. I liked the risk. I led him on for the excitement. What I should have really liked was to have been an explorer, like those Victorian women. Or to be the first woman on the moon. I really envy Neil Armstrong. And your brother's wife, Karin, in Biafra. She was wise not to get trapped with babies.'

'Didn't you love Gordon?'

'Oh, I suppose I did, but it was the risk, and sailing close to the wind, and then when I got pregnant and once Mother knew, and Gordon's mother, they couldn't rush us into marriage fast enough.'

'Still,' Van was adjusting to this new concept of Wendy, 'you could have done a lot worse. Gordon's successful,' she searched in her mind for his other attributes, 'I was dippy about him when I was fourteen or thereabouts.'

'I know. So were lots of girls. Maybe that was his attraction for me. Oh well, I'll never be a woman explorer now, but maybe the children will when they grow up. I expect I'll have another two at least. Or maybe they'll live in different parts of the world and I'll be able to go and visit them and see the countries where they live.'

'Well, be sure and see that they get around while they're growing up – they do nowadays – or they'll end up by marrying Glaswegians and staying put.'

'Yes, I've thought of that. On the other hand there are your parents. I've always admired them. They went away and came back, at the right time fortunately. They're in that new Glasgow Society, your father told me, they lead interesting lives and meet interesting people. And they're both gorgeous to look at. They've cut themselves off from the old bigoted Glasgow ideas. The way they dealt with you when you got pregnant was so different from my mother and Gordon's.'

'Hey, wait a minute, they're not perfect! Well, my father is, nearly, but Mother objected for years when we lived near London to my style of life. She couldn't ever take Eb. I think it must have been a relief to her when he died – no, that's not fair. They gave me shelter, and Sam, she fed me and clothed me – am I quoting the Bible? But it always turns out fine for my mother. Aunt Jean is the one who gets the blows. Mother adores Hal, so everything is all right.'

'She likes exciting men. Don't be hard on her. But she's beautiful herself. You're not a bit like her.'

'Thanks.' Van laughed. 'I was just about to pay *you* a compliment, say that you're different from what I thought.'

'That's because you never asked. You lumped me with the Pettigrews.' They laughed together. 'But I think I can see what Hal likes in you. You're beguiling, different, with your dark eyes and that hair. Look at me, all gold and pink. You're like your Aunt Jean. There's a mystery which Hal must see . . . will you have children if you get married?'

'Perhaps.'

'Now at least we can choose.' Gordon and Sam came rushing into the room, Gordon with his school cap on at a rakish angle, his tie screwed to one side, looking with his fairness and handsomeness like a replica of his father.

'Gordon's been fighting all the rough boys on his

way home from school!' Sam announced, different from his cousin in his brown litheness.

'I punched one on the nose.' Gordon stood with his head back, chest out, feet apart. 'Gave him as good as he handed out.' Van heard his father. 'Mummy, I'm starving!'

'All right. Off you go to the kitchen with Sam. I don't want crumbs on my Wilton.' Now it was Wendy's mother speaking, that imposing matron of the West End and Helensburgh. She gave them each a plate of sandwiches and coffee cake and they went off together.

'She's a bit meenjy with the coffee cake.' Gordon's remark came back to them as he went out of the room, followed by an adoring Sam.

Wendy looked at Van. 'Sometimes I don't like my son,' she said. 'He reminds me of his father.'

Van looked at Wendy with a new respect.

Twenty-Eight

When Van came downstairs with Sam the following morning she found Anna in the kitchen. She was preparing breakfast. Ritchie, she said, was having a shower – a recent innovation which he had grown to like. Showers were for extroverts, Van had told him. 'Where's Bessie?' she asked, going towards the cupboard for Sam's cereal, chosen for its jazzy packet and its free plastic aeroplanes.

'She isn't up yet. I'll just let her have a lie-in.'

'She needs it. You take Bessie a cup of tea, Sam, while I heat your milk.' She poured out the tea which Anna had already made. 'Carry it carefully, and remember to say, "Good morning, Bessie."'

Anna was now sitting at the table, her hands round a large cup of coffee. 'We'll have to have a talk about the Christmas thing, Van. Ritchie and I have decided we'll have a party, all the relatives, of course, but really for Hal coming home. A kind of pre-wedding feast since you don't know the date.'

'No, but it will be as soon as he can fix up the Special Licence. And it might be London.'

'Well, Christmas Eve, do you think?'

'That would be great, but it will be an awful lot of work, though I'll help. And Bessie can't do so much now.'

'I'll hire help. But I really want to see the house filled. We've plenty of bedrooms. It will be a real humdinger of a party. And it'll make up to Sam as well for the pantomime.' They had decided it would be too exciting for him. She looked up. Sam was back. 'That didn't take long.'

'Bessie wouldn't sit up for her tea, Mummy,' he said. 'I just left it.' Van looked at Anna.

'I'll go and see her.' Van got up and went swiftly to the little room off the kitchen.

The old woman was lying on her back, her eyes closed. She opened them when she heard Van.

'Did the wee lad clipe?' she asked.

'What's wrong, Bessie?' Van sat down on her bed. There was a familiar smell, a hospital smell which could sometimes seep through antiseptics. She felt fear. 'It's not like you to refuse a cup of tea.'

'I'm that tired. Stupid, isn't it? But I'll be awright when I summon masel. It's . . .' Her mouth screwed up with pain.

'You're not well, Bessie. Why didn't you say?'

'I knew you'd fuss. Don't tell Anna. You're both fussers. You widnae gie a body a meenit's peace.' Van rose, her mind made up.

'Right, we'll give you peace. You lie there and have a rest and I'll come back when I've had my breakfast and see if you want a fresh cup.' She pulled up the bedclothes and tucked them round Bessie's chin. Bessie gave Van a sheepish look.

She went back to the kitchen. 'There's something wrong with Bessie, Mother. I'm going to phone the doctor.'

'Are you sure? Maybe all she needs is a morning in bed?'

'She called you "Anna" to me. It's . . . significant.'

Anna smiled at her. 'There speaks the budding almoner. All right, you go and phone Dr Reid, provided you can also thole the coals of fire Bessie will heap on your head.'

'Eat up your cornflakes, Sam,' Van said, passing him. He was playing with one of the red plastic aeroplanes from the cereal packet.

'I am. I was listening at the same time. Bessie smells funny.'

'Get on with your breakfast.' She remembered how a young doctor had said to her he'd been told to use his nose as well as his stethoscope.

Dr Reid was just going on his rounds, but as he lived nearby in Clevedon Drive his ladylike wife promised he would call *en passant*. He arrived while they were still talking about Bessie and agreeing that if she stayed in bed voluntarily she *must* be ill.

Dr Reid was with Bessie for a long time. Van was tidying upstairs and Ritchie was busy working. This was conveyed succinctly by the notice which he had pinned to his studio door, 'Danger. Man at Work.' She heard the door shut and went running downstairs. Anna was in the hall.

'Bessie's got cancer,' she said.

'Oh, no!' A fear confirmed.

'Yes, a lump on her breast. She'd let it . . . spread. She didn't say a word to me, ever!' She sounded aggrieved. Her eyes were tragic. 'There's to be a mastectomy immediately. We've to get her ready for tomorrow morning. The sooner the better, Dr Reid says.'

'We'd better go in and talk to her, Mother.'

'I was just going.'

Bessie was no longer lying down. She was propped

up by pillows and there were two spots of red on either cheek.

'Oh, Bessie, I'm so sorry!' Van sat down on the bed, Anna on the other side. Bessie looked guilty, like a lad caught stealing apples.

'For a wee lump!' she said indignantly. 'I've been . . . attending to it.' Her voice rose. 'Whit fur would they want to take the whole thing off?'

'It's medical practice,' Van said.

'So you're the doctor now that you're going to your classes! Wonders will never cease.' She was laying on the sarcasm.

Anna said, 'You should have told me, Bessie. You've known for ages, haven't you?'

'I don't go feelin' masel every time I wash under the oxters. It was only when it started . . . leaking.'

'But you'd have pain! I don't know what to do with you, really.' Anna bit her lip. 'Anyhow, you have a nice rest today. Sam will be your waiter and I'll bring in the television we have upstairs. That'll be a treat for you, watching television in the afternoon.'

'Maybe. I'm no' in favour of this goin' into hospital, Anna. When your time comes, that's it. If I take a lie-in for a few days it'll settle.'

'It won't.' Anna got to her feet, leaned over and put her arms round her. Van saw there were tears running down her face. 'We don't want to lose you, Bessie. We couldn't do without you. My mother would have told you to go in. You know that.'

'Ye think so, dae ye? Your ma kept herself pretty quiet on the same subject, I remember. Didn't want ony o' you crew to know a thing aboot it. Now you're aw roon me like a swarm o' bees.' She had shaken herself free of Anna. 'I canna get daein' a thing . . .'

'Oh, Bessie, I can't bear it! You're part of us.'

295

Van got up and left them together. She had never seen her mother break down like that, even when Ritchie had gone off with Maria in Barcelona.

She went upstairs to see that Sam was all right, and from there up again to Ritchie's studio. Urgent commission or not, he had to know. Besides, Anna would need some comfort.

It was the first time in sixty-four years that the house had been without Bessie. Anna worked it out. Bessie had come to Clevedon Crescent when she was fourteen to work for Anna's grandmother, then for her mother, then for herself.

She accepted the removal of her breast the way she accepted everything in life. The prothesis, in the shape of a stuffed muslin bag to be worn inside her bust bodice – she had never used the word 'brassiere' – would make a good pin cushion, she said, still using sarcasm as her staff.

Van visited her daily in the Western. The college was shut for the Christmas holidays and she had more time than Anna. Sam enjoyed the daily trips.Each day saw him stronger and more in need of a disciplined structure to his life. He would have to wait until after the New Year to go to his new school. The visit to see Bessie filled part of his day.

They brought her home a week before Christmas, cocky because of the different world she had inhabited, and with a new topic of conversation about patients and nurses which would keep her going for a long time. She had acquired a new vocabulary, 'Time to take your temp.', 'Tidy beds, please, for visitors,' and had listened in shamelessly to the conversation of the night nurses when they thought the

296

patients were asleep. 'They've got men on the brain,' she informed Anna and Van. The surgeon's round had seemed to her like 'wee dugs barkin' roon the heels o' the man takin' them for a walk.' The Matron thought she was 'Lady Belheeven', the Sister 'sucked up to her', and 'the nicest o' the lot were the men wi' the barrows – even if it was a corpse,' she added.

The house was going to be full, but Ritchie and Anna had told her that she would be one of the guests. No one expected her to do any work. They had a daily woman now, Mrs Fairbairn, whose bark was worse than her bite, and who promised to spend part of the day with Bessie, who would be glad of the company.

Invitations were issued for the grand pre-nuptial party to be held on Christmas Eve. Jean and John would be there, and would stay on for Christmas and Boxing Day. Alastair would be standing in for John at the practice, and Sarah preferred to stay at home with him since she was in the early stages of a third pregnancy.

Wendy and Gordon had accepted but would leave the new baby with the nurse. Young Gordon would come with them as company for Sam. Nancy, of course, would be there. She had already bought a new outfit for the affair, she told Anna.

There would be friends from the Art School, and, of course, Hal, who was moving heaven and earth to arrange the Special Licence.

The caterers were booked, the Christmas decorations were up, chiefly Sam and Van's work, and she was in a fever of excitement now at the thought of seeing Hal again. There was another letter from him. 'I can hardly wait. Now that I know we're going to be married soon, life is bloody marvellous. And to think I never believed in rose-coloured spectacles! Tell your chap he can come on the honeymoon with us. That's how marvellous it is.'

She thought of that summer at her father's house at Arenys de Mar when Manuel Folguera had introduced her to two of his friends, one of whom had explained to her the meaning of the word 'imago'. And when Hal had appeared and held out his arms to her to dance, how she had known that that moment was the peak of her existence.

Now she saw there were many peaks, and the one ahead was even higher. She was waiting for her lover who was coming home to marry her. Physically, mentally and psychologically it felt right . . . *maduramente*. She breathed deeply, closing her eyes. This is it, she thought, the highest peak. Or was there always a higher one?

'My, I never thought you could look so bonny,' Bessie said to her when she took in her morning cup of tea. 'I've always been that used to beauties roon aboot me, first your Granny Rose, then the three sisters. No wonder I gave up the idea early of ever catchin' a man.'

'Was there ever anyone you felt fond of?' Van asked her.

'No,' she shook her head. 'You see, wi' the men it was just as bad as far as looks went. Your Grandpa Mackintosh, a grand-standing fella he was wi' his Highland darkness, then your mother's man, well, you know what he does to women – so does your mother – and Nancy's, he's a handsome man as well, or was till Nancy squeezed the juice oot o' him. You can see why I widna gie tuppence fur the milkman.'

'Not to mention Gordon, Nancy's son?'

'Ach, no,' she shook her head, 'no' ma type. He's

jist like a dummy in Burton's. But the yin that took the biscuit for looks was that furriner who was after Jean, the yin she had the puir wean tae that died. Oh, he would have made any lass sigh at her supper! His eyes, wicked eyes they were, an' him wi' a wife an' three bairns.'

'He was the love of her life.'

'Aye, you're right there. If you had seen the face on her the day he was drowned! I opened the door to her and there she was, standing with yon taxi driver, fair drookit and wi' eyes that put the fear of God in me. Anna took her in charge. Aye, Anna's always the yin. And the screaming that went on when the pills the doctor geid her wore off, like an animal caught in a trap. They went through your heid. The only yin she wanted was Anna. Aye, they're close, they two. You can't beat twins for closeness, men or no men, there's a link there aw right, as strong as steel. Wee Nancy was aye jealous o' that closeness.'

'They even know what's happening to each other when they're miles apart. If Mother's edgy, it means there's something wrong with Jean. I think they even have the same headaches . . .' She looked at Bessie. Her eyes were closed. Perhaps she was no longer listening. Her skin was like putty, the lines round her mouth made tiny pleats.

'I'll leave you to have a rest,' she said, getting up. 'Mother will be needing help. Father's gone to the airport to pick up the American contingent.'

'Wi' your man amongst them?' She didn't open her eyes.

'Yes. With Mish. His wife's in Biafra. Oh, Bessie, Hal and I are going to be married, just as soon as we can arrange it.'

299

'He's another beauty that yin, like Anna's. Full of devilment. He'll keep you hoppin'.'

'Maybe you're right.' The thrill levelled out into a steady joy. 'Have a sleep now. You'll need all your strength for the Highland fling.'

'Och aye, I'm a fair dab at the Highland fling.' The mouth stretched, ironing out the tiny pleats round it for an instant. Her eyes remained closed. Van heard her murmur, 'Biafra . . .' She said it as if it were completely new to her. 'Whatever next?'

Twenty-Nine

There was the noise of the front door opening.

'There they are!' Anna said. They were both in the kitchen and they dropped what they were doing and rushed into the hall, Sam at their heels. He had a white moustache on his brown face from the bowl of cream he had been whipping.

'Hal!' Van said, and went like a bird into his out-held arms.

'Karin!' she heard her mother say.

'Hi, Sam!' This was Hal to Sam who was clinging round his legs, 'You'll have my trousers off! I want to kiss your mother!' He did, and Van released herself, laughing, going towards Mish and Karin.

'You never said a word, Mish!'

'I didn't know.' There was an American intonation in his voice now. 'She arrived on our doorstep two days ago. I wondered whether to let her in or not.' Karin laughed at him. Her eyes were brimming over with love.

'I wanted to see if I could shake that English *savoir-faire* of his.'

'Did you succeed?' Van asked, looking at her. She had altered. She was thinner, more taut, but with a sweetness in her expression which hadn't been there before, a look of experience, and perhaps wisdom, a hint in her eyes of suffering seen at close quarters. She would ask her later all about it.

'I succeeded. But I had scarcely time to preen myself before we were off to Kennedy Airport.'

'Let's get upstairs and dump this stuff, and all have a drink,' Ritchie said, his face brimming with pleasure. 'Did you put the champagne in the fridge, Anna?'

'Yes, two bottles. You go and help him with the glasses, Mish. There's a tray in the kitchen.'

'Bessie's in bed,' Van said. 'Do you and Karin want to go in and say hello?'

'Sure. Is it serious?'

'I'll tell you later. Would you like to come too, Hal?'

'It's a bit of a crowd. I'll go upstairs with Sam.'

'All right.' She met his eyes. Bliss, she thought.

Bessie was awake and lying still. Karin bent and kissed her on the cheek. She spoke softly. 'I'm Karin, Bessie.'

'I'm that ashamed.' She struggled to rise. 'They wouldn't let me get up . . .'

'You look just dandy lying there. Here's Mish, dying to say hi!' He came forward, and Van saw the small boy again, the prim sweetness as he bent over to kiss Bessie.

'It's not often we catch *you* in bed!'

'I'm fair ashamed. I was just saying to your wumman . . .'

'Karin.' He hid a smile.

'Aye, Karin. But I thocht she was in another place. A funny name . . .'

'Biafra.'

'That's it.' She was sitting up now, looking from one to the other. 'My goodness, I've never known onything like this, an' me in ma bed.'

302

'Well you're going to have a glass of champagne to celebrate.'

She looked at him, shocked. 'A haveny come to *that* yet, Hamish.' They laughed.

'Would she be able to come upstairs in her dressing gown?' Mish asked Van.

'Do you feel able, Bessie? You know you're always in on our family celebrations.'

'Aye, your grandpa was a great yin for that. Onything would be better than lyin' here and being gawped at. Away you go, Hamish, and the lassies will help me. I've never had a man in ma room yet when I'm in ma nichtgoon, except the doctor.'

'There's always a first time. Okay. I'll leave you to put on your warpaint.'

Karin and Van helped Bessie into her dressing gown and put on her slippers. Karin combed her hair.

'You've been away helping they black yins, then?' she said as Karin coiled the long thin hair in a bun on the top of her head.

'Yes, the Biafrans. I've been in a place called Umuahia helping the children and the wounded to get away.'

'Were they bein' chased?'

'Yes, they came from the Ibo tribe. The Nigerian Government are trying to prevent the Red Cross from flying in with food. They think they're bringing in arms.'

'I've seen pictures o' these puir wee skinny things. Whit is the world comin' tae, eh? When nobody in their senses would prevent them gettin' food in their bellies?'

'Yes, it's terrible. But we have to look on the bright side. Just look at that girl, happy as a sandboy now her Hal's home. Are you ready to go upstairs and drink their health?'

'Och aye, there's life in the auld dug yet.' She got shakily to her feet, helped by Van. 'I'm glad you've got yersel a guid man at last, but time will tell.'

'Oh, Van's got the right idea of things,' Karin laughed. 'Come on, then, Van, you take one arm and I'll take the other.'

'Afterwards we'll get you back to bed with a nice tray with your dinner on it,' Van said. 'Sam will be your waiter.'

'Is ma hair aw right?' She gave it a pat.

'Right as rain.'

It was an easy rising staircase and the drawing room was on the first landing. Bessie managed it with a little help from the two girls. How often she must have carried heavy trays up here, Van thought. The whole thing was a nonsense, this rigmarole of service, at least to the able-bodied, when down in Maryhill they were lucky to get a cup of stewed tea in a mug if they made it themselves, or a swig from a bottle. She was sure the thought had never occurred to Bessie. The idea of service was engrained in her.

Hal joined Van at the serving table when she had settled Bessie with her champagne. Sam was with Ritchie and Mish, looking very important with his fizzy lemonade in a champagne glass. Bessie was looking bemused, sitting between Karin and Anna. She had always liked what she called 'a wee dram'.

'The wedding's fixed for next week,' he told her.

'Next week!' She was astonished. 'How did you manage it?'

'Ritchie, chiefly. He's got important connections in Glasgow. It will be in the Register Office, then I thought we'd have a weekend in Paris for our honeymoon.'

'Mother will look after Sam, if we ask her.' There was a balloon of happiness inside her.

'Oh, no. He's coming with us. Right from the beginning he's to be part of the family.'

'Mother says you can stay here until we're married. They wouldn't ask any questions.'

He kissed her on the mouth. 'No, let's be proper. I can wait, if you can.'

'So what's in a week?' Their eyes met and held.

He took her arm. 'For God's sake, let's get somewhere. There must be something in the kitchen you can stir.'

'Come on . . .' The piercing, shivering thrill again. She stopped at the door, dowsing her eyes as she looked across the room to Anna. 'We'll go down to the kitchen and see how the turkey's getting on.'

'Thanks. Baste it, please, Van.'

'Do you want the potatoes turning now?'

'Yes, please. Such thoughtfulness!' She was laughing at them. 'You could give the soup a stir, Hal, if you don't mind. And check that the gas is turned down low.'

'On my way.'

'I hope it's a decent pot of soup, Anna, and no that tinned muck.' The champagne was making Bessie brash.

'It's your recipe. Mish, give Bessie another vol-au-vent. She likes them.'

They raced downstairs and when they were in the kitchen Hal swept her into his arms and waltzed round the kitchen with her, at first like a whirlwind, then slowly, and even more slowly, looking down at her upturned face.

305

'This reminds me of that time in Arenys de Mar,' she said. 'We were dancing, and when you held out your arms to me I went into them like a doo into a doo-cote. I bet you don't know what a doo-cote is.'

'A house for keeping doos, obviously. Are they bees?'

'Oh, ignorant Sassenach! No, doves!'

They kissed, they danced and kissed until she broke free and said, 'My God, the turkey! I can smell it burning!'

Hal helped her to baste it, to turn the potatoes in the fat in which the bird sizzled. He stirred the soup while she took plates out of the dresser and put them on top of the cooker to warm. His eyes scarcely left her.

'It's nice,' he said, 'when reality exceeds expectation. I've imagined you all the time I've been away. You've changed. More composed, and yet your eyes belie it.'

'That's because I'm like a live wire when you touch me.'

'At that rate you're going to be electrocuted a week from today.'

'I can't believe it,' she said, standing beside him as he stirred. He put an arm round her waist.

'Can't believe what?'

'That you're here and that we're going to be together for ever and ever. Will you want us to live in London? I have to find out if there's a similar college near your flat.' He didn't answer.

'What is it, Hal?' she asked.

He put the wooden spoon down, turned to her and drew her towards him. His eyes were serious. 'I've accepted another six months in America. The project I'm working on isn't finished, and they've offered me

306

more money to see it through. The money isn't the bait. It's the satisfaction, and the acclaim.'

She drew away. 'How does that affect me?' She tried to steady her voice.

'I'm hoping not at all. We'll get married as planned and live in New York instead of London.'

'But there's my course, and Sam's schooling.' She drew in a breath.

'Six months,' he said, 'that's all. It would be an experience for both of you. I thought you wouldn't mind postponing your course . . . or finding a similar one there.'

She told herself she must be reasonable at all costs. She wanted to be feminine, female, throw herself on him, weeping, because her plans for herself would be swept aside if she went to New York. '*He*'ll keep you hopping,' Bessie had said. And there was Anna, who'd had the same thing with Ritchie, but had decided it was worth it. Men like Ritchie and Hal were special, she had said, but you had to be your own woman if you chose men like them.

He pulled her against him, rocked her gently, his cheek against hers. 'I had to make up my mind quickly, tell the firm whether I'd be back again. I felt like a heel, and then I thought, you're the one for taking a chance, and you had Mish and Karin there, and it would only be for six months.'

'I'm sitting my Diploma in six months.'

'These things can be arranged.' Oh, Ritchie-like Hal! 'There are hospitals in New York which have a training course attached to them, probably more advanced than Glasgow. Let's take it one step at a time, Van. Get married, have our weekend in Paris, talk it out.'

She drew away to look at him. And was beguiled

by everything about him, his insouciance, the love in his eyes, the promise of the richness of living with him, being his wife. There would never be anyone else. Anna and Jean were one-man women, as she was, Jean hadn't had the good fortune to marry hers, but she had made a good second choice in John. What had sustained her was her painting, her ability to fulfil herself apart from him.

There was a small volcano in the soup. She saw the bubbles. 'Hey!' she said laughing, 'Vesuvius's erupting!' She quickly turned off the gas and pulled the pot away from the heat. 'We'd better have a look at the turkey as well.' Talking about the food steadied her. 'Everybody will be starving.'

'I'm starving,' he said, 'but not for food.'

'Pass me the big platter.' She was a Mrs Beeton.

'Okay.' He saluted. When they had the turkey safely settled and surrounded by its border of golden brown roasted potatoes, he kissed her, hard and long. Seriously. 'We're meant for each other, don't forget. Nothing will ever part us.'

'I know that.' She felt calm. She felt she understood him, how life offered so much to him and how he had to take it. She felt she was beginning to understand herself.

The door opened, and Jean was there, beautiful as always, with that extra quality to her beauty because it was only one small part of her. 'Am I interrupting anything?'

'Oh, Jean!' She went forward to greet her. 'And Uncle John! I didn't hear the bell.'

'Nancy arrived at the same time with Wendy and Gordon. And wee Gordon, in a kilt. They've gone upstairs but we thought we'd have a look at Bessie first. Anna told me.' She looked at Hal, eyes smiling.

'We took her upstairs. But you haven't met Hal! I forgot. This is my Aunt Jean and Uncle John, Hal. He's heard plenty about *you*.'

'I thought it must be,' Jean said, 'or someone who liked you.'

'I'm helping Van with the cooking,' Hal said.

'So I saw.' They exchanged smiling glances.

'Well, the results look pretty succulent,' John said, and they all laughed.

'You've come just at the right time.' Van returned to her Mrs Beeton role. 'You go upstairs and tell them everything's ready. Bring Bessie down with you. She's going to have hers in bed with a tray.'

'We'll do that,' Jean said. 'How is she, really, Van?'

'Very frail, but game.'

'Anna says she's only about six months to go.' She was grave.

'Oh, no, she can't have!' Van was outraged. 'She didn't say that to me.'

'Perhaps she didn't want to spoil your celebration.'

'Come on, Jean,' John said. 'We'll do what Van asks.'

'Bosky,' Jean said. 'Each Glasgow park could have its own adjective. Rouken Glen is bosky, Queen's Park is elegant, as befits a queen's park, Kelvingrove is gracious.'

'Why did you want to come to this one?' Van asked her. They were sitting on a seat near the waterfall. Anna had volunteered to stay with Bessie, Ritchie had taken Hal to meet the bigwig who had organized the Register Office arrangements. Sam had been collected by Wendy to spend the day with young Gordon.

'It has memories for me, long-ago memories. I came

here with Frederick when we were seeing each other, clandestine meetings when he was teaching at the Art School and I was a student. It would be,' she counted on her fingers, 'thirty-four years ago, a lifetime. The tram, they were still running then, was like a galleon sailing through the suburbs of Glasgow, Pollokshaws Road, Kilmarnock Road, Fenwick Road, to Rouken Glen. It was its boskiness which appealed to me. I hoped we would find a place amongst the trees where he could kiss me.'

'Did you?'

'It was difficult. We were guilty lovers, the world full of spies. We had to sit on a park bench eventually. I had envisaged lying on the grass. That came later . . .' She looked away.

'Will you ever forget him?' Jean shook her head. Van didn't think it would be the same bench. That would be sacred.

'No, never. My whole life is partly expiation, partly an expression of love.'

'It seems unfair to John.'

'I hope not. I've tried hard.' Van thought of that talk she had had with him when he had advised her to choose passion.

'And we have a good relationship, solid, respectful. We're like close friends, cemented by sex now and then. That's why I never thought Alan McAlpine would suit you. I didn't think he was capable of passion.'

'Maybe he will be with Cissie Crichton. Did you know he ditched me for her?'

'The best thing he ever did.' She shuddered. 'It's cold here, yet lovely. Glasgow light's better in winter, clearer skies, that lovely northern light . . . Is Hal passionate?' Van liked how she slipped that one in.

'You bet. I've chosen my father.'

'The same charm?'

'The same unpredictability. He wants me to marry him, but he's going back right away to New York to work. He's forgotten about my beautiful career.'

'Have you?'

She didn't answer immediately. 'It's a crossroads. I can't bear the thought of being without him, and yet if I throw up the course I'll bear him a grudge for ever and that wouldn't be good.'

'You have to think it through. Anna and I did.'

'Yes, you're alike as two peas. And neither of you gives advice.'

'She tried when you lived in Renton but it didn't work. It never does.' Jean got up, beautiful in her long fur coat and fur hat, boots, a Russian princess, hair tucked away, the beautiful line of her jaw revealed. Van smiled up at her.

'All you need is a troika.' She got to her feet. 'Are you game to race me to the gate?'

'I'm always one for a dare!'

They set off, laughing, bumping into each other as they ran. An old man watching them said, 'Tchk! Tchk!'

Thirty

Only Anna, Ritchie, Jean and John came to the Register Office with them, and Sam, of course. He was the best man, Hal told him, and he wore a new navy suit with a white carnation in his buttonhole, like Hal's. Van was in red, for passion, she told them, both sisters wore fur coats and hats and looked like *two* Russian princesses.

They had lunch in Ritchie's club, then he and Anna drove them to Renfrew Airport. Jean and John were leaving for Kirkcudbright right away. The Pettigrews hadn't minded not receiving an invitation as they were spending a few days with Wendy's parents in their Helensburgh mansion. 'We couldn't refuse an invitation from the *Armours*,' Nancy had said.

The Paris hotel was small and elegant, and after Sam had been tucked in they sat at the window of their bedroom looking down on rue St Honoré. Hal was like a boy at a shop window.

'City lights always excite me,' he said. 'In New York you get the noises as well, sirens wailing, cabs hooting . . . no sirens here. Paris is too dignified.'

'I'm staying on in Glasgow, Hal,' Van said, 'to take my exams in June. I won't be coming to New York.'

He sat very still for a second or two. His voice was shaking when he spoke. 'Of course, I see now. The selfishness of it! Carried away by the idea of showing you and Sam New York. The joy of living with you. Coming home to you each night. Visiting Karin and Mish. I'd forgotten how much this Diploma means to you.'

'It's my insurance, you see.' Her voice was also shaking. 'I bought it from the man from the Prue.' He didn't laugh at her little joke. Perhaps they only knocked on Glasgow doors.

'I'll miss you like mad,' he said. 'You're my wife now. The legal feeling is good, right.'

'I know, and you're my husband. I must be mad to let you go off when I've just acquired you. A funny marriage.'

'You were always unconventional.' He tried to laugh. 'Mish told me all about you. Cats having kittens in your bed.'

'One cat.'

'Have you told your mother?'

'Yes, I had to ask her if she was jumping with joy at the thought of getting rid of me, but she said, no. There's Bessie, you see, on her way out. We would nurse her between us, and that would give her a chance to get some of her own work done.'

'And Ritchie?'

'Ritchie's like you, *complaisant*, since we're in Paris.'

'I'm not complaisant at this moment. I'm castigating myself, and desperate at the thought of not having you beside me for six months. But I respect your decision.'

'That's it, then,' she said, and put her hand out to him. She felt his close, warm grasp. 'We won't make a big thing out of this. There's always Renfrew Airport. "Things maun be some way," as Bessie says.'

*   *   *

313

She said afterwards that if they hadn't known they were to be parted, their first married night would not have been so breathtaking. There were no words you could use without being sentimental. She was convinced her heart had stopped for a second or two with the wonder of it all. It would have stopped for ever had their parting been for a year.

Lying side by side, weak with loving, Hal said, stroking her cheek, 'Tomorrow we'll take Sam up the Eiffel Tower . . .'

She laughed, weakly. 'I've been, there and back.'